EAST OF TROOST

EAST OF TROOST

A NOVEL

Ellen Barker

SHE WRITES PRESS

Published 2022

Printed in the United States of America

Print ISBN: 978-1-64742-229-5
E-ISBN: 978-1-64742-230-1
Library of Congress Control Number: 2022907076

For information, address:
She Writes Press
1569 Solano Ave #546
Berkeley, CA 94707

She Writes Press is a division of SparkPoint Studio, LLC.

To all the residents of the east of Troost neighborhood,
both those who lived there in the sixties,
when the Civil Rights movement played counterpoint
to Peace, Love, and Rock and Roll,
and those who live there now and call it home.

CHAPTER 1

God, what have I done? I'm standing just outside the front door of the house I had closed on less than an hour ago. This is a moment of truth. As soon as I open the door, I will know if this is a complete disaster or just a potential one. I'll be able to see half of the house without actually stepping inside, so the first look will tell all. Or enough, anyway.

Okay, open the door. The late-afternoon sun, warm on my back, streams in around me and lights the room. Walls and ceiling are stained from a roof leak, and I can see plaster rubble on the floor. The room smells of damp and cigarette smoke and something else, maybe mice. It does not smell like home.

I back up a step and take a deep breath, trying not to panic, not to second guess what I have just done: bought my childhood home thirty-seven years after moving out to go to college and thirty-four years after my parents sold the house and fled the increasingly dangerous and unfamiliar neighborhood where they had spent their entire married life. I close my eyes, loosen my grip on the doorknob, and step inside.

Turning around, I close the door and look at that doorknob, set in a 1930s doorplate. The doorplate looks and feels familiar. I look at the key still in my right hand. It could almost be the very key I carried all through high school and even taken off to college. Impossible. The locks have surely been changed a dozen times. But the doorknob, that is the same one that I, and my brother and my parents, had turned a thousand times. I focus on that for a moment and not on the smell and the stains and whatever else the house has in store.

Another deep breath, then I move forward to open some windows and take stock. I can see immediately that the living room has a lot of ceiling plaster missing. At least it isn't all on the floor—the sellers must have cleaned up a bit. I can see most of the kitchen and on through to the room behind. There is a refrigerator, although the door is standing open. So maybe it works, maybe it doesn't. Ten steps forward and I see a stove too. Not surprising. Tenants don't often own the big heavy appliances. Maybe one of them will work, at least for a while. The room beyond seems empty and therefore more familiar. It has the same gray wall paneling, anyway.

So far, I think, it's no worse than I imagined, although I had allowed myself to imagine only the worst. I step into the kitchen to open a window. There are two umbrella windows, one over the other, which my dad installed when he redid the kitchen the year I was in kindergarten. You push out the bottom of the window and lock it open, and the rain won't blow in: ingenious. The mechanism is broken on the lower one. No worries. The top one works and air floods in.

I reach over to flip the switch on the exhaust fan over the stove, another Dad project. Nothing happens, but I am not surprised. It is, after all, fifty years old. Or . . . is the electricity off? Ah. Yes. No lights—but that could be burned-out or missing bulbs, right? So where is the electrical service? Basement. I'm not sure I am ready for the basement. I try more switches and finally a light comes on. I'll try my phone charger later and make sure some outlets work.

Electricity is a good start. What about water? Kitchen

sink—yes! Water is forthcoming. I leave the hot water running until I know the water heater is working and then head for the bathroom. Okay, this doesn't smell so good. Lavatory? Water on and drain works. Flush? Yes again. Bathtub? Water is brown but flowing. Oh, but not draining very quickly. Maybe that's not a huge problem. The familiar turquoise linoleum floor tiles are chipped and cracked, curled up along the tub, probably harboring mildew.

So—electricity and water on, plus hot water tank and drains mostly working. Good signs. It even smells better with the window open and water in the drain traps. Maybe a lot of the bad smell was just because the traps were dry. I can tour the rest of the house and then decide what absolutely has to be done before I can sleep in here.

I had known that it was a risk, a big risk, buying this house and thinking I could live in it. The neighborhood is not what anyone would call good. Crime is high, although maybe not as bad as when my parents moved out. I know from my research that owner occupancy is low, and from driving around that neighborhood businesses have been reduced to liquor stores, beauty shops, storefront churches, and one fast-food place. At least as many are boarded up as are in business.

It hadn't been that way when I was a child, of course. The three- and four-room houses built in the 1930s were set on forty-foot-wide lots on streets lined with elm trees. Most were owner-occupied when my parents bought the house in 1950. Flowers bloomed, hedges bordered the front yards, people sat out on their porches in the evenings. But within fifteen years, times were already changing. Talk of building a freeway through the neighborhood began. Redevelopment efforts downtown pushed Black residents out of crowded tenements, and those who could afford it began testing the policies that made it hard for them to buy houses. Four decades on, the freeway has been built, the demographics are completely different, the crime rate is concerning.

It's a risk, but my choices are limited and here I am, home again, maybe.

I peek into the back bedroom. Hey, look, the red lantern ceiling fixture is still here. The room is darker than I remember, and tiny—like the size of an office cubicle. The closet door is missing. At least I don't have to open the closet door wondering what might be inside. The room smells a bit. Cigarette smoke maybe. Anyway, there is nothing here to keep me out of the house. I step back and turn around to look into the front bedroom.

This room is even smaller. It was mine from age six until I left for college. It still has no closet, but also no water damage, and is fairly clean. I can dust and mop and set up the inflatable bed waiting in my car. I had last slept in this room in a cot-sized trundle bed. Will my borrowed queen-size inflatable leave any floor space at all? I measure with my arms. Yes, but not much.

The kitchen is vital, so I take a closer look. The ceiling is water stained but mostly intact. I look in the open refrigerator and see that it is empty and, if not exactly clean, it doesn't seem to contain anything lethal. I close the door and plug it in. No sound of a refrigerator coming to life. I poke around and find the control and reset the temperature. Still nothing. The image of my brother giving his garage refrigerator a good shake comes to mind. It can't hurt to try. I shake it as hard as I can and hear the reassuring sound of the compressor coming on. Maybe it does work, but I am not going to depend on it yet.

The top of the stove is clean(ish), but the burners don't click or light. Oh, duh, this thing is old enough to have pilots, which are not lit. Either it doesn't work or the gas is shut off. I decide to save looking for the gas valve for another day, a day when I have matches. Kitchen cupboards—did we really manage to keep everything in just these few drawers and cabinets? Obviously we had. Might as well take a look inside while there is still daylight and I can see what I am dealing with. The overheads are okay, with a few random boxes and empty containers. Dirty but cleanable. The drawers are less clean but at least they all work and the fronts are solidly attached to the sides. The under-sink cabinet is a mess, having seen some water over the years. It will need serious attention somehow, sometime. The fifth room, the addition my dad built on the back in 1959, is empty. I don't feel compelled to examine the closet or cupboards today. There is nothing here to keep me away.

I consider my options. Can I buy lightbulbs and cleaning supplies and get one room clean enough to sleep here tonight? Is it even secure? I have not looked up motels that will allow a dog, especially one as big as the German Shepherd that is waiting in the car, and I am a long way from being ready to show up on the doorstep of anyone I still know in town and explain my situation. I know that sleep will be elusive anyway. So I check the window and door locks, let Boris out of the car to pee, and head out for food and a few cleaning supplies.

Without thinking, I turn west at the corner and head for Prospect, the commercial street three blocks away. As soon as I turn, I am slapped again with the reality that an expressway now blocks the side street. I knew it was there. I had driven on it earlier that day. I sigh at another indicator that I am not firing on all cylinders then turn on the next street. My stomach lurches with the realization that it will be a long walk now to any shops still in business on Prospect, and that makes me question my decision yet again. I like to walk on my daily errands, not drive. Deep breath, change the channel, focus on the moment.

Traffic on Prospect is nothing like it used to be. Many buildings are boarded up or empty. I decide to drive five or six blocks in each direction and see what my new neighborhood has to offer. I had taken an online tour weeks ago using Streetview, so my expectations are low.

The changes are so dramatic I have a hard time orienting myself. Driving south, nothing remains from my past, nothing at all. I find a chicken restaurant (*hurrah*), a sketchy food mart (*hmm*), and wonder of wonders, a hardware store (*double hurrah*). The hardware store seems promising, both for my own convenience and for what I imagine it says about the neighborhood. Heading north, I find that the local hospital has grown considerably. Maybe medical care won't be an issue. I also find a Dollar Store, a CVS, and a few storefronts advertised as food marts. None of them looks like it has a wide selection of cheeses or anything like fresh broccoli, but I decide to remain hopeful. The Dollar Store seems like the best place for cleaning supplies and light bulbs, followed by take-out chicken for dinner. I can begin patronizing the hardware store and investigate the food marts tomorrow.

The Dollar Store does not disappoint—I find cleaners and rags. Walking up and down the aisles, it occurs to me that I will need coffee to face the morning. Coffee they have, but how will I brew it? I move on to CVS, which has a perfectly good drip pot, along with filters. I do not want to buy schlocky things out of desperation. But I do it anyway, knowing that this is just the first of many compromises I will make, so I might as well get the first one out of the way.

It's evening commute time, so there is a line at the checkout. While I wait, I pick up a flashlight, put it back, pick it up again. I add two granola bars for breakfast, wondering what else I am forgetting. Surely I can get through twelve hours with what I have.

I sigh, frustrated at my indecision. I'm hungry and worried and rethinking every decision I have ever made. The woman behind me in line gives me a knowing smile.

"It's always like this at six o'clock," she says.

My mind stops rehashing history and scrambles to figure out what she's talking about. "Oh," is all I manage to say, but I smile back like I know what she means.

"The lines," she says, nodding to indicate the people ahead of us. "Everyone stops on the way home. Including me." She sighs and shakes her head, as though the line is her fault, and then smiles again. I realize she thinks I was sighing about the line. She's being friendly, passing the time.

Her smile cheers me up, just enough to feel it. I smile back for real this time.

"Yeah, I guess I could have done this earlier."

Then it's my turn, and I pay and collect my bag of essentials and wave goodbye to the clerk and the woman behind me in line.

"Nice talkin' to you," she says, and I briefly feel like an ordinary person doing an ordinary thing. On the way home I remember to go around the expressway.

In early 1960s, when the Watkins expressway was just a distant plan, we called it "The Freeway" and, being grade schoolers, didn't think much about it. The idea was already more than ten years old, and it was referred to as the Mid-Town Freeway at that time. The configuration we heard about was pretty much what was finally built, with the critical change from a freeway with cloverleaf interchanges to a boulevard, with only a few at-grade cross streets. It's officially the Watkins Boulevard, but it's not like the other boulevards for which Kansas City is famous. It is an expressway in all but name.

What we already knew back then was that my best friend's house was definitely in the path of the freeway and would be demolished, and that ours would be demolished only if a cloverleaf interchange was built at Gregory Boulevard. Angie was four when her family moved there, and the real estate agent had assured her parents that even though the house was a bit small for their large family, it would be fine because "the freeway will take your house" in a few years and they would make money on the sale. The agent also told them that the kids could walk to the Catholic grade school, which was technically true but she didn't mention that the walk was two miles each way. We all took a school bus as it turned out.

What our parents probably began to realize early on was that if "The Freeway" did come, the impact would be enormous. If their houses were in the acquisition path, they would get a fair purchase price with no need to repair or upgrade anything, plus moving expenses. If their houses were not acquired, they would be living next to a massive freeway and their property value would plummet.

Meanwhile, nothing was actually happening. Years would go by with no information. Then, maybe there would be a meeting. There would be talk for a while or an article in the *Star* or the *Times*, and then everyone would forget about it again, almost.

Back at the house, I eat the delicious chicken and passable cole slaw and am relieved to find that the refrigerator is at least cooler than the kitchen. There is nothing to sit on, so I eat just enough to keep the hunger pangs at bay and start cleaning my old room at the front of the house, which seems to be less disgusting than the other rooms and easier to tackle. Plus, the ceiling light works. The room also has miniblinds. They are in bad shape but with some bending and tying up I decide they will be fine for at least the first night.

The bathroom also gets a wipe down and a promise of more tomorrow. Yikes, no toilet paper. I scrounge enough Kleenex to last overnight.

It is dark now, so I hurry to bring in everything from the car, inflate the bed, feed the dog, and sit on the bed to finish eating. I try to pretend I'm in a hotel having room service, but that doesn't work. Boris puts his chin on the bed and looks at me soulfully. "What do you think, Boris? Was this a crazy idea?" He wags his tail once and trots off on another tour of the house. I hear him slurping water from his bowl and then hear a long sigh as he thumps himself down somewhere. Thoroughly exhausted myself, that's what I'd like to do too. But I still have to make a list for tomorrow; otherwise I know sleep will be impossible.

I find a pen and something to write on and sit on the bed under the glare of the ceiling light, listing food and kitchen essentials. Within a few minutes, I'm too tired to go on. I write down "lamp" and give it up. I take Boris out for a last pee, using the front door. There are dogs in the back yard next door and I don't want to deal with that in the dark. Time for shower and sleep.

Shower? Seriously, after thirty-four years there is still no shower in the bathroom? I know there was a basement shower, "was" meaning it was working in 1975. But I am not going down there tonight. I add "check shower" to the to-do list. And I start a mental "Much Later" list with remodel bathroom at the top.

The sad truth is that I'm afraid of the dark. I may seem to be courageous, moving across the country and into a sketchy neighborhood. Things like that don't scare me. And introverted I may be, but public speaking doesn't worry me, either. What I'm afraid of are dark places, especially basements with no lights. That kind of darkness is more than absence of light. It is thick and dense. I can feel and hear and smell the dangerous darkness of a basement at night.

Right now, I'm also a little afraid of sleeping alone in a house that is one step above derelict in a neighborhood where I know exactly no one. I remind myself that I have a dog, and that he's big and has a scary, business-like bark. I can at least get in bed and pretend to sleep. But I am not going down in the basement tonight, even with Boris. I give the tub a scrub and take a bath, and then curl up in bed and wait for sleep to come.

CHAPTER 2

I wake up to the mingled scents of Murphy's Oil soap and fresh chilly air coming through the (slightly) open window, the sound of birdsong, and some traffic noise (damn that expressway). I guess I can sleep in this house after all, at least when I'm exhausted.

I take Boris out, wash the new coffeemaker, eat a granola bar, check the refrigerator. Good, it's still cold. I need to find something to put water in to see if the freezer actually freezes. I rummage around in the cupboards and find a plastic glass and an empty margarine container.

Rats, I forgot to charge my phone. I go out to the car and find that it's almost eight o'clock. If I don't buy a microwave today, maybe I can find a bedside clock. Not from the Dollar Store, though. Well, maybe. The last few I bought from reputable stores didn't last long anyway.

Boris needs a real walk, so I decide to start with that before distractions make me put it off for another day. First, we creep out into the back yard to see if there is any potential for letting Boris out sometimes without a leash. I know those next-door dogs are there because I've heard barking and can see them from the back window. Sure enough, the two of us set off a barking frenzy. No real snarling, though, and they are securely caged in chain link at the back of the lot. Boris stays by my side, hair up, but his tail is waving hopefully. We back off. Enough for the first look at each other. No one appears at the door of the house.

We exit down the driveway and pause. I decide to go a long block north, a short block east, then south two blocks, west to my street, and back to home base. These are the streets I knew best, other than the streets that don't exist anymore. We start off downhill.

It hardly seems like much of a hill now, on foot instead of roller skates or a bicycle or a sled. The sidewalk is in better shape, no longer heaved by those stately elms and repaired bit by bit by homeowners selling up. The first house I pass actually looks much the same as it did in the 1970s and is in great shape. The second still has a beautiful pine tree that takes up much of the front yard. I always wanted to climb that tree, but we were a little scared of the man who lived there. Kind of a Boo Radley in our imaginations. All we ever knew about him was that his name was Pete, and he left in the first wave of white flight.

The third house was always called the Scurlock house, for the simple reason that after the Scurlocks left, no renter stayed long enough for us to associate their name with the house. After that was the Alewine house, where Bonnie and Francie lived when we were very young. The lot is at the lowest point on the block, and the basement flooded regularly until the city put in a larger storm sewer.

Starting up the steeper end of the street, the houses on both sides are less familiar but look better than mine. There are more mature trees too. I'm happy about this. A couple of houses are missing, though, including the one two-story house I remember. Friends of ours lived there, on a double lot with a large vegetable garden.

I turn the corner and go around to the next street, the one behind my house. It's one block farther from the expressway and is faring maybe a little better than my street, although there are some gaps between houses here too. A few people are out, leaving for work or school or putting out trash. I smile and say "hello," and they wave back. I don't stop or try to start a conversation. Time for that another day. I have forgotten that this street didn't have sidewalks and wonder why I never thought about it before. Probably because this street was where we sledded and rode bikes—the hill is steeper than ours, and therefore more fun.

Back at the house, I get my list, lean on the kitchen counter, and think. I have to go downstairs, and I have to check the closets and cupboards in the rest of the house. My shopping list is getting longer and it will take some time to run today's errands. If I am going to live here, I have to have Wi-Fi so that I can start working again. I've told my boss I'll be back online on Monday, six days away. I will probably just bundle it with a landline, even though most people don't have landlines anymore. Somehow a landline feels like a lifeline, plus conference calls are easier with a landline. Getting that set up could take time and will certainly be an expense, a commitment. Before I commit, I need to get past the hurdle of the basement. I open the door.

The basement light switch doesn't do anything, but there is enough light coming through the basement windows to see the steps. On the other hand, it isn't really that much light. I remember the flashlight I bought and go back to the kitchen for it. The stairs are solid, but I go down carefully anyway, remembering the short step at the bottom that had irritated my mother so much. As I step onto the concrete floor, the basement smell comes to me, familiar, with only a hint of dampness, typical of Midwestern basements. Maybe the upstairs just needs cleaning and airing.

To the left, the electrical box is just where my dad had installed it, the new service required for the Federal Housing Administration sale when they finally found a buyer back in 1975. I take a quick look around. So far, it seems junky, but nothing too scary. So small, though. The basement is the size of the original house before my parents added on. The whole thing would have fit in the great room of most suburban houses.

The furnace, chimney, and hot water tank are all in the middle of the space, creating four corner areas. The first, on my right, was my dad's workshop. I expect to see his workbench, but of course he moved it. Still, I step into the space where it had been, shelves all around and a light with a pull cord. At last, a working light bulb. A few boxes and paint cans, lots of cobwebs, some toys.

I move on to the laundry area, reaching for the light switch without even thinking about it. Someone has left a washer. I check to make sure the hoses and drain are connected and turn it on. Water starts flowing. I turn it off, hopeful. I will run it later when I have time to keep an eye on it. The shelves that used to hold laundry products are gone, but easily replaceable. Now, what about the shower?

Who knew why it was where it was, with the faucets fastened to the chimney and the shower head tucked up between the floor joints, the whole thing out in the open? No one in our family ever used it until I was a teenager in the late sixties, tired of washing my long hair in the kitchen sink. I wheedled and pleaded until my dad replaced the showerhead and my mother helped me rig up an enclosure of shower curtains. She even put a curtain on the basement window in that corner and brought home a shower caddy, which we attached to the plumbing somehow. It was all very tacky, and I loved it. The plumbing is still there. Someone has added a partial enclosure of plastic panels, along with a shower curtain. A sliver of soap sits on a shower caddy. This will do.

I loop around to the southwest section, where we used to sit on folding chairs during tornado warnings. It was also one of my favorite reading spots on hot summer days. Now, there is a ratty broom, some boxes, a garden hose that is probably rotted, a car tire, a television on a stained and rusted card table. An egg crate I can stand on to replace ceiling lightbulbs. I nudge the boxes with my foot. They seem to be full. No bugs, no dead mice, no cracks in the foundation. One window is boarded up but seems secure. It's all quite dirty, but nothing I can't deal with. I pick up the hose and drag the end to the faucets over the floor drain, thinking I'll test it. Then I think better of that plan and drag it back. I'll test it outside some other day.

Turning back toward the stairs, the light catches the silvery furnace duct overhead. Look at that, one of the clotheslines still there just under the duct. I snap the line against the duct, just to hear the long-ago sound of my mother hanging laundry in the basement on a day too wet or cold to hang it outside. So—there is a dryer after all; it's just made of wire and is slower than I am used to.

I inventory the lightbulbs, check to make sure all the breakers are on, walk around once more looking for cracks in the foundation or evidence that the gutters have failed and water has crept in through the walls. I'd like to open the windows and air it out, but that will have to wait until I'm going to be home all day. Boris is waiting for me at the top of the stairs. "You're going to have to figure out the stairs, buddy," I say. "We have stairs now."

In the kitchen, I work on my to-do list and my shopping list, then go back over both, marking the things that have to be done today. Wi-Fi is first. There is a satellite dish on the roof, so I start there. The cost seems high, but maybe they don't really have an internet-only deal, and I'm not interested in cable television. I realize that the operator who took my call may have never talked to a customer who didn't want TV. I tell her I'll get back to her. I have to call the phone company anyway, since I also want a landline. It turns out that the phone company has a better bundled deal, even after the wiring fee. They will be out on Thursday. I'm happy with that. I start to call the dish company back and tell them to come get it, but decide to see how the phone company thing works out. This isn't my first experience with home Wi-Fi.

Next, the kitchen stove. The gas must be working since I have hot water. Unless the hot water has been switched to electric. Down to the basement, no fear now. It's gas, so I just have to figure out what's going on with the stove. Back upstairs, I get out the matches and uncover the pilot light. I squeeze between the stove and the wall—*eww, need to do some cleaning here*—and find a gas valve. Everything seems to be connected. Still, I'm alone here so I need to be cautious. I squeeze back out and open the window, then go back and turn the valve. I strike a match quickly and hold it over the left pilot. It lights, as does the right-side one. What about the oven? I open the door—*yuck, another cleaning job*—and see the "light here" hole. Okay, that means the oven doesn't have a pilot, right? It's been a long time since I saw one of these. I examine the controls, strike another match, turn the oven control to "light" and hold the match to the hole. I hear the familiar whoosh of the oven lighting. So far, so good. Can I assume it's all okay? I light the burners, then turn everything off. I'll give it a few minutes, to see if I smell gas. Meanwhile, I'll check the rest of the closets, the ones in the back room.

When my parents added onto the house, they demolished the tiny mud room and built one larger room the full width of the house. This let them build a new basement stairway in the addition and expand the tiny kitchen. They moved into the new room, which was bigger than the other bedrooms, with a large closet and lots of storage. With no furniture the space feels open and . . . well, not exactly big, but bigger than any other space in the house. I decide on the spot that I won't sleep there, even if it is the room farthest from the freeway. I will use this as workspace, with its extra windows and view of the backyard. Maybe someday I will dig out my watercolors and paint back here. Ouch. The watercolors are part of the ash heap in California. I hate it when the loss leaps out at me like that. Tears well up, not so much about easily replaceable watercolors as at the vision of that smoldering pile of everything I owned.

Change the channel. Things to do. I will let myself mourn for a little while later on. Right now I am checking the double closet in the addition (*which I'll just call "the back room" from now on*), the coat closet by the back door, and the other cupboards in the back room. I try not to cringe when I open the doors, not knowing what I might find. One of the sliding doors on the double closet is off its track, and the other has a hole in the veneer. I slide it open, shine the flashlight. A few hangers (*I can use those*), some bits of clothing on the floor (*more rags*), an ant trap (*I hope they all have moved on*). A shoe box. Bits of paper. I add garbage bags to the list.

The coat closet is empty except for a few hangers and one kid's shoe. I'll have to wait until I have something to stand on before I can check the two cupboards over the closet. I move on to the more spacious cupboards adjacent to the kitchen. My dad built all of these to my mother's specifications. On the left is a pantry, and the lower shelves are empty. Oh, not quite empty. Mousetrap, complete with dead mouse. Ick, but at least it is dead, and seems to be alone. The upper shelves have some half-empty cereal and cracker boxes. On the right is a large deep cupboard built over the descending stairway. We kept luggage there. It is also the access to the attic crawlspace, which I have never actually seen, now that I think about it.

I open the cupboard door warily, flashlight on and pointed up. Having remembered the scuttle hole, I want to make sure it is closed. It is not. I can smell damp too. That is not surprising, given the obvious roof leaks. I need to figure out how to dry out the attic space and how to close that scuttle hole. But for now, I can't even get to it—I need a chair or ladder. I close the door on the damp smell.

Argh, I have already forgotten that I am supposed to be checking for gas leaks. I step back into the kitchen. No obvious gas smell, but then the window is open and I have a nose full of basement and damp attic. I close the window and go out to the front porch for a breath of fresh air. Three houses down, across the street, a man gets out of a shiny red pickup truck and goes in the front door. He is the first neighbor I have seen. Maybe later I'll knock on that door. Maybe not. I try to remember the etiquette from other moves I've made. In California, the neighbor across the street appeared with wine and flowers within the first two hours. In Massachusetts, it was weeks before we met anyone at all. Not much to go on, so I should just wait a bit and keep an eye out for an opportunity.

The gas—I've forgotten again. I go back in, and everything seems fine. I set a timer on my phone to remind me to check again in five minutes. I won't die in five minutes, will I? The house won't explode in five minutes, will it? Aauuuugh. Change the channel again. Back to the list.

After my house in California burned down last winter, I stayed with my friends, Rita and Hugh, and purposely accumulated as little as possible. I knew that I'd have to fit everything in the car for the trip to wherever I ended up, along with a large dog. Plus I didn't want anything I had to worry about losing. So I had a few clothes, my rain jacket, toiletries, and my laptop. I didn't want much more. I just didn't want the responsibility, as pathetic as that sounds. I didn't want to have to rummage around looking for anything—even that tiny bit of stress was painful. I was still unsure that I should even take the dog when I had friends who would love to have him, but after worrying myself sick about it, I had decided that the best thing was to take him and just stop thinking about it. But that was all, no more stuff until I am settled somewhere permanent.

My friends were wiser than I. The day before I set out, they handed me a smallish duffle and told me that I was taking it, no matter what I said. Inside were towels, an afghan that I knew Rita had made, and a few bowls from Hugh's pottery studio. And a pillow. They said I might need it if my back hurt from hours of driving, but I knew they were really sending me off with comfort. None of it was new and it all felt like love. Now I have my own place, even if it feels unsettled. I'm not sure that I can stay here, but I don't have a Plan B, so it is time to add a few more things to the collection. I feel like I can take responsibility for at least a pot and some spoons.

I tell Boris to watch the place and leave to run errands. I get one block and stop. I should turn off the gas, just in case. The dog can't even escape since there isn't (and won't be) a dog door. No, it's fine, I'll only be a few minutes, and the kitchen window is open. *But remember, you weren't gone that long when your last house burned down.* I close my eyes, take a deep breath, and say out loud, "I am going to the Dollar Store for toilet paper, then I will go home and take it from there. Small step." I open my eyes. A woman is looking at me from her driveway across the street. I smile, wave, and pull away from the curb. I don't look back.

As I get in line at the checkout at the Dollar Store, I remember seeing trash at the neighbors' curb, and it occurs to me that if I go straight home I might be able to get some of my own trash out to the curb before the truck arrives. I have no idea if I need special bags or stickers, but it seems like it is worth a try—and a good excuse to go home and make sure the house is still standing and not full of fumes. I add rubber gloves and pay.

Putting the trash out was a great idea, I'd just had it thirty minutes too late. I follow the truck down my street. At least I know that Tuesday is trash day. I just need to find out how it works. But I don't need to know that today.

The dog is fine and there is still no gas odor. I light a burner just to be sure, and all is well. Now I can go out and do the next round of shopping. I have my list, I just need to figure out where to go. Groceries are easy so I decide to start there—my cell phone tells me there is an Aldi on Troost, which I know is the next commercial street west of Prospect. As I am locking up the car in the Aldi lot, though, it occurs to me that I didn't recheck the refrigerator to make sure it is still cold, and I don't have any cooking or eating gear, so the food shopping is premature. I get back in the car. No, I'm going in there. I'm going to buy some food, even if it's a can of peaches and a potato I can bake in my oven. And apples and bananas, maybe oranges. I will take a risk and buy a carton of yogurt. I am buying enough food for the next twenty-four hours, and I am going to eat it from the bowl my friends in California sent me off with. In I go.

I guess I haven't been in an Aldi for a while. I remember a store selling mostly produce, with no free bags and with seats for the cashiers. People tended to shop in bulk. That is all still the case, but they also sell cookware and dishes. I reach for a skillet and remember my decision to buy used. Crap. Do I really need these kinds of principles right now? I guess I do. Besides, I remember seeing a cluster of resale shops near my old high school, just off Troost. I buy butter, bread, peanut butter, and produce, put them in a box (*still no free bags at Aldi*), and get back in the car.

Blackstone Thrift is a great discovery. I find a few dishes, a few pans, some sturdy utensils, and some glasses that will do for now. By this time I am starving and decide to go home and try things out before I break down and stop for chicken again. As I struggle in the door with the boxes and bags, Boris gets up, stretches, and saunters over to meet me. He seems relaxed, so I decide that he is settling in. I unpack so I can wash the new dishes and fix my first meal.

No dish soap, no sponges, no towels, no dish pan, and no dish-rack. I need to plan a little better, which I will do when I have some food in me. A peanut butter sandwich and fruit will be a fantastic lunch, nothing needed but a knife and a plate. When I'm finished, I collect the cleaning supplies and rag bag. I scrub the sink again, wash the dishes, and lay them out on the clean rags. I consider the little collection, realizing how small it is compared to what was in my old kitchen, my mother's kitchen in this house, and, in fact, anyone's kitchen. Before I can cook anything, I need a chef's knife, a cutting board. An omelet would be warm and delicious. Eggs need refrigeration. I check my cups of water and find the one in the freezer is frozen and the one in the refrigerator compartment is . . . also frozen, or at least icy on top. I find the controls, adjust them a bit, and refill the cups. Too cold is probably a better sign than too warm. Eggs will be okay.

Now, I really want a table and at least one chair. Or if that fails, a stool. I've remembered that the kitchen counter has a pull-out bread board. It looks like most of the house's occupants have missed it or failed to find a use for it, because it's not looking too bad. I can scrub it (*add scrub brush to the list*) and use it as a temporary table if I have to. Assuming I find a stool to sit on.

The problem with furniture shopping when you are starting from literally nothing is that everything you see is something you could use somewhere. A furniture store is ADHD-inducing in this situation. Table! Chest of drawers! Hey, I need a bookcase! A desk! That end table! This dish cupboard! I have to make myself focus. I really must have a bedside table so I can stop putting my glasses on the floor near the bed, exactly where I will step on them, or Boris will. I need lamps and I need tables to put the lamps on. I need a kitchen table and a work table or desk. And, I realize, I need to be able to get them home in my VW station wagon.

All my plans for buying just the right thing go out the window. I had scoped out another resale shop, and there I find a serviceable kitchen table that I sort of like and that can be worried apart and put in my car. I find a side table that can be used anywhere, and two wooden chairs that do not wobble and are comfortable enough. I promise myself a trip to World Market for cushions. Tomorrow. Right now, I desperately need a lamp. A lamp has become critical to my emotional well-being. I cannot face the evening with ceiling lights shining on the top of my head. I want to do a little more cleaning, cook myself a potato and eggs, take a shower, crawl into bed with a book, and read by the light of a lamp. But the lamps in this shop are filthy, missing a shade, plastic, or too ugly for words. I look up the nearest Target and go buy a new lamp. I'll figure out a better shopping plan tomorrow.

Maybe the lamp thing is related to my fear of the dark, maybe I'm just a morning person, or maybe I have sundown syndrome—lately I have certainly felt like I have dementia. But ever since my dual tragedies, or the double-whammy as I call it to myself when I'm trying not to be dramatic about it, I get anxious when it starts getting dark. I'm counting on this getting better eventually. The grief counselor I met with in California assured me that forgetfulness and anxiety are normal—and temporary—side effects of grief. She also warned me that the stress of moving to another state would probably make it worse for a while. She did not, however, discourage the move. She knew full well that I couldn't possibly afford to live within a hundred miles of where I was living, and if I was moving farther than one hundred miles to an area I could barely afford, I might as well move two thousand miles to a place where finances wouldn't be so tight. Especially since I was going somewhere familiar. Sort of familiar. I didn't give her enough information for her to object to what I was really doing.

It's also possible that my lamp meltdown was just fatigue and hunger and sensory overload. I don't think I had ever before spent most of a day shopping. I made one more stop, for dish soap, a cutting board, and ice cream.

One can cut up potatoes quite well with a table knife if one wants fried potatoes badly enough, which I do. Potatoes and eggs, plus a salad, and polished off with vanilla ice cream. I sit in my new chair (newly cleaned with Murphy's) at my new table (ditto), with the lamp glowing. It's a lovely lamp. Why didn't I get two, so I don't have to move this one to the bedroom later? It's not quite dark yet, but it will be soon, and I don't want to shower off the day's trials in the dark basement. Yes, I have lights working down there now, but the window in that part of the basement is almost visible from the street and doesn't have a curtain yet. So downstairs I go, leaving Boris looking worriedly down the steps but not trying to follow. After sluicing in warm water, I forget about anything else I thought I should do and curl up in bed next to my new, relocated lamp, which is beginning to feel like a trusty sidekick. I fall asleep early and sleep fairly well, with Boris between me and the bedroom door.

CHAPTER 3

I wake up thinking. I won't have internet for at least another twenty-four hours, and possibly thirty-six hours (or more, but I'm not going to think about that). So it makes sense to run as many errands as possible today. Again, I start the day by walking Boris. Okay, I start the day with coffee and toast, but I don't linger. I wish I had a newspaper, but that would probably just take up more of the morning. I set off. It's a beautiful day, sunny and cool. Trees are leafing out, tulips are up.

Today Boris and I walk west toward the expressway. It's just bizarre to saunter down an almost-familiar side street and run into a wall. I walked and biked along that side street a thousand times, thousands of times. I walked that way to kindergarten, to run errands with (and later for) my mother, to the grocery, the post office, the shoe shop, the pharmacy. I went to my best friend's house. And I walked home from high school every day on that street, always on the south side, which had a sidewalk. The sidewalk seems utterly unchanged except for the new ADA curb cuts. At some intersections, the old blue-and-white street name tiles are still there, or at least remnants of them. At Chestnut, the gutter has the same mud puddle, where we occasionally found tadpoles in the spring. Some yards have the same chain-link fences they always had, some fences are gone.

And then—the wall. I turn right and walk along Chestnut, houses on one side and the expressway on the other, behind the wall. Some bits are familiar, but of course a lot of houses have changed, and some are gone. The neighborhood storefront at the next corner, which had once housed a little beauty shop, is a vacant lot. On the next block, where another childhood friend lived, the expressway returns to grade level and runs along next to Chestnut. They have planted trees, which help, but it will take me a while to get used to this thing. I breathe deeply and enjoy the morning, putting aside everything else. At least the last six months have given me a lot of practice letting go of whatever I don't need to be thinking about, at least for the moment.

I turn around after a few blocks and return the way I came. I want to approach my house the way I did so many times, see it from the sidewalk. In spite of the changes, the shapes of the houses, streets, and sidewalks are so engrained that they look familiar, they feel safe. Even though my front porch has been altered poorly and needs repair, and a flowering shrub has grown taller than the house, as I walk up to the front door, it feels like home. Work needs to be done, and soon, or I will have the shabbiest property on the block, if I don't already. But once again, I let that thought go and get on with today's needs. Top priorities are thoroughly cleaning and taking stock in the kitchen. A clean sink and bit of counter isn't good enough. I put my hair in a braid, get out the trash bags, and open all the cupboards, plus the oven and the broiler. Ah, the first surprise of today, a dead mouse in the broiler. Thank goodness I didn't leave the oven on when I was testing the gas, or attempt to bake a potato. I take the broiler apart, put the pieces in the sink and spray them with cleaner. Peering into the nether regions, I sigh. It's probably no dirtier than under any other stove, but still. I go after it with rags and cleaner. The storage compartment next to the oven has a better surprise: a few cookie sheets and a cast iron skillet that might be salvageable.

Once the stove is shining, I degrease the wall next to it and don't let myself think about stripping the wallpaper and painting it to make it more washable. I reassemble the cleaned broiler and turn the oven on to make sure it works and doesn't smell of something I've missed. And open the window. Chilly is better than stinky or smoky. I'm still comfortable ignoring the broken but securely locked latch on the lower window, but I would like a curtain. I remind myself that no one can see in. The window is high, it has an awning, and my car is parked just under it. At this point, curtains are for windows that make me feel exposed.

Maybe because she grew up in the country, my mother was religious about closing curtains at night and, for that matter, about opening and closing them in the summer as the sun moved around the house, to keep out the heat. "Babe, close up the curtains" still resounds in my head as the sun sets. But the days are fairly long now, and I have only two usable rooms at the moment, so I've been putting that voice on mute. Curtains are on my "soon" list, not on my "right now" list.

I clear out the rest of the kitchen cupboards and drawers and get them as clean as I can. A few jars and dishes go in the sink. I now own a ceramic Garfield mug and a plastic insulated mug from H&R Block. I add shelf liner to the shopping list, along with basic tools. I move on to the pantry and clean those cupboards, standing on my new chair to clean the top shelves.

Break time—peanut butter never tasted so good, but I really want a toaster, so that goes on the "right now" list. I also make a list of basic tools so I don't get distracted at the hardware store. Pliers, adjustable wrench, hammer, measuring tape, putty knife, wood filler, work gloves, WD-40, and duct tape. And I might as well get a garden hose for outdoor cleaning. I'm excited about my trip to the hardware store. It's definitely a way to shop local, and I want to know how well stocked it is, since I expect to be a regular customer. Before I head out, though, I take a tour of the backyard. I haven't had time for that yet, although in reality I know I'm also a little nervous. Just looking out the back windows reminds me of how neglected this property is. The garden shed is gone, as though it never existed. The swings are gone. The rose arbor is gone. Mostly, though, the maple tree in the middle of the yard is gone. That tree was my refuge, my reading room, and my escape from my brother, who didn't like climbing as much as I did. Even on chilly autumn Sundays, when the leaves had already fallen, I would take a book and a blanket, climb as high as I could, and read until it rained or got dark or I got hungry. No one ever looked up and saw me. Even my parents would call out the back door for me and not think to look up.

It is no surprise that the tree is gone. It died while I was in college, shortly before my parents moved. But in my head, it is still there. Now that vision will have to be updated. Maybe I will plant another maple. It did shade the house from the morning sun on hot summer days. The good thing, I suppose, is that the yard is so altered that I can start over and make anything I want of it. Out we go.

Again, the dogs next door bark in their pen, and again Boris holds back, tail waving but held low. I hold his leash and wait. I can see that there is little left of the fence on that side of my yard, just a few cedar pickets and the wires that hold them more or less upright. There is a drop from my yard to the next one, with a stone retaining wall that I can't see but that is apparently still retaining, since the yard seems level. After a minute or two, I drop the leash. I know I can call Boris back. The pen next door seems secure enough. Boris drops his nose to the ground and starts sniffing around the yard, pretending to ignore the other dogs. They stop barking and watch. I explore.

Exploring is maybe too strong a word for a level city yard that is maybe forty by forty feet with no buildings. But I once knew every square foot, having examined it from toddler level up. The only real remnants from my childhood here are the clotheslines along the ragtag cedar fence, the stone fireplace in the southeast corner, and the teeter-totter base near it. The fireplace had been used for burning trash until the neighbor on that side built a garage right on the property line and then called the city to report that we were burning trash too close to his garage. The inspector who came out told my mother that, yes, his new garage was too close to the property line, but he couldn't make him move the garage now that it was built, so we would have to move the fireplace or burn our trash in a barrel set the proper distance away. Relations were never good with that neighbor anyway, and they sank to a new low after that. No outright animosity, but no friendliness, either. Well, his grandchildren were my age, so I am pretty sure he doesn't live there anymore. Maybe I can get along a little better with whoever lives there now.

The chain-link fence on that side is still in place, so I know where to look for the row of peonies and poppies and iris, plus sweet peas and raspberries, at the back of the troublesome garage. No sign of anything except the berries, but I am glad to see them. Some years we got enough for a pie or two. I had not expected any of the other flowers, but I was hopeful that at least one of the lilac bushes flanking the fireplace would still be thriving. As it turns out, both are still there and in bud.

The wire fence across the back of the yard is gone, and I will need to put something up before I can let Boris out unsupervised. In the northeast corner, where my dad grew tomatoes and peppers behind the now-missing garden shed, there is nothing. I peer into the next yard, where the Duperes used to grow a larger garden, including a grapevine and asparagus. Nothing. The dogs in the pen bark, just enough to remind me that they are there and watching. Boris, who is nosing around near the fireplace, also looks up. "Hey Boris," I say, to distract him. He goes back to sniffing while I look for day lilies and tulips and the spirea and firefly bushes. Maybe they are here, maybe not. A lot of weedy-looking trees have been allowed to sprout along the edges. I do find the concrete slab that had been in front of the shed door. Well, maybe there will be a shed there again someday.

Hearing a whimper, I look up to see that Boris has squirmed through the pitiful excuse of a fence, dropped over the wall, and gone over to greet the neighboring dogs. I look around a little more, noting that I will need a lot of fencing, and call him back. There are really no usable tools here—not a rake or hoe or scrap of hose, that I can see. I am going to need garden tools, and soon. And a place to keep them. With no shed or garage, everything will have to go in the basement. So a lawnmower is out of the question. I'll have to find someone to mow. Do kids still mow lawns? In California, everyone hired a mow-and-blow guy. I will have to ask a neighbor—this is one thing I can't look up on the internet. I can also keep an eye out for what the neighbors do. Maybe mow-and-blow is a thing here too. Meanwhile, I add pruners to the list.

The hardware store is a gem—and it is nearby, on Prospect. It has been there a long time and it is everything a hardware store should be. It even smells like a hardware store instead of like a giant chain store, which often smells of the taco truck out front. I find what I need and ask about paint. They tell me that the Troost store has more stock. Sigh. Why would the Troost store be different? But this store does have locksmith services, so I arrange to have my doors rekeyed. I ask the clerk, a middle-aged man with the confidence of a long-time employee, or perhaps the owner, about contractors who could help me with the living room ceiling, my top priority in the repair department. "Kansas side?" he asks, looking at me a little more closely than he had before.

"Nope. Missouri side," I said.

"East of Troost?" He seems a little hesitant.

"Um, yes. Does it matter?" I give him an open, nonaccusatory look. I want to find out what he's thinking without making a big deal. Curious, not snooty.

He pauses. I'm working the credit card reader so I can look away and let him decide what he wants to say.

"Well, some guys are a little cautious is all." I wonder if they are worried about safety or getting paid, or both, or something else, but decide not to ask. It also occurs to me that he might be trying to work out whether I am a landlord or a resident. I decide on a direct approach. It can't hurt for him to know a little about me since I do intend to keep shopping here.

"I live about four or five blocks from here," I say, looking up to gauge his reaction. "Actually, I used to live here, and I've just moved back." That raises an eyebrow. Moving back is probably not a regular occurrence. I suddenly wonder where he lives.

"And the house needs a bit of attention," I continue, so he doesn't have to respond to the moving-back comment. "I can do a lot of things, but I know I can't fix that ceiling. I think it's lath and plaster, if that matters. It's a small room, so maybe it should just be replaced with sheetrock, but I was hoping to avoid a tear out."

That puts him on firm ground and he picks out a business card from a stack he's pulled out from under the counter.

"In that case, try this guy. Jimmy Cooper. He lives around

here and does a lot of handyman work. I don't know if he's up for plastering a ceiling, but you can ask. Anyway, you'll have his number if something else comes up."

"Good idea, and thanks for everything. I'm sure I'll be back."

I take a quick look around, vowing to always shop here first for anything they sell, even if it costs a little more. I need to keep these guys in business. I assume that their location on the corner of Gregory and visible from the expressway makes it a little easier for them to hang on. I note that they rent hand tools and repair glass. Outside is a rack of seedlings. I go back in for a shovel and then remember the fence and ask the clerk what they carry. I am hoping for something I can manage myself (i.e., not chain link) and that will last a good long while. He recommends cedar snow fencing but suggests that I look around the neighborhood for something I like and come back with a picture. I buy the shovel and some tomato plants. I know full well that I am getting ahead of myself, but home-grown tomatoes are a weakness of mine. As I get into the car, it occurs to me that a fence is nothing without a gate, which I definitely can't manage. One thing at a time. I'll explore the neighborhood a bit more.

The next stop is World Market for the cushions I had promised myself, and maybe a second lamp. I feel a little bad about buying a new lamp but I also know that I will be buying more lamps and for those I can take my time and find used ones that I like. I have no compunction about new cushions. I also buy a nice soft bed-side rug—I am feeling bad for Boris, sleeping on the old towel we always kept on the backseat of the car. I make sure it is not too heavy for me to haul outside and shake, given that I don't yet have a vacuum cleaner. I buy kitchen towels too—the white rags make me feel like I'm camping. Actually, the store is full of things I need, but it is all too much to deal with. I am happy with what I buy.

After the World Market stop, I decide to call Jimmy about the ceiling. Whatever it takes to repair it, there is going to be a mess involving insidious plaster dust, which I hate. The sooner that's over with, the better. Especially because I am starting to accumulate things, and I will have to keep them out of the way of the dust. Jimmy asks if I want him to come in the evening or on the weekend. I tell him I am home most of the time, or can be, and that daytime might be better if that's okay with him. I am thinking that there will be no light in that room if he comes too late in the day.

"Oh, okay," he says. "How about Friday morning around ten o'clock, then?"

"Works for me." I thank him and hang up. I guess most people are working and want to get estimates in the evening.

I take everything home and go on a cleaning binge for the rest of the day. At six o'clock I realize that I haven't planned supper and that going out for a few groceries is a bigger deal than it used to be. I rummage around and come up with pasta and a jar of sauce, plus a salad. I will need to do a real grocery shop soon.

CHAPTER 4

The next morning I get up at six thirty and set out with Boris right away, not knowing when the phone guy might be coming. This time I go east, away from the freeway.

This was what we called a side street, by which we specifically meant the short numbered blocks connecting the long named blocks that all the houses face. From here, I can look up and down the back yards, at least most of them. On my own corner the back yard has a tall wooden fence along the side street, blocking the view downhill into my yard. It's a pretty ratty fence and has No Trespassing signs. I don't want a fence like that. The yard is too small, for one thing. It would feel claustrophobic. I have to laugh at that idea, because my new back yard is bigger than the one I had in California, which was mostly patio and surrounded by privacy fence. All the yards in California that I can think of are surrounded by privacy fences. Interesting that open fences or no fences are more common here.

I come to the first missing house pretty quickly, on the south side of the street. I remember this place. A family with several kids moved in when I was still young enough to want to roam around on my bike after school and on summer days, going nowhere and hanging out with anyone else who might be outside. The family was Black, one of the first Black families to move in. Imogene was a few years younger than me and would hang out with the rest of us. And then one night a few weeks later, the house burned down and we never saw Imogene again. Forty years on, the lot is weedy and empty.

Strolling on, I see a few more empty lots, but mostly houses like mine. Some better, a few worse, most not really familiar. I probably didn't pay much attention to the houses back then, and of course a certain amount of remodeling has occurred. I do recognize the stone retaining walls that appear now and then, built to even out the rolling topography. I'm pleased to see so many mature trees, especially maples, which have grown up since Dutch elm disease denuded the neighborhood in the 1960s.

I meander up and down a few streets, occasionally taken aback by something particularly familiar and sometimes wondering where I am when nothing is familiar. Some streets have larger, nicer homes than mine, and some have pockets of true blight. This makes me laugh too, because even my expensive California neighborhood was a mix of 1950s tract houses in good condition, new monuments-to-pride that replaced the original houses, and rentals that were unkempt messes. Plus holes in the ground where someone had scrapped the old and was building new. In some ways, not all that different from this.

At one house, I am surprised to see wrought iron covering the windows and doors. I am not surprised that they are *there*, I am surprised that it is the first house I have seen that shows any concern about break-ins. I decide to pay more attention to see if there are more houses with bars. Intent on this, I am surprised when I see bigger houses and I realize that I have reached Meyer Boulevard.

One of the great charms of Kansas City is its fountains. Another is its boulevards, which are all lined with large homes, often brick, and have wide landscaped strips—usually wide enough to serve as parks—down the middle. Meyer was only a few blocks from my house, and we took it to my grade school, the public library, church, and Swope Park, with its zoo and outdoor summer theater. It's lovely to stroll home along Meyer, where the houses are almost all well-kept and unchanged.

I turn toward home, where the street becomes more recognizable as I go. I keep an eye out for security systems and bars on windows (*none*). I also inspect gates and fences. A few houses have chain link, and one or two have picket fences along the front. But mostly, no fences. I stop in front of my own house and give it a critical look. Mine is one of the few with a gravel driveway. How I had envied my neighbors their paved driveways in my roller-skating years. Well, maybe I can pave mine, and I can even think about adding a carport to keep the sun and snow off the car. The next-door neighbor has one that my mother had coveted, even though they used it mostly as a sort of shaded patio. Still, it would be nice to be able to get out of the car and into the house without tracking through mud and snow. I'll put that on the "nice-to-have" list.

Turning up my concrete walk, I brush past the mailbox, fastened to a post at the public sidewalk. Palm to forehead—this is my third full day here and I have not even thought about mail. And what is the mailbox doing out here instead of being attached to the house, like all the others? Okay, now I see that there are remnants of a chain-link fence across the front. Someone must have had dogs loose during the day and been made to move the mailbox out of the dogs' range. The box is tightly packed. I clear it out and make a mental note to figure out how to move the box to the front porch. Maybe I can catch the carrier and ask if I need to notify the post office.

Going up the front steps, I realize that I have mostly avoided the front door since I arrived, probably because of the dismal state of the living room it opens into. Now I take a good look at the front porch. Someone has attempted to duplicate the screened or glassed-in porches that most of the neighboring houses have, by extending it to the north and enclosing it. I love those porches, and some shade from the afternoon sun on hot summer days will be a relief. But mine is looking a little rickety from the street. Up close, it looks fairly sound. Mostly it needs paint. It is hard to tell if it had been screened or glassed, since the frames are gone.

I need to stay home now until the phone guy shows up, so I decide this is the day to test the washer in the basement. I gather up the used rags, along with the stray T-shirts and other clothing detritus, usable as rags, from the closets. I throw them in the washer with detergent and a good dose of bleach and turn it on. It starts to fill and nothing leaks, so I go upstairs and leave the basement door open, resolving to keep checking on it. I can't stay down there in case the phone guy comes, so maybe this wasn't a great idea. I set my iPhone timer for five minutes to make sure I'm not distracted long enough for a disaster to occur. Maybe I shouldn't have used bleach, either; that will be a mess if I have to bail out the washer. Also if it leaks on the floor. I can't afford bleach stains on the few clothes and shoes I own. I run back down and reset it to a small load. Less to deal with in case of trouble. It starts to agitate and seems fine. I go back upstairs.

I'm expecting the doorbell to ring, but does it even work? The button is still there, at least it looks like the same button. I can't remember where the ringer was. Kitchen, maybe? I haven't noticed it anywhere. I push the button but don't hear anything, so I try to hunt it down. I find it in the basement stairwell. The wires seem frayed. That will be hard to sort out since it's in the stairwell—hard to just stand on a chair. I start a new list for the handyman: living room ceiling, basement windows, doorbell wiring.

Jingling noise—a moment of disorientation and then I realize it's my phone timer. I run downstairs, where all seems fine. It's in a rinse cycle now. Reset the timer and back upstairs in case phone guy has come and is ringing the useless doorbell button. Okay, chill. This is no kind of crisis. I'll wash the kitchen walls while I wait, which will finish the kitchen cleaning and make me happy. I put a note on the doorbell (Out of order. Please knock). I decide to risk leaving the inside door open and locking the storm door. My mother, who was not a worrywart but didn't believe in taking unnecessary chances, never worried about leaving the inside door open during the day, as long as the storm door was locked. Of course, that was a sturdy wooden door, now gone. The lightweight aluminum replacement seems too flimsy. But I leave the inside door open anyway, reasoning that I have a ninety-pound German Shepherd at my feet, and the kitchen where I will be working is approximately thirteen feet from the front door, in full view. The kitchen in this house is connected to the living room through a wide doorway with narrow sidewalls. It's practically all one room.

Soon the rags are washed and hanging on the line in the basement (*I'll investigate the outside clothesline another day, when I'm not worried about missing the phone guy*). I wash my new jars, put down the new rug, and put the cushions on the chairs. The phone guy arrives just after one o'clock and I am connected to the internet. I will need to buy a phone to connect to my landline. I wonder where you even buy those anymore. Why didn't I think about that yesterday, so I could be sure it worked before he left? I head out for groceries and decide to buy flour and sugar and other pantry staples, adding large Ziploc bags to protect against humidity and ants, and maybe mice. Then I stop at the resale shop and score some large glass jars to use as canisters. I'll keep an eye out for more of the extra-large-mouth kind. I also find a phone that has a speaker and a mute button and is not too grimy with crumbs and coffee spills. I ask the clerk if it works, and she shrugs. She lets me have it for a dollar.

The phone does work and I wish I had asked for my childhood number. Maybe it's not too late, although I don't relish punching through menus at the phone company trying to find a choice for "change number to one you had forty years ago." Instead, I dial the number to see if it's in service. Someone answers and I ask for myself. I'm not there, of course, so I say, "Oh, I must have an old number. I'm so sorry." and hang up. I've saved myself a morning of frustration. My second call is to the people who sold me the house. I want to thank them for cleaning up the fallen plaster and generally sweeping out most of the debris from the former occupants (*who might be them, so I don't use those words*), and clearing out the yard. My thanks are met with silence, followed by "Oh, we didn't do much." Okay, that's true.

"Well, I just wanted you to know that I thought it would be a real mess, and it's not as bad as I thought it might be."

Another pause, and then, "I'm not sure what to say. We really didn't do anything. There was plaster on the floor and quite a lot of trash and even an old mattress on the porch from the last tenants. I have been feeling kind of bad about it."

That stops me, especially the mattress on the porch, which I picture crawling with bedbugs. I said "Well, maybe the tenants felt bad and came back to clean up." I'm trying to get off the phone so I can process this.

"Oh, I'm pretty sure that didn't happen." She doesn't elaborate.

"Well, anyway, things are going well, so thank you again for selling me the house and for getting the roof replaced so quickly."

That she can deal with, and we wish each other good night.

I am a little spooked, but I tell myself that the last tenants really could have come back to clean. Plus anyone who came in and cleaned up was unlikely to come back and rob me, right? *Anyway, the locksmith is coming soon, and don't forget that you have a really big scary-looking dog.* Still, I take the two chairs and wedge them under the front and back doorknobs. I have never done that and don't know if it works, but I don't have any other ideas, and it makes me feel at least 5 percent better.

CHAPTER 5

I wake up to a rumble of thunder, which was so foreign during my sojourn in California that I don't immediately recognize it. I was dreaming that someone was breaking in and scraping the chair across the floor. Fully awake, a distant crack of lightning brings me to my senses. I am safe from burglars. The rumble that follows feels more familiar, and I catch the lovely scent of spring rain on grass. But the next crack of lightning and crash of thunder send a shock of terror through me, straight from childhood.

One of my clear preschool memories is of a particularly violent thunderstorm during tornado season. Kansas City is in Tornado Alley, and it has dozens of outdoor sirens that blare when a tornado is sighted, warning us to take cover. I knew about this from an early age. Mother took my brother and me to the southwest corner of the basement and read stories to us. If Dad was home, he usually stood on the front porch watching for funnel clouds. He joined us only in extreme situations. The most extreme tornado situation I can remember was in the spring of 1957, when I was three years old. It became known as the Ruskin Heights tornado, and thirty-seven people died in Ruskin Heights and Hickman Mills. Kansas City didn't observe Daylight Savings Time in 1957, so it was dark when the sirens began. It's possible that the power went out too. I don't remember. The storm had been tracked across Kansas for most of the day, continually spawning tornados. By the time it crossed into Missouri, police cars were roaming the streets with sirens blaring to warn people to take cover. The combination of storm and sirens terrified me, as did the talk for weeks after of the death toll in Ruskin Heights, especially in areas where houses had no basements. I don't know where Ruskin Heights is, but for me it always signified danger and destruction. And it puzzled me that adults didn't know that houses needed basements.

By the time I was in school, my fear of storms had subsided. And I had no terror of atomic bomb drills, either, since for us they were the same as tornado drills: when the alarm sounded, we went to the basement rooms and corridors of the convent attached to our school and sat on the floor. Fear of storms in those years manifested itself in the person of Dorothy, a close family friend who lived on our block. On thundery weekday mornings like this, even if we had no tornado threat, she would scoot across the street and hang out with us until the noise passed. "Oh, murder," she would say when we were shaken by a particularly loud clap of thunder. Her fear made me brave, I think. Today, it makes me smile just to remember her.

Now that I'm connected to the internet, I need some information. First I verify that the tornado siren system is still in place. It is, tested on the first Wednesday of the month at 11:00 a.m. I would have put money on Tuesday. Next, I look up garbage collection, since I haven't managed to knock on a neighbor's door yet. It's easy to find not only my trash day and details, but also who owns every property in the city. I check mine to verify accuracy, and sure enough, there is my name. I'm a little taken aback by the square footage: 798, on 0.13 acres. That's um . . . twenty-five feet by thirty-two, or a bit less. Quite a bit less after accounting for walls. Before the addition it was even smaller, about the size of the living room in my rather ordinary tract house in California. But then, that house is now ash and this house is 798 square feet of real.

I click on the houses nearest mine. A lot of them are owned by investment companies or by people who live elsewhere in the city or beyond. But a lot are owner-occupied too, and one neighbor apparently owns several houses on the street. That seems like a good sign. But overall, what I am seeing sounds like instability. Which I, now that I think about it, am contributing to. One more change of ownership, one more move-in, which might soon be a move-out. Not that I am thinking that far ahead, but I know that's what it might look like to neighbors sensitive to changes.

That website leads me to the area's crime statistics, with pop-up ads offering to show me houses in safer neighborhoods. And from there I can click on race statistics, probably from census data. And one more thing. It tells me that I now live in a neighborhood called "Self Help Neighborhood Council." That sets me back on my heels. The nearby neighborhoods are called things like "Swope Park Campus" and "Foxtown." "Self Help Neighborhood Council" sounds like we have hit bottom and been left to founder and perish or figure it out for ourselves. Of course, I made all that up in an instant. I just want a name like "Foxtown" instead of "Self Help." I can't find out anything about an actual council. That doesn't really bother me, though. Everything doesn't have to be on the internet. I can find out from actual neighbors.

Other than the self-help thing, I am not surprised by any of this. If anything, the crime statistics seemed better to me than they had been when I left for college. And instability? It couldn't be less stable than when the prime movers of "The Freeway" and blockbusting smacked us in the mid-1960s.

I take a break to mix cookie dough. I don't have a bowl that's big enough, and it has not occurred to me to buy measuring cups and spoons. But I want the cookies, so I wing it, and cobble together enough flat surfaces to bake them. Again, I set the timer repeatedly for five minutes to be sure the oven is running close to its temperature setting.

While I'm stirring and hovering, I keep clicking on city data, and trying to figure out how we got to this point. Around 1964, after a lifetime (my ten-year lifetime) of no one in the neighborhood ever moving, the neighbors across the street put their house on the market. The Walshes had one son, who was at least ten years older than my twelve-year-old brother, so we barely knew him. After he graduated from high school, the parents had been spending nine months a year at their lake house (to Kansas Citians, at least of that era, "the lake" meant the Lake of the Ozarks, a 1931 hydroelectric project that gave rise to tens of thousands of vacation homes). Now, they told us, they were going to live at the lake year-round. That made sense, right?

But something else was going on in 1960s Kansas City besides bellbottoms and war protests and rock music in the parks (*all of which I was into*). It was blockbusting, and its close cousins redlining and housing discrimination. I knew a lot about these things, and they are forever intertwined with Sixties music and antiwar demonstrations in my memory. Three years after Vatican II, the Sisters of Charity who taught in my grade school and high school were fired up to teach us more of Catholic theology than the Baltimore Catechism. They were teaching us about social justice and how inseparable it is from being Catholic.

By the time I was in seventh grade, the neighborhood surrounding my school, about ten blocks north of my home, had changed from mostly white to a mix of Black and white. But integration is fluid and fragile. In the run-up to the Fair Housing Act passing in 1968, our civics class was studying the tactics of redlining (banks refusing loans to nonwhite applicants in areas considered "white") and blockbusting (real estate agents stealthily negotiating the sale of a house on an all-white block to a Black family, then quietly speaking to everyone else on the block, warning them that "Blacks" were moving in, all in an attempt to get them to list their house and sell quickly "before prices drop"). Together, these tactics did two things: They opened up home ownership to Black families much faster than had ever happened before, which was good in the big picture; but they determined exactly which part of the city they would be allowed to live in, which was not so good. To many, it was a way to let off some of the pressure of the market demand for housing by middle-class Black families while still keeping the races separate.

There we were in our classrooms watching it happen all around us, and to us. Our school was integrated, as were the public schools nearby, although the integration statistics changed year by year as white families left the area. But that didn't mean that Black families could buy houses anywhere they wanted. We studied the issue in civics class, and after school we started a social action club that wrote and mimeographed leaflets supporting the proposed Fair Housing Act, and we handed them out door-to-door in the immediate neighborhood.

To idealistic young teens, this was noble work. I don't know what our parents thought. My own parents were brought up under segregation, my mother in a whites-only farming county and my father in a farming village where white and Black people mingled daily but with a clear class distinction. In 1967, they were already middle-aged, and my father was ill. The mixed threat of "the freeway" and "the Blacks" must have kept them up nights, worrying about where they would go if their primary investment, our paid-off house, lost its value. But they never said a word to me about Fair Housing being unfair to them.

There was talk on our block about Black families buying houses closer and closer to us. But all of our neighbors said "we aren't selling, we are staying here," and so everyone felt like nothing would change on our block. Or so it seemed to me. I was probably nine when I heard that line, and I almost always believed adults. Meanwhile, Black families did start moving into nearby neighborhoods. On the street, hanging out with neighborhood kids, I began to hear language I had never heard before, hateful language. Sometimes rocks went through windows, and sometimes the houses mysteriously caught fire and burned to the ground. Or not so mysteriously: one neighborhood kid in particular always "knew someone who knew someone" who had lit the match. That was what happened to the family of the girl named Imogene, who briefly lived a few blocks away. Hers was not the only family that moved out in the night, or was burned out, and was never seen again.

Back to the Walshes. Mr. Walsh is the one I remember insisting the loudest that they were going nowhere. When the For Sale sign went up in their front yard, I was still young enough to be puzzled but old enough to begin to wonder if he was making sure that they got their money and got out first. I just don't know. They did have that lake house, and they were retirement age, and, well, it's complicated. They sold the house, which was about the same size as ours but on a double lot with a garage and a lovely screened porch, to a woman who lived in a different part of the city. She rented it to a young white couple with three young kids, and I got my first babysitting jobs. That couple soon divorced and moved away, and I got a new client, another white couple with twin toddlers. The dad sometimes came home soused, something I had never seen in my thirteen or so years.

Their house had gotten just a bit run down by then, with plumbing problems and a torn screen that flapped in the wind. That was new to me too, something broken and not immediately repaired. Then one morning before dawn, a house-moving truck appeared and deposited an entire house on the open lot that had been flower garden. Once it was placed on a new foundation, it was rented to a Black family with several kids, who immediately started hanging out with other kids on the block. Black families living in our neighborhood was normal by then. The only things that stood out about the house were that it had two stories and no driveway, both anomalies in that area. Meanwhile, the neighbors next to us moved away and rented their house to another neighbor's newly married daughter. Another family moved and rented their house to another young couple. The moved-away owners seemed to lose interest in maintaining the properties, which took on the look of rentals (sagging gutters, peeling paint). Maybe they were busy with their new suburban houses, maybe they were waiting to see if the freeway was coming through, maybe they didn't think anyone cared. Gradually the renters changed from mostly white families to mostly Black families. The transition occurred peacefully on my block, once the kid "who knew someone" moved away. Burnouts still happened, but farther away now.

As more families on Montgall moved away and houses were razed for the freeway, crime in general increased. Drug deals in the empty houses, break-ins nearby. One night I woke to the sound of breaking glass. Peeking through the curtains, I could see someone smashing a window in the house next door, where a young mother lived with her eight-year-old son. I'm embarrassed to say that I woke up my parents before I called the police. By the time they got there, mother and son had run out the front door and down the street. The burglar broke through the back door, took the mother's purse, and ran off through the backyard. Maybe he knew about the gap in the back fence, which we would slip through and then go down a driveway to get to the next street, instead of walking around. I didn't recognize him, so maybe he didn't know. What I know is that Kevin and his mother never spent another night in that house. They moved in with a relative in another part of town and we only saw them once more, when they came to pack up their things. Kevin's mother was heartbroken. "We finally got to live in a house, with a yard and kids for Kevin to play with," she told my mother. "I had this dream that I'd buy the house and we could stay put. But now? I just can't."

As a high schooler, I was beginning to see that the Fair Housing Act may have opened up more housing choices for Black families, but it was already clear that they were not necessarily able to buy their homes or live safely in them. Of course, in that particular part of town, the freeway plan was still lurking. Maybe those neighbors who moved but held onto their houses and rented them were hedging on the freeway buyout bringing more cash. Maybe it didn't happen the same way in other areas.

But I was noticing another thing too. Walking home from my high school, it was clear that the change was happening east of Troost and mostly east of Prospect. I noticed, but it didn't really register with me for a long time that what I was seeing was a deliberate act, quiet policies at work keeping west of Troost white while east of Troost was allowed to "turn Black." I figured it out in college, studying sociology and political science. But I still assumed that it was the unrelated work of real estate companies and banks, not a concerted effort. Only much later did I hear the term "East of Troost" and "the Troost Wall" and discover that it wasn't just a direction, it was a thing, it had a name, and it was a disgrace.

Well, it was and it wasn't. It did not work out so well for my parents, and it did not work out well for many of the first Black families who were courageous enough to face white fear and sometimes outrage and actually move into white neighborhoods. Let's just say that it was an unequivocal disgrace but that it did eventually open up one affordable neighborhood to Black home ownership. At the same time, other factors were at work. Larger, newer houses were being built farther out. Many white families had outgrown what were by this time considered starter homes, and with more choices available to them, some would have moved on anyway. The World War II housing shortage was well over. And that's fine. But the suburban option (and the west of Troost option) was still a white-only option open to those who had equity because they had not been denied the right to buy a house a generation earlier.

My parents stayed put for a long time, probably because the house was paid for, my brother and I were still in school, and my dad was too old to find a job somewhere else. They stayed until my brother was drafted, I went off to college, and my dad was old enough for Social Security. At that point most of their friends were gone. The elderly widow who lived behind us was constantly troubled by petty thievery and at least one break-in. A block to the west, houses were being bought and torn down for the coming freeway. The cloverleaf at Gregory was not in the plan, or at least not in the land acquisition plan. So my parents called a real estate agency and began the long process of selling up. When they finally found a buyer and jumped through all the hoops to qualify the buyer for an FHA loan, they moved three hours away to a small town in the Ozarks. The house they bought there was smaller and in much worse condition, but it was all they could afford with the proceeds from the sale in Kansas City. They made a new life and were happy enough there, but it still breaks my heart.

The timer goes off just as the doorbell rings, as familiar as if I've heard it every day of my life. Simultaneously, Boris barks and moves into the living room. I jump, heart racing. Cookies! I fumble for something to use as a potholder and take them out of the oven.

"Hello?" I hear knocking and jump again. Oh! Doorbell! *Wait, the doorbell doesn't work.* Well, someone is at the door. I run to the door. Well, walk fast—it's not far enough to get up to a run.

"Sorry about that. I didn't realize the doorbell worked," I say, sounding ridiculous.

"Well, maybe I can take a look. I'm Jimmy, the guy you called about a ceiling job."

"Of course. Come in. Thank you for coming." I step aside to let him in. "You can see the problem right here."

He looks up. "Yes, you got a problem there. I was looking at your roof—it's new?"

"Yes, the last owners replaced it before I bought the house. I couldn't face a leaky roof."

He looks at me for a couple of seconds and takes in the failed plaster, the smell of baking, and the fact that a middle-aged white woman has bought this house. He may be surprised, but he doesn't quite show it.

"Well, the roof looks good. Dry in here?" He peers at the ceiling again, reaches up, and feels the lath where the plaster has fallen away. He's a tall man, but then the ceiling isn't all that high.

He doesn't wait for an answer from me.

"Feels dry, and all this rain we've had—it would be wet by now if the flashing leaked around that chimney." He nods his head at the corner where I know the chimney to be. I wonder how he knows.

"I can take it all down and put up sheet rock, or just patch this area. Whatever you like." And he tells me how much it will cost, just like that. I'm surprised, then not surprised. It's a small room and absolutely regular, no fiddly corners or anything. He knows what drywall costs and what it takes to put it up.

"What about insulation? Isn't the lath holding it up?" I ask.

"It was, but it looks like some of it has come down." He pokes at the hole again.

"Looks like you've got some old rock wool and then some pink foil-faced on top of it. I'd want to go up and take a look, make sure the flashing is alright. I can see if any of the insulation is still wet while I'm up there. With it open like this, it probably dried out, long as the heat's been on." A question in his eyebrows.

"Um, I don't know." I'm embarrassed. "I just moved in this week." I walk over and check the thermostat. "It's on and set at sixty. I guess it's been warm enough this week that it just hasn't come on." I nudge it up until I hear the whoosh of gas lighting, then wait for the sound of air moving in the ducts. I keep my poker face on, pretending that I'm not worried about whether the furnace works or doesn't work or will explode or gas us. I'm glad I've left the door open.

He has his poker face on too, but I can see that he is processing the fact that I have just moved in. I'm not sure if he's wondering why a middle-aged white woman whose accent is not quite Kansas City would move into this neighborhood, or if he's puzzling over my definition of "moving in," given the utter lack of furniture and decor. There is the table and one chair in the kitchen (the other chair is off somewhere filling in as a table), and I'm sure he can smell the freshly baked cookies, but still. I've looked in the mirror and I know it's a stretch. He definitely thought I was the landlady and not a particularly well-heeled one.

I give him a wry grin, hunch my shoulders a bit.

"Well, your price sounds okay. I'd sort of like to just take it all down now and be done with it. Would you leave the lath?" I've moved on to business-like.

"That's what I would do, but I could patch it if you'd rather. Patching's a bit cheaper. There are some other cracks, though."

"Let's drywall the whole thing then. Do you want to go up in the attic? I have to admit that I have never been up there." I wonder why I said that. Why on earth would I have gone up there if I've lived here only four days? I'm not ready to tell him my whole story.

"Sure. Where is the access?" He's looking around for the hallway or maybe a closet. I lead him to the giant cupboard and open the door.

"You have to climb up in this cupboard first. Let me get a chair."

"Interesting, I've never seen one like this. Sometimes there's a pulldown somewhere."

"Yeah, I think my parents thought this would be a good place to store big things like suitcases and my dad's army footlocker. It's not like we actually used the attic—it's too low, I think. Like I said, it never occurred to me to go up there. I can't even remember what the hatch is like. Although I did see that it's missing." And there I am telling him my whole story but in a completely unintelligible way.

He shakes his head, gives me a questioning look. "So, you just moved in?"

"Well, *back* in. My folks left around 1975, after my dad retired. I was already grown and gone. I've just come back to Kansas City and I thought . . . well, I thought I'd like to live here again." Maybe I can just shut up and not go into all the details. I smile and shrug, trying to give him a clue that he doesn't have to pursue this topic. On the other hand, he's in and out of all kinds of people's lives. Maybe he collects stories. Also maybe this story isn't all that interesting compared to some things he's heard.

He produces an "Ah" that could mean anything and steps up on the chair and into the opening, then pulls the chair up into the cupboard with him. He whips out a giant flashlight that I immediately covet, steps on the chair, and shines the light around. His voice is lost now, but he may be pointing out that the chimney is in the old part of the house and that the old exterior wall is between him and it.

He hoists himself up, and I can hear creaking as he moves around. A minute or two later, he's back.

"Well, the flashing is tight at the chimney and the plumbing vents, and it's pretty dry up there. We might give it another week or two, though, and maybe you could run the furnace a bit at night to hurry it along. Or you could put a fan in the living room and point it at the ceiling." He looks around as if a fan might appear in the emptiness. Or as if I am a long way from owning any kind of fan.

"Okay, good. I'll do that." I don't say which one I'll do but I'm thinking that I will want a fan sooner or later anyway. "When would you like to start? Do you have a standard contract?"

He grins and shakes his head. "Give me half down when I deliver the drywall and the rest when it's finished." Then, "I can paint it for you too, if you get the paint." He knows I have no painting equipment.

"It's a deal," I tell him, and reach out to shake his hand. "Will you take a check?" I don't mind a cash arrangement, I'll just need to have enough on hand.

"Sure," he says, "long as it's local." He grins in a way that makes me suspect that he has figured me out.

"I'll see you in two weeks, then," I say.

He nods. "Your dad did a good job," he says, and lets himself out. I wish I had offered him cookies, but I don't go after him. I'm relishing his last comment.

He wants a local check, and of course I'm going to need a local bank. The internet is not helpful. Or rather it is helpful, it's just telling me there isn't much to choose from. When I was eighteen and got my first real paycheck and income-tax-withholding sort of job, I opened a checking account at Suburban Bank, a few blocks away—on Prospect, of course. I closed it three years later when I was living in an apartment in St. Louis. I didn't really expect my old bank to be on Prospect anymore, and I wasn't sure it even existed. A lot of banks have merged, changed names, and folded. Suburban Bank seems to have vanished, leaving not even a Wikipedia entry detailing its demise.

No big deal. I was just curious anyway. I am mostly looking for FDIC coverage and a convenient location at this point. There is only one choice, a Bank of America in the general area of the hospital campus. I'll drive by the ATM to decide if it is in a place I'll feel safe collecting cash or if I just need to drive farther every time I need money.

I sit down with some cookies and coffee and get out my lists.

"Check BoA ATM" gets added to the list, along with "buy toaster." Peanut butter sandwiches are fine, but peanut butter toast is a basic human need. Then I reluctantly add vacuum cleaner to the shopping list. I've been going back and forth about that. I have alternately wanted a shop vac (*for the basement, plaster debris*), a cordless hand vac (*for the cupboards*), and a regular floor vacuum cleaner. I waver. I don't want to spend money on three appliances to keep 798 square feet clean. But I can't see going after the basement dirt with a household vacuum, and a shop vac certainly won't do upstairs. A hand vac would do upstairs for now, along with a broom and dust mop, but eventually I'll want a rug or two that will need vacuuming. And the moment I turned on the furnace and smelled its unmistakable dusty odor, I knew I needed to vacuum the floor vents and the cold air return. I could attack the basement with broom and dustpan for now and then decide on a shop vac later. So now, which to buy? And why do I find this so hard?

I should have set a timer to keep myself out of the rabbit hole that is online product research. Time melts away while I ponder features and reviews. Too many cookies later, I have my answer. I make notes on what I intend to buy at Target, the closest biggish retailer, and head off to see if the hardware store has anything reasonably close. I need a rake too, before I can deal with planting those new tomato seedlings. Since all of my destinations are pretty close to home, I cruise past the bank first. Wow, bright and shiny and in the middle of a large parking lot, next to a chain drugstore in the middle of its own large parking lot. Maybe they were paving a safety zone, but to me it looks godawful. No one will ever walk to this bank. But it will do for me, and there is no time like the present, so I go in and open a checking account. No, I don't need a credit card to go with that. And I don't need a safe-deposit box, either. Then I remember the pile of ash in California and the difficulty that was causing me for things like next year's taxes. I rent the box. I've got nothing to put in it other than the deed to the house and the extra copies of my husband's death certificate, but even that will be safer there. I'll also try to back up my personal files on a thumb drive and put that in occasionally. I've learned my lesson there too.

My new best friend at the hardware store shows me the garden rakes, and I go for sturdy. Rakes should last a long time. I briefly remember the pile of junk in the basement and wonder if I should have looked through that first.

"I need to check something before I buy this," I say, realizing as I say it that it sounds like "I'm going to go home and buy this from Amazon." So I add, "I just remembered that there are a lot of things in the basement that I haven't had the courage to look through."

Maybe he believed that.

"I definitely need a vacuum cleaner, though," and I explain my quandary.

The man knows his stuff and convinces me pretty easily that buying all three is not a luxury, especially given what I have taken on, buying a decrepit house with piles of junk I haven't even looked at yet. His prices are good. I feel ridiculous for worrying so much about such a trivial thing and also ridiculous for buying three vacuums when I have only four pieces of furniture and not even a microwave. He carries only shop vacs, so I buy one from him and will find the others elsewhere.

"The big trash pickup day around here is usually in July, if it's too much for regular trash day. And I've got a kid who can help you haul it out if there's a lot. He's usually up for making a little extra cash."

"Oh, thanks. Does the kid mow? He'd have to have his own mower. . . ."

"That he does. I'll send him over on Saturday. Tomorrow, maybe nine o'clock if he's up. His name is Matt."

At home, I have a small panic that I've burned through five days and will have to log in and start working again on Monday. I need a list of what has to be done before Monday. Technically, I can log in and work: I've got a table, a chair (now with cushion), a telephone, an internet connection, and my laptop. Also a lamp, although a desk lamp would be nicer. But the idea of spending entire days in the fairly dark kitchen depresses me. A work table of some sort, and maybe an actual desk chair suitable for hours of sitting, are prime needs. I can work in the back part of the house, looking out at my back yard, which may be messy but is at least green. A vintage furniture store called Urban Mining keeps coming up in my internet searches, so I decide to try it for furniture and maybe Target for a microwave. I'll do that tomorrow.

Once the lights are all on in the basement and the missing bulbs replaced, I see that yes, it's messy too. I'm tickled that someone has spray painted the "ceiling," which is really the floor beams and subfloor of the upstairs. It's now white, or white with an overglaze of cobwebs. But I can see that it does make it a little lighter down here. I take the broom and start poking, moving things around, assessing the extent of the dirt and debris. I start shoving lighter things in heavy-duty trash bags and stacking heavier things to carry up in boxes. I'm clearing out the laundry and shower quarter first, staging the junk near the bottom of the stairs. It's going to take a lot of trash bags. I'll have to check the city website again for details on getting rid of this. Or maybe I'll have to hire someone with a truck to make a run to the dump. Leaning against the wall in a corner of the workshop area are some poles that turn out to be a cracked snow shovel, a garden rake with a split handle, some bent and broken curtain rods, and a hoe. Cool. I've got my rake. I'll just need to tape the handle. They all are dirty, but they are now mine. I take the hoe and rake upstairs and lean them next to the back door, then go back down to survey my trash pile and think about how to get it to the dump.

Ah, the dump. It used to be just a few miles south. In the days when garbage collection really meant just garbage, we burned paper trash, saved newspapers for the Boy Scouts, and kept empty cans and bottles in cardboard boxes until it was time for a dump run. On a Saturday morning, we'd load up the trunk of the car and head for the dump. Dad worked long hours, so we didn't have much time with him during the week. I guess any outing with him on a weekend was an adventure we were up for. And Mother got a bit of time to herself. By the mid-sixties, trash burning was banned, the weekly garbage collection became trash collection, and the dump runs ended. We'd outgrown them by that time anyway.

CHAPTER 6

I wake to low barking from Boris and the slam of a car door very close to my head. I peek outside through a space in the crappy miniblinds. There is a car in the driveway next door, only a few feet away from my bedroom. It's a few feet lower, but it sounded like it was in my room.

I realize that I have never seen anyone next door and never seen or heard a car in the driveway. I can't remember if I have seen any lights, but then I haven't spent much time on this side of the house.

Two people get out; they look like a couple, both a little younger than me. They go up to the door and apparently ring the bell, since they don't disappear inside right away. Moments later, I hear voices and then the window shade on the living room window, which is directly across from me and my miniblinds, snaps up. I see the couple and an older woman.

I suddenly feel like a voyeur, or at least a snoop, and I jump back, which means I hit the bed and fall down, luckily onto the bed since it takes up most of the room. *Geez.* I get dressed and hit the button on the coffee maker, feed Boris. He wants out, so I take my coffee and go out the back door, into the dewy yard. I take my rake and poke around in the weedy sprouts along the chain link fence, still hoping to find a peony or an iris peeking out of the ground. I also want to make sure there aren't any hazards when Matt gets here with the mower.

After five days, I've stopped worrying about fencing Boris in, as long as I'm out here with him. As usual, he's sniffed around, peed, and sauntered over to catch up with his pals in the pen next door. I pivot away from the thought that he knows more neighbors than I do. I hear a screen door opening, and voices. The people next door—I have forgotten already. I scurry over to call Boris back. I don't know if he considers that yard his territory now and will want to defend it. He's just watching them, though, tail waving slowly. The couple I had seen earlier is helping the older woman down the two steps to the carport. Boris heads toward them as though he knows them. The other dogs are watching, tails wagging.

"Boris," I call softly, not wanting to startle anyone.

The older woman looks up, and the others spin around to face me.

"Oh, hi," I say from about fifteen feet away. These yards are so much smaller with people in them. "I, uh, I've just moved in. Sorry about the dog." By now Boris is sniffing the older woman's hand, and she is petting him. The others are staring at me. They are processing the fact that a middle-aged white woman in jeans and t-shirt, holding a coffee mug and a rake, is looking down on them from a yard that their eyes tell me has not been occupied in their presence before. Or maybe that's not it at all, but I am going with that for now.

"Oh!" the younger woman says. I wonder how we would get by without the all-purpose "oh" to fill these gaps.

"Well . . ." Another useful filler.

"We, uh . . . I mean, welcome! I didn't know anyone was moving in. It's been empty for so long. After. . . . And the roof. . . ." She trails off again. I know now that there is a story, but I don't know if I'm going to get it just yet. I will let her off the hook for now.

I go for the elevator speech about why I'm here and give them the high points: I arrived on Monday, the previous owners had agreed to replace the roof before they sold it to me, and I lived here a long time ago and just felt like coming back. Now they know that I own it and am living in it and I have a history here. That's enough for now. It may or may not reassure them that I'm a suitable neighbor. Time for a new topic.

"Boris seems to have made friends with your dogs." I smile and nod toward Boris and the older woman. Dogs are an easy topic. "He's friendly," I add for no good reason, since it's abundantly obvious that he's not going to take a bite out of anyone.

"Oh, those aren't our dogs. I mean, not my mother's dogs, either." Clearly we are both trying to get our thoughts together. I wish I weren't standing two feet higher, that can't be helping, but it seems wrong to hop down into the other yard.

Now it's my turn to look befuddled. I hope she's going to finish the paragraph and tell me whose they are, and maybe we can work this into a more normal conversation.

"They seem friendly," I say, encouragingly, although I have not actually gone over to the pen, not knowing whose yard I'd be trespassing in.

"They belong to the guy back there." She nods toward the house behind. "He has a garden in his yard, so he keeps them over here when he's at work. He takes them home at night. Mom likes having them. She gives them treats and talks to them sometimes."

"Sounds like a great arrangement," I say, not adding "and the last thing I was expecting." I want to say, "Hey, let's just fence both yards and let all the dogs run around together," but that's pretty presumptuous. Besides, she's still talking.

"He put in a gate on his side."

Her gate comment reminds me that long ago, when the fence was new, there was a gate between my yard and hers, with steps down to their carport. I start to say this, but realize it's a dead end and may somehow seem creepy, as if I want access to their carport again. They haven't even told me their names yet.

The mother must have read my thoughts. "I'm Josie Fawcett," she tells me. "You must have thought no one lived here. I just got back home after a hip replacement. These two think I'm still an invalid but I'm fine. Six weeks in rehab—that was wonderful, having maids and meals fixed. But I'm glad to be home. And I'm real happy to have a neighbor again."

I'm feeling better, like I've passed a test.

"I'm Sue, and this is my husband Joel. We live in Columbia."

I smile and nod and start to say that it's so nice to meet them all, when a car door slams and we all turn toward the street.

"Oh, it's Matt. He takes care of Mom's yard." It's always a yard here, I've noticed. Not a lawn. That works for me because my yard is a long way from lawn.

I can't see him, but they apparently see him walk toward my door instead of toward them.

"Is Matt doing your yard too?" This from Joel.

"Yes, if it's the same Matt. I talked to his dad, I think, at the hardware store the other day and he said he would send him over on Saturday." I'm assuming today is Saturday. I'm a little confused at this point.

"I'd better go meet him. I hope he likes dogs." I go around the house, on the side away from them, because there is no gate in the fence between my front and back yards on their side. I roll my eyes. There are no gates on either side now, and not much fence either. Muscle memory, I guess.

Matt is tall and skinny and looks barely fifteen, but he must be at least sixteen since he's driving a truck. He's clearly the hardware-store guy's son. Same build, same eyes and smile. He tells me who he is and asks if this is a good time.

"I mow next door too," he says, nodding toward Josie's house. "I can do that one if you aren't ready yet." Very polite for a sixteen-year-old.

"Now is fine. Oh, and this is Boris—are you okay with dogs?" He's already nose-to-nose with Boris, scratching behind his ears, so he doesn't bother to answer.

"There isn't much to mow in front, huh?" I point out the obvious. A multi-trunked tree, or maybe it's an overgrown shrub, is growing in the middle of the yard, shading out whatever grass would be growing there. It's flowering at the moment, but I don't recognize it at all. It's tall enough to shade the porch a little, which I think I'll be grateful for in the summer. But it's also blocking the view and looking a bit out of place.

"So maybe just around the edges," he says.

"Yes, that would be great. I might trim this thing up some. I haven't decided." He doesn't offer an opinion on that, so I gesture toward the back.

"Mostly I want to get the back mowed before it gets out of control." We walk down the drive and around the corner of the house. The neighbors are petting the dogs in the pen and feeding them treats, so Boris abandons us.

"I poked around and didn't find any flowers or anything," I tell him. Then I backtrack: "I just moved in, maybe you knew that."

"Yeah, I figured. It's looked empty for a while." He doesn't elaborate, so I go back to the business at hand.

"So, anyway, don't worry about mowing anything down, just do what you can. I'll figure out these bushes later. Also, I've picked up cans and whatever else I found in the grass, but you might keep an eye out. I could have missed some things."

"Yeah, I'm ready for that." I see that he has goggles hanging on a tool belt.

"So, the only other thing is back here. There used to be a toolshed here; you can see the concrete doorstep. And behind that was a little vegetable garden, so the soil may be loose." I should have checked that already. I still have my little six-pack of tomatoes to plant.

"No worries. I'll get started," he says, and names his price. Well, he doesn't exactly name it. He asks if it's okay.

"That sounds good to me. I'll just pay you now." I was thinking I'd pay him and then I could go on with errands, but I decide to stick around just in case he runs into something, literally or figuratively.

I call Boris and we go inside. I take the cash out to Matt then refill my coffee mug and start the washing machine.

I don't have many clothes because I didn't want much to move and I didn't want to decide what to wear every day. I've reverted to schoolgirl days, when I wore a uniform and never thought at all about what to wear. In college, I might as well have worn a uniform, since I was always in bell-bottom jeans and a T-shirt or a thrift-store flannel shirt. You could wear basically the same clothing for days and no one would notice. By the time I was ready for the working world, the pivot to dressing for the office caught me off guard. I had no style skills at all. Zero. Pair that with an extreme lack of options for a tall woman (basically, it was Lane Bryant's Tall Girl catalogue or make it myself), and the result was adequate but dull. It's probably a key factor in my inability to take the business world by storm, or at least it's a good excuse.

So I have the jeans I was wearing when the house burned down, plus a second pair of jeans and one pair of all-purpose black pants. The duplicate pair is in the ash heap. Plus five T-shirts (black, white, and shades of blue) in short, long, and three-quarter length sleeves. Underwear, a couple of sweaters, and a hoodie. Socks, hiking boots I was wearing on fire day, sneakers, and a pair of flip-flops. When I list them like that, they seem like plenty. But the jeans and t-shirts get dirty pretty quickly these days, so I need to wash them often. I also need to buy some summer clothes—it's pretty warm today. The sound of the washer makes me happy—it was such a relief to find it working. Maybe I can hang things outside to dry once the mowing is finished.

It doesn't take Matt long to finish both yards. I offer him a cold drink, but he declines and tells me to let him know if I need him to mow again or want help hauling trash. He gives me a card with his phone number and email address. It's bright green and says, "Matt's Mowing and Math."

"Mowing and Math?" I ask.

"Yeah, I'm a math major at UMKC. I tutor on the side. There's not much mowing in the winter."

Okay, so he's not sixteen.

"Oh, and I think that garden area was used lately. There's something sprouting that looks like marijuana. I can spade it up for you if you like, but I just left it for now." I must look like the aging hippy I sort of am, and his diplomacy is impeccable.

Matt takes off and I have a look at my potential cash crop. Marijuana is certainly not legal in Missouri. I wonder if the marijuana crop has anything to do with the whisper of past trouble I heard in Sue's comments. Seems pretty lame in the scandal department. If someone was serious about growing, there would have been fluorescent lights in the basement and all the basement windows would have been boarded up to hide the 24-hour-a-day grow lights.

Anyway, I'm not interested, but if someone bothered to plant any kind of crop last summer, the soil should be easy enough to dig up for my tomatoes. I wonder now exactly how long the house was empty. Whoever planted this apparently wasn't around to harvest it, since it must have gone to seed and self-sown the current crop.

Gardening is a good Sunday afternoon activity. I've got errands to do today.

I pass the hardware store on my way to look for furniture, and I see a sign in the window that I had missed before: BEDBUG SUPPLIES. Drug bust forgotten, I immediately wonder if my house was abandoned because of bedbugs. I can't risk used furniture. Worse, the bugs are probably still in the house. I've read that they can live for months without feeding. Or maybe that's ticks. Still. But they have had five nights to find me—can I assume I'm safe?

Okay, I'll go to Surplus Sales first and then maybe go to Urban Mining. I like that it is family owned and lists both office chairs and microwave ovens on its web site. It's a bit of a drive, but I find the chair and microwave I want. The chair costs a little more than most, but I want one that adjusts a little higher than many of them do, and I'm not going to find that used. I want a microwave that fits the space at the end of the counter, under the overhead cabinets where a metal breadbox used to sit. And it has to have a silent setting, so I can turn off the beeps when I'm reheating coffee while talking on a conference call. When I tell the clerk these things, I feel like a secret shopper giving her a test, but she doesn't bat an eye. She takes me to the microwave that fits my critiera, I pay, and she even gets someone to load my new things in the car. It's a tight fit, so a work table is out of the question for today. Well, I can work at the kitchen table for the first week. By then I'll be over the bedbug scare (*or else deep into remediation*) and might be willing to risk a used work table. It's not like I'm planning to buy a used bed or sofa.

I lug the chair and microwave into the kitchen. I bounce on my desk chair, remove the tags, and read the instructions for all the adjustments. They are rudimentary, mostly directing me to a website. That's a new one—a chair with a user manual so extensive that it's online. I test the microwave, make sure it heats water, set the clock, and mute the beeper. Then I wonder where to store the microwave manual. I'd file it if I had a folder and a file drawer. But I don't, although I instantly rethink my work table concept. Should I get a real desk instead, one with a file drawer? Or maybe a metal file box at a resale shop. A metal file box can't harbor bedbugs, can it? I drop the manual in the kitchen towel drawer, which has no kitchen towels in it because there are only two, and one of those is on the counter and the other is in the laundry.

Oh no, the laundry. It's getting pretty late to hang it outside, plus it seems to be clouding up out there. I hang it all in the basement, where it falls limply and wrinkly from the line. Not much chance these jeans will be dry by tomorrow. I want a dryer.

Upstairs, I sit down to have a talk with myself. About money.

When my husband died, our finances were in bad shape. That was an appalling situation to me, because we were both well-paid and we were both frugal, the children of Depression-era parents who were taught early to spend wisely. Moving to California at age forty had been a carefully considered decision. He had a good job offer in Silicon Valley, and I could move with my company. We had enough equity in our existing home to buy a house we could be happy with. The mortgage was not onerous given our salaries, and we were not otherwise high maintenance.

Then he got sick, with a form of Parkinson's whose symptoms included an obscure form of dementia. He stopped going to work without telling me. He still left the house every day. His salary had been going into savings and mine into checking, which was the account I kept track of. Only when I went to pay the real estate taxes did I discover that he had not been paid for nearly a year.

At the same time, he was tweaking our investments, but not with the care he had previously put into that exercise. As a result, much of the money he had made over the previous years was gone. By then, I had to hire help to take care of him while I worked. I couldn't quit to stay home and care for him myself. We needed my health insurance. That, along with California property taxes and some remodeling to make it easier for him to navigate in a wheelchair, ate up most of our nest egg. Eventually, I stepped down from my management job into a staff position so that I could work thirty-two hours a week, enough to keep my insurance while giving me more time to cope with medical crises. By the time he died, the recession had reduced the value of our house to just about what was left on the mortgage. I had no equity. On a single income, I would have had to move anyway, and probably out of California, to someplace with a lower mortgage and taxes. By then I was telecommuting, so location didn't really matter, as long as I could occasionally get to an airport. I knew full well that leaving Silicon Valley would mean that I might never get my management job back, and I knew that I was at an age at which the odds of finding a new management job there were close to zero. So I'd already been thinking about where to move. A new place or a familiar one? Closer to family or to a new life in a new place? I gave myself a couple of months to settle the estate, file the taxes, and get through the first stages of my new reality.

And then the house burned down.

The fire was caused by a fluke during a January rainstorm. A branch broke off a neighbor's tree and got hung up on the high-voltage line. Water streamed down the branch, which blew back and forth in the wind, hitting the neutral wire below. Each time it hit, there was a small explosion, and voltage shot into my house (and one neighbor's house) on the neutral, something surge protection did not anticipate and could not block. Sparks shot out of electrical outlets. I called 911 about the fire on the power line, and they sent police, fire, and the power company. The neighbors came out to watch, Pacific Gas & Electric shut off power on the line, the fire team extinguished the flames, and everyone left.

I walked through my house, noting the outlets and appliances I would have to replace, including the microwave oven, the router, and worst of all my laptop. I called the local computer shop to see if they could retrieve my files. They said they would try, so I took the laptop and drove to the shop. I knew it would take a while, so I took Boris with me and went for a mind-clearing hike. By the time I got home with my files on a thumb drive, there was no home. Apparently in the confusion, someone—fireman, power company, a helpful neighbor—had turned off the gas and then turned it back on. The house filled with gas, and a smoldering outlet set off an explosion.

I had the clothes I was wearing, plus my wallet and phone. I had Boris and his leash. I had my VW station wagon and whatever was in it. Maps, mints, a first-aid kit, a coffee mug; I had a tire iron but no toothbrush.

All that misadventure had been like frugality steroids to my psyche. Friends took me in, but I was nervous about spending any money. I tried to keep up my work schedule because I was frantic about losing my job, losing my insurance. I worked thirty-two hours and spent Fridays coping with estate and insurance paperwork. I realized I needed professional help and contacted the local hospice, which set me up with grief counseling and financial counseling.

That saved me. We worked through the insurance claims and disposal of the property, all of which took a lot of time. The insurance company had to be sure I hadn't burned down the house because the mortgage was underwater (it wasn't, but it was in a dead-man's float) or because I was depressed. They had to assess the value of an ash heap. In that neighborhood, buyers often want to build new, so the ash heap shouldn't have been considered a problem, except that fire turns some household items into toxic waste that has to be remediated. While all that slowly perked along, the insurance company paid me for the contents. Thank goodness we had opted for replacement value. I got enough money to buy the house in Kansas City and furnish it. Plus I had most of my own retirement account and whatever was left of our diminished investments.

So I do have money, just not a lot. And I do have my job to return to on Monday. Facing me from across the table are all my worries and fears.

I let them all have their say: the worries, the fears, the needs, but also the little optimistic voice that points out how much is left of the insurance money that was always intended to allow us (*or now me*) to replace clothing, furniture, cooking utensils, rakes, books, rugs, serving spoons, and lamps. And a dryer. Fergodsake, the dryer that burned in California had been purchased in 1977 by my mother-in-law and we had inherited it when she died. I can certainly justify a new one.

I feel better now, and although it's getting late I call Surplus Sales and order a dryer. I don't even go there to look at one. I tell them what I want and they tell me what they have, and they promise to deliver it on Wednesday. I give them my address and ask if they deliver to that neighborhood. They say "yes," and I go out and pick up a rotisserie chicken and a bottle of wine to celebrate. I decide to have a little chat with myself every Saturday.

CHAPTER 7

I sleep a little later the next morning, maybe because of the wine, maybe because of the talk. I wake up feeling not quite so panicky. Mass at St. Louis Church is at ten o'clock. I pick through my clothes. The only dry pants are the black ones, and they are the only nondenim ones I own anyway. I have one clean sweater that isn't too wintery. Flip-flops are actually the dressiest shoes I have. At least they are strappy and black. It will have to do.

The drive is twenty minutes, so I leave at 9:35. I want to drive around just a little, look at the old school building and convent (sold long ago and now a residential treatment facility). I want to time my arrival for 9:59, so that I'm not late but also won't be trapped by an overzealous welcoming committee. In general, Catholic churches don't overdo the welcoming thing, but I want to be sure. I'm keeping my options open about church or no church, this church or some other one.

I have no idea that today is Palm Sunday.

As I drive north past the church on Swope Parkway, I see a mob of people on the steps and sidewalk outside the front door. Oh, no—big social event? Or am I late? Did Mass just get out? I'm an introvert. I don't do well walking into a crowd of strangers. I consider heading to Christ the King.

I make a U-turn at the old school building and head back on

the southbound side of Swope Parkway. I drive past the church again and realize that everyone is holding palms. Of course. So much for slipping in at the last minute.

I park and walk back, joining the edge of the throng and noting that it is a mixed bag of black, brown, and white faces. That feels safe. I'm greeted with a smile and a palm and no talk. The service has begun.

When I last attended Palm Sunday services here, I am pretty sure that Palm and Passion Sunday were separate events. I don't know when they joined them, probably while I was looking the other way, in college or early adulthood. However it came to be, I can appreciate the purposeful irony of celebrating both on the same Sunday.

We stand outside with the palms and listen to the Gospel story of Jesus riding into town on a donkey, met by hosannas and waving palms.

The Palm Sunday story complete, we process into the church and listen to the Gospel story of betrayal, indictment, humiliation, torture, and death, all in one week. I have had weeks like that, not so gruesome, of course, but alternating days of honor and humiliation. Sometimes I bring them on myself, sometimes they come from outside. Sometimes I cause others to glory or suffer. Some are better and some are worse. But I am not alone in this. You can believe the details of these stories or not, but the big picture is surely a basic human truth.

Without really planning, I had pictured myself sitting in the general vicinity of where my family sat, halfway up in the left section, near the outside aisle. In the Palm Sunday scenario, everyone just goes with the flow. I end up on the other side, about two-thirds of the way back. I manage to get as close as I can to the outside aisle. Just in case. Of what, I don't know.

I want to pay attention, but I can't help looking around. First I am struck by the shape. In my head, it was the long rectangular shape of most traditional churches. But it's actually almost square. The altar, the cross, wood paneling, everything about the sanctuary is as familiar to me as my own face. It's exactly as it was in 1964, when the post-Vatican II changes were complete, with the altar facing the congregation. The lights and the pews are the same. The Stations of the Cross are the same. The fans are still in place, high on the walls. There are new pictures of different saints, a minor alteration. Same floor, but I had completely forgotten that it was anything other than a standard church floor: wood or a bland terrazzo or carpet. This floor is a Moorish pattern of dark red, cream, and dark brown. I can't stop looking at it. It is familiar, but had vanished from my memory. Best of all are the windows. I'm a sucker for stained glass, and these were originally just opaque waves of yellow and white. I always thought we had been cheated. But now they are beautiful, true stained glass with deep rich colors. I am buoyed that they have managed to do this. I'm also happy to see that they have removed quite a few of the front pews. Most churches take out one or two to make space for wheelchairs. These guys have moved the band and choir up front.

I settle down and pay attention to the Passion Sunday readings and the rest of the service. The music is both modern and soulful. I feel like this is a good place for me. As the traditional service ends, it arcs off into louder and more emotional music and prayer. I sit back and let it wash over me. I need this.

After another forty-five minutes or so, the service seems to be ending and I start to slip out. Most people are staying, but I'm not the first to go. I'm feeling refreshed and don't want to tell my story. An usher is waiting with the parish bulletin. He hands me one and we exchange a few words in soft voices. He knows I'm not a regular, of course. I tell him only that I grew up here and that I'll be back. He smiles and nods and says that I will always be welcome.

Driving south toward Meyer Boulevard, I take a detour into Swope Park. I need this Sunday to be a day of rest in the traditional sense. I've had a long week and am exhausted emotionally and physically. I need a break before logging in tomorrow. A long walk in a park seems like a good idea, but I have no idea if it's safe, if it's done, if dogs are allowed. It's noon now, on a lovely spring Sunday. If ever the park is used, now would be the time.

I don't have to go far to see that it's full of people, kids, and dogs. I go home, make a peanut butter sandwich and an iced coffee with plenty of sugar and milk, and drive back with Boris for a long relaxing walk. We go at his pace, so we amble along, stopping a lot. I'm feeling better than I have for a long time.

The good feeling lasts until I drive up my street and see a car in my driveway. I drive past, turn around, park in front of the house uphill from mine, and get out my phone. I can see that my back door is open. I am almost panicking. I think—*this can't be something bad going on in broad daylight, can it?* Car parked in the driveway? This isn't how burglars operate, is it? But I'm not willing to face down anyone, even with a large dog. I dial 911.

While I wait for the cops to arrive, the dispatcher tells me to read her the license number on the car in the driveway and then to move my car a little farther away and stay in it with the doors locked. She wants my name, phone number, and vehicle description. I cringe when I give her my California license plate number, but she reacts as if every caller has an out-of-state license plate. She tells me that if anyone comes out, I'm not to look at them, and I should be prepared to drive away.

Two police cars arrive within an extremely long ninety seconds. Both park in front of my house, one blocking the driveway, the other in front of the first. They are SUVs, the big black kind with windows you can't see through. They clearly mean business. I find them intimidating but also reassuring.

Four cops get out. They are armed and in flak jackets, and they take their time. I have the feeling they want to be seen, they want whoever is in there to know that they have arrived. They don't want any panicked shooting, I suppose. Two cops go down Josie's driveway. One stops in my front yard, but well back from the door. The other is walking down my driveway.

I hear another vehicle behind me and look in the mirror. Another police SUV has parked behind me and a cop is circling the house uphill from me. Another one appears at my window. Boris growls softly, so I lower the window, only about an inch.

The cop asks if I'm the one who called. The dispatcher verifies that the officers have arrived and are talking to me, and she hangs up. I'm finding it hard to speak. I don't even want to look at the officer. My vision seems fraught, everything vibrating a bit. I take a deep breath. The officer at the window asks me a few more questions, things I've already covered with the dispatcher but maybe he's just trying to reassure me. He tells me they know who the car belongs to; that search was probably done as soon as I read the dispatcher the number. He tells me that they know the owner, implying that they have had business with him before.

"I don't think he's dangerous," he tells me, "but we need to be cautious. I'm going to stay here with you. I think the other officers are talking to him now."

Boris has stopped growling and is wagging his tail, which uses up most of the space in the car. I suppose he senses that I have calmed down. I open the back window a few inches, and the officer reaches in and scratches Boris's ear.

More voices, and two officers are walking out of my driveway with a thin, rather ragged man between them in handcuffs. He is talking in a loud and animated voice, but he isn't struggling. He has dirt on his face and cobwebs in his hair—no question he was in my basement. They say nothing and put him in one of the cars, then come over to talk to my officer.

"He's cooling off for a minute. He says that he lives here and is looking for his stuff." This stops me cold. "We know this guy, and he did live here at one time. He's been in jail for the last six months, but he claims that the rent was paid."

"Do you have proof of ownership?" one of them asks me. He's seen my license plate.

"I do, it's inside. I closed last Monday." Now I have a new reason to panic. What if this guy did pay the rent and the landlord sold the house to me anyway? What are his tenant's rights? How can I be in this situation? At least he's not a burglar. Although he could be. And the door was open—he has a key.

"Should I go inside and get it?"

Two officers stay with their car and my keeper goes in with me, leaving Boris in my car. Two cops are still in the house; they seem to be inspecting it thoroughly. Another one is in the back yard. Seeing my derelict living room and sparse furnishings through their eyes, I feel the urge to babble, but I keep my mouth shut. I find my closing papers and hand them over.

"What brought you here?" I can't tell if he's being conversational or suspicious.

I cut straight to the bottom line: "I grew up in this house and wanted to live here again." They all look at me. They seem to believe me. How could they not, it's not the sort of thing you'd make up.

One of them asks if I have a phone number for the previous owner. He takes it and goes outside.

Another one comes up from the basement and asks me questions about what's down there. I think it should be abundantly obvious that very little of what's down there could be mine, given the dirt and dust and cobwebs, but I take the questions as they come and answer them as simply as possible.

The backyard cop comes in and asks me if I know there is marijuana growing in the back yard. I come clean and tell him that I found out yesterday from a kid I hired to mow. It's obvious that the yard was just mowed, and that I have no mower. I think it's also obvious that the plants have been there since before last Monday. But I don't say any of that.

The basement and backyard cops leave by the front door, telling my keeper that they are going to talk to the guy. My keeper stays with me and we make small talk, mostly about the weather. I thank him for the quick response to my 911 call. I'm confident that they don't really suspect me of any wrongdoing, but I can't think what is going to happen next. Basement guy finally comes back looking cheerful.

He opens with "We've figured this out," which I think is a good start. I look up expectantly from my office chair, which I realize I've been rocking back and forth with nervousness.

It turns out that Mr. Forsythe, as they are now calling him, did indeed live here at one time, with a wife or girlfriend and her, or maybe their, child. He's been gone for more than a year, for reasons unknown or not relevant. He lived rough for a while, got into trouble, was in jail last summer and fall. He's been at the VA for the last six months. He got a part-time job and told the VA that he had rented this house. When his key didn't work, he got in through that basement window.

"I figured it out because there's a sort of skid mark in the dirt where he slid over the window sill," basement cop says. "And the pipes have cleanish marks where he grabbed them on the way down. Also, there are damp clothes on the floor by the window. I was pretty sure he didn't come over here to do laundry." He laughs. He knows they are my clothes. "I reconnected the clothesline, but your stuff is probably kind of dirty."

Great. I get to do laundry again and will have to wear the black pants for another day while the jeans dry. On the other hand, the perp doesn't have a key to my house. It's a reasonable tradeoff.

"So, what next?" I ask. "And can I get my dog?" Boris is probably in a panic by now, and although he's never damaged anything before, he's also never been tested this far. They tell me that they will book Mr. Forsythe for breaking and entering, and that I should let them know if anything is missing. They ask if I have a gun. They ask this in several different ways, and I finally realize that they want to make sure that he didn't find it and stash it somewhere to pick up later. I assure them that I don't, but I also point out that I haven't been through all the junk in the basement and can't vouch for what may be there. They all laugh and we go outside.

I needn't have worried about Boris. He's out of the car and hanging out with Josie in her driveway. The two of them are holding court with what must be everyone else on the block, plus two of the cops. Boris sees me but doesn't bother to check on me. He's clearly got better things to do.

My handler is talking so I turn back to him.

"Josie next door is feeling pretty bad about this," he is saying. "She's hated having this house empty for so long and now she's afraid you'll leave. Also, she thinks she should have noticed that something was wrong and called us sooner."

I am touched, and instantly become Josie's defender. "Well, his car is red too, and it is pulled in pretty far." His is fire-engine red and mine is dark red, but I'm ready to cut her a lot of slack.

"Um . . . what about his car? How do we get it out of here?" This can't be my problem.

"No worries. A tow is on the way. One of us will stay until they take it to impound. We have to sign for it." Well, yeah, duh. I'm glad they will be around a bit longer, at least until my heart stops pounding.

Someone starts talking on the radio in one police car, and two of the cops get in and take off, waving at the neighborhood gathering. The car with Mr. Forsythe in it takes off too. The tow truck appears and my officer goes to meet the driver. I cross the front yard and hop over the retaining wall into Josie's driveway.

"Hi, Josie," I say. I'm not quite sure where to start. About ten faces turn toward me. "Thanks for getting Boris out of the car."

"Oh, Michael did that. He wanted to make sure Bud knows you have a German Shepherd. Boris certainly looks like a police dog." My frazzled mind grasps that Michael is one of the cops and Bud is Mr. Forsythe. I am not sure if it's good that she's on a first-name basis with both of them, but she looks cheerful so I decide it is at least okay.

While I'm getting my brain to function in a social situation, Josie has started introducing the neighbors. I repeat the names hoping to retain them but knowing I won't. I'll drop in on Josie and get the full roster later. Mostly, I am feeling a little teary just to be standing in the sun surrounded by neighbors who seem happy to meet me, whoever I am and regardless of how I came to be there.

One of them, Dave I think his name is, tells me that he'll board up the basement window. Clearly they all have gotten the story from Michael the cop. Chances are, they know more than I do. Dave heads across the street to his house for tools. So now I can associate Dave with what was once the Hughsons' house.

It's a start. I give the crowd as much of my story as Josie already knows. She's probably just been filling them in, but hearing it from me means they can acknowledge it without implying that she's been gossiping.

Bud's car departs with the tow truck and the last cop comes over to me. My new best friends hang around to hear what he has to say.

"I'll be back sometime tomorrow to take a statement," he says. "You can let me know then if anything is missing. Here's my card if anything comes up before I get here."

I ask if he can come in the evening. I don't want to risk being on a work call and having to say that I have to answer the door because the police are knocking. That also lets everyone know that I'm working, although I may have to explain that I telecommute. We agree on five o'clock and he gives Boris a final scratch.

"See you tomorrow," he says. "Oh, and be sure to get that marijuana out of there."

I give him a look, then realize that I shouldn't give a cop "a look." And then I think, what the heck. The neighbors are laughing. I'm guessing that Michael already told them about the marijuana and that neither they nor the cops are surprised. My house has a history, and I'm confident that I'll get it from my neighbors. But not today. I've had enough input for one day.

Dave appears and tells me that no one will be getting through that window. I thank him profusely, but he waves me off.

"I feel real bad that this happened," he says. "We had no idea that anyone was moving in here. We saw your car but we didn't know if you were just cleaning it up or what. I should have come over and said hello before this."

I'm already overwrought and this makes me tear up.

"Well, I could have introduced myself," I say, with a little head waggle. I guess I'm ready to defend all my new neighbors, even against themselves.

The neighborhood meeting breaks up and I go inside to deal with the laundry and get out of the basement before dark. I tell myself that I'm going to get over my fear of the night-time basement soon, just not today.

Alone in the house, my skin crawls. The rooms feel alien. My mind wants to escape, but I can think of nowhere to go. I consider crawling into bed and pulling the covers over my head, but first I have to deal with the kitchen. Bud had helped himself to a snack, which creeps me out. I hate the idea that a stranger has been in my kitchen, taken food out of my refrigerator, maybe opened the cupboards and drawers.

The milk carton is open on the counter, and I picture him drinking from it. I pour out the milk and toss the carton. The bread is out too, the twist tie removed. I picture his hand in the bag. I really want toast. I remove a few slices and toss them. I still see his hand in the bag. I know it's silly, but I toss the bag. The peanut butter is out but the lid is still on. So I wipe it off and put it back in the refrigerator. I'll probably toss it in the end. I sigh but leave it. I scrub the counter and wipe all the knobs and handles in the room. It's only symbolic, but it helps.

Where else has he been? I peek in the bathroom, cringing as I look around. The toilet seat and lid are down, which tells me that he has not been in here. The bathmat, or rather the white rag I've designated as temporary bathmat, is undisturbed. The sink is dry and the towels appear to be untouched. I take them all with me to the basement, where I take everything off the line that was broken and restart the washer.

I'm not hungry, but I slice an apple and some cheese and sit down with the Sunday paper, hoping I can calm down enough to sleep.

Maybe it's the fact that cops had been all over my house, plus the fact that the perp was caught, and on top of that I now know some of my neighbors, but I do start to feel drowsy. Or maybe I'm beyond exhausted. I crawl into bed and try to clear my head. I remember the morning message of Palm Sunday, hosannas and disgrace. I tell myself that the good has outweighed the bad for me today. I have good neighbors and in spite of everything I feel more secure than I have since I arrived. Boris has had his best day in weeks, with both a long walk and a lot of new people petting him. He chases bunnies in his sleep on the floor next to me. Eventually I fall asleep too.

CHAPTER 8

I've set an alarm to make sure I'm logged in early for my first day back on the job. My boss, Cathy, is an old friend and knows of my recent tribulations, although not the fact that I'm living in what any of my co-workers would call squalor. I've made sure no one has my new home address. I don't want them driving down my street on Google Street View and making judgments.

I put on the same clothes I was wearing yesterday, reminding myself that I have to hang my wet laundry out to dry if I ever want to wear anything else. I head for the coffee maker and remember that I didn't go shopping last night. No milk, no bread. Also no actual grocery store within a mile. The closest store of any kind is an Xpress Mart at a Shell station. It will have to do.

I'm relieved to find this place. It's mostly a liquor store, but it's clean and the clerk is friendly. I get bread, milk, cereal, and bananas. I pick up a can of soup too, just in case. Good to have a few emergency rations. I race back home. Next time I'll walk. It's only four blocks, even if I do have to cross the expressway. It's directly across the street from the public school where I went to kindergarten, and I walked there by myself every day for nine months.

I can see that Cathy is logged in—she's one time zone east and also telecommutes—so I chat on line with her for a bit and let her know that all is going well (*everything is relative, right?*). We've agreed that I'll continue working thirty-two hours a week for the time being, although we both know that it will be more than that because that's how telecommuting is—you're always at the office. But however long I work Monday through Thursday, I'm officially not working on Fridays, with the time blocked out on my Outlook calendar so no one will schedule a meeting that I absolutely have to attend. Well, they will, but only once or twice. The list of things I need the Fridays for is getting longer. It starts with car registration and driver's license, moves on through things like notarizing signatures on unfinished business in California and investigating permits and regulations for fences and toolsheds. Finding a local grief counsellor is on the list too, but I don't write that down.

I have "All-Day Meeting" on my calendar for today so that I can slog through my backlog of email without any conference calls, and that has worked, except for Cathy's normal Monday staff call. I tell her I'll dial into that. The rest of the team members know I've taken two weeks off to move, but they don't know where. I also had two weeks off when my husband died, and two weeks after the fire, so I have to think that while they are very kind, they are probably a little tired of my absences. When anyone is missing, everyone else has to pick up some of the slack.

After the call, I concentrate on email and don't notice how dark it has gotten until I hear a crack of thunder followed by rain spattering the kitchen window. It's also chilly. I remember the laundry that is not drying in the basement and that I promised Jimmy the ceiling guy that I would run the furnace or at least a fan to dry out the living-room ceiling. I have not bought the fan, so I go into the living room to turn the furnace on, only to realize that the dust and dirt in the living room are just going to sneak off to the cold air return in the tiny hallway between the bedrooms and the bathroom.

By now it's almost noon, I'm hungry. I open the can of soup, pour it into one of my two bowls, and put it in the microwave. I am lucky that the can had a pop-top. I find my list and add can opener to it. While it's heating, I shop vac the ceiling, walls, windows, and floor in the living room. Now I am grateful that the room is so tiny and glad the hardware store guy talked me into the shop vac. I follow up with damp rags. This makes it 100 percent nicer in here and I wonder why I didn't do it sooner. I'm hot now from all that cleaning, but the thermostat says it is sixty-two degrees inside, so I turn on the furnace anyway. The shop vac goes back to the basement and I take the laundry out of the washer. I had completely forgotten that I was going to hang it outside this morning.

And now it's raining, so I smooth out the shirts as much as I can and hang them on hangers in front of the basement furnace duct. Mother had pounded nails into the joists just for that purpose, and they are still there, although a bit cobwebby. The jeans go upstairs on the bathroom towel bars. This is the best I can do until the weather clears or the dryer arrives on Wednesday.

By now my soup is cold, but thanks to my new microwave that is easily fixed. I make toast and sit back down at my computer. The furnace cycles, the email buildup shrinks, and my incoming email slows down as my colleagues gradually end their workdays.

At 5:00 p.m. sharp, a car door slams and Boris barks. I remember the cop and wait until he knocks, which reminds me that my intermittently working doorbell needs attention. At the same time, I remember that I didn't go through my pitiful collection of belongings to see if Bud took anything.

I open the door, trying to remember the officer's name. I can't quite picture it on his card, which I put in my pocket last night but can't very well pull out right in front of him.

"Officer Benning," I say, reading his name badge. He can see that I'm looking at it, but maybe he's used to flaky burglary victims. Or flakes in general. He steps in and I'm grateful that the living room is cleaner and warmer than it was yesterday, even if it's just as empty. It smells of Murphy's, which I'm beginning to love.

"Come on in to the kitchen. I'm holding off on furnishing this room until the ceiling is repaired," I tell him, adding "next week" as if that will make me seem like I have things under control. Of course, he's seen that most of my rooms are just as empty.

"I've seen it worse," he says, looking around the living room. I can't tell if "it" means my living room or living situations in general.

I offer him one of my two kitchen chairs, sitting down in my desk chair and pushing my laptop aside. I'm glad I've moved the remains of my lunch to the sink, but I'm realizing the benefit of a dishwasher as a place to hide dirty dishes. I wonder how my mother kept it all looking neat.

Officer Benning tells me to call him Carl and asks if everything is okay. I tell him that one of the neighbors secured the basement window and that I felt like they would be watching out for me. I said that Josie, in particular, seemed like a great neighbor. I was fishing a little.

"Oh, yes. Aunt Josie keeps an eye out," he says, with a big smile, sort of laughing to himself.

I give him a moment to continue along those lines, but he doesn't. I'm wondering if "aunt" is a term of respect or family relationship, and decide to pry a little.

"Oh, is she your aunt?" I ask, in a tone that I hope indicates that she fulfills my idea of a perfect aunt.

"My mom's cousin, or second cousin, I guess. It's easier to just call her my aunt."

"That's nice. My cousin's kids do that to me sometimes, and I like it."

Niceties complete, Carl opens the zip case he's brought with him and takes out a form.

"I apologize, but we need to take your official statement about what happened," he says. "We took notes yesterday, and I can have you sign those, but I want to go over it again now that you've had a chance to calm down. Sometimes it's hard to think clearly when you've just been confronted with a home break-in, especially since you've just moved in."

I see that he has switched to his business face. I wonder if there is something I don't know, or if he suspects something. I realize that this incident is not over, and I suddenly feel alone and anxious. Boris comes over and puts his head on my lap, and I scratch his ears. Carl reads from the notes, starting with my 911 call. He's got a complete transcript and asks me to read it and verify that it accurately represents my conversation to the best of my knowledge. I tell him that it does. I'm relieved to see that I didn't say anything too wacky.

He then reads me the other officers' notes detailing their questions and my answers. I tell him that I can't remember exactly what I said, but that it sounds okay. I'm a little concerned that the marijuana plants are in the record, but I think it's best not to call any more attention to that. I'm getting the sense that he is a little tense, which makes me even more tense. So much for his coming back when I'm calmer. I take a few slow, deep, quiet breaths. Carl is quiet, so I keep my mouth shut too. If I had gotten a clock, we'd be listening to it tick. Instead, the furnace kicks on.

Carl seems to come to a decision.

"This should be an easy case," he finally says. "We caught

Bud in your house, and it's obvious how he got in. He makes a pretty good case for why he targeted this house." He pauses.

"And all he did was have a snack, right?" he continues. "He didn't have anything in his pockets, just his own wallet and some change. We didn't find anything in his car that could have been stolen, and he didn't stash anything outside that we could find. Did you notice anything missing, or see anything outside that you had left inside?"

I told him I hadn't, and although I hadn't tried to inventory everything, there just wasn't very much. I had my phone and purse with me, and he didn't touch my laptop. I think about my extra key and go check. It's still on its nail in a cupboard.

"I really don't have anything else worth stealing," I tell him. "I hardly have anything, period." And I go ahead and give him the short version of my recent history of sickness and death and fire.

I can tell that he doesn't want to ask the next question, but I guess he has to: "Can you verify all of that?" He looks at me and sees . . . I don't know what he sees, but he does add "for the record." I guess I am relieved that he's asked a question with an easy answer. It doesn't feel as bad as he thinks it does. I sort of want to laugh and say, "You have no idea." But I stick with the serious demeanor. I've learned a lot about dealing with authorities in the last year.

"I can," I say, pulling my laptop toward me. It doesn't take long to find the main newspaper article about the explosion, which has a couple of photos of me. I spin the laptop around and show it to him.

"I can send you the link, or you can just search for my name and 'explosion'." I reclaim the screen and scroll down a few inches, then turn it back to him.

"Here is the name of the officer who responded. You can get records from him, I would think." I know the story references the

Parkinson's part of my history, and he can track that down on his own if he wants further verification.

He's looking a little embarrassed and sorry he asked, but isn't letting on. "Thank you. That should take care of it."

I've had twelve years of Catholic school, and I know how to press the guilt button. This is the moment to ask my own question.

"Of course you need to know who I am, but is there anything you're especially concerned about?"

He pauses before he answers.

"The judge is inclined to let him out on his own recognizance since nothing was stolen and he says that he lives here and that the house was empty. It's hard make the case that this place was obviously occupied." He swirls his eyes around the room. "The VA will take him in and find housing. But I have the feeling he's going to keep coming back here, and I am trying to figure out why, so we can make sure he doesn't come back."

I sigh audibly. Why couldn't this have been just a smash-and-grab crime?

"We've confirmed that you own it and that the former owners sold it to you legally and that his name was never on a lease if he did live here." He pauses again. "But also, he says that he knows you."

My modicum of cool drains away. "How could he? He didn't even see me. And I don't know anyone named Bud." I sputter, which gives my brain time to remind me that hysterics are valuable sometimes, but not here.

Carl is still cool. He looks me in the eye. "He may have been watching you this week. We don't know that, but we're going to ask around, see if his car has been here."

"And his name is actually Craig. Craig Forsythe. Do you know that name?"

I don't, but I tell him that I'm pretty sure there were Forsythes in either my grade school or high school. Or both.

He asks where I went to school and I tell him St. Louis grade school and Hogan High School. "Back when it was Bishop Hogan."

"Catholic schools," he says. I don't know if that's good or bad. It may just mean that he knows they've been closed for a while, and it might take some time to find school records.

"Well, I went to public school for kindergarten, but Blenheim is closed now too," I say, thinking but not saying that it wasn't just Catholic schools that were choked out by the freeway and the demographics.

"Yeah," he says, pretty much to himself, "I went to Hogan." He doesn't say if it was before or after it was no longer Catholic and the Bishop part was dropped. "All east of Troost." He says it; I don't.

He gets back to business. "You don't have your high school yearbooks, do you?"

I actually roll my eyes and look askance, hands out and palms up.

He half groans, half laughs. "Yeah, I guess not. Sorry." He sighs.

"One more thing. The judge isn't happy about those marijuana plants. Are they still there?"

"Not for long," I say. A little fresh air and drama are in order. I grab a trash bag from under the sink. "Care to watch?" Not a trace of sarcasm.

I grab the shovel from its spot by the back door and the three of us troop outside. Boris goes to visit his pals next door. Josie pops out her back door and waves, but then busies herself with the dogs. I use the shovel to chop up all the sprouts I see so that I can't possibly replant them after Carl leaves. I shovel them in the bag.

"Okay if I put this out for the trash tonight?" I'd just as soon not compost them. "And I do have those tomatoes to plant here." The sad little six-pack is sitting by the back door. He agrees, and I'm relieved that he doesn't want the weed for the evidence file. Although it's likely that the backyard cop took photos yesterday anyway.

He seems satisfied and his mood has lightened a bit. We go back in the house. I stay standing and ask if there is anything else. I'm hungry and my head is starting to ache.

"If we need you to, can you prove that you were not in Kansas City before last Monday? Or rather, demonstrate that you were someplace else?"

I mention my cousins in Joplin. He doesn't look like he thinks that cousins are trustworthy, but he takes their names and phone numbers.

"What about receipts? Gas, motels, food?"

I could have so easily spent cash for those things. Leaving California to drive east, I had been a little anxious about a big credit card bill. But when I got out of the car to pump gas at my first stop in Needles, a thought went through my head that I would be able to deduct moving expenses. If I hadn't just filed my previous year's taxes the week before, I might never have thought of it. And I knew that keeping paper receipts of cash purchases was a lost cause in my current frazzled state. I didn't even have an envelope and wouldn't know where to keep it if I did. Years of corporate expense reporting had taught me that a lost cash receipt is lost forever, but a credit card receipt is always somewhere on the internet.

"Yes," I say. "I don't know that I can collect all the paper receipts, but I charged everything, so they'll be online." I am really getting hungry, and I sigh with frustration. "I don't have a printer, but I could pdf them and email them to you. Or wherever."

He realizes that I am exhausted and he doesn't really think I am guilty of anything.

"Just hold onto it for now. I'll let you know if we need it."

"Okay, thanks," I say, adding "please go now" in my head. "And since tomorrow is trash day, can I take out everything in the basement that's bagged up?"

"Would you mind keeping it till next week?"

I do mind, but I say "no problem" in a way that I hope conveys "goodbye."

He walks toward the front door, then does that cop thing where they turn back and ask one more thing. Except he doesn't ask a question. Instead, he says, "This neighborhood has started to come around lately. People are feeling safer and more confident. So we're trying to check out everything that happens and make sure that. . . ." He doesn't finish the sentence. I wait.

"This property has been a bit of a problem. . . ." He doesn't finish that sentence, either, but he says, "You know what, talk to the neighbors. Better that they fill you in. Start with Josie."

He walks out onto the porch, and then he does the cop leaving thing one more time.

"Don't worry too much. This was all probably nothing. And I'll check in with you in a few days." With that, he really does leave.

Crap crap crap. Don't worry? Is he nuts? What is there to NOT worry about?

When I'm stressed, especially late in the day, I get a little manic about finishing up whatever needs doing. That's particularly true about dinner. I'll fix and eat whatever is easiest, then immediately clean up the kitchen, put everything away, as though neatness will protect me from something more than clutter. I get out the eggs and lettuce. Scrambled eggs over salad with a side of toast. Ten minutes tops.

Before the eggs are out of their shells, the doorbell rings. Boris doesn't bark. He just goes over to the door and wags his tail. He whimpers impatiently. That makes me suspect it's Josie, and it is.

"Honey, I just talked to Carl. Don't you worry. Things will be fine. You just come over some evening this week and we'll talk. Tomorrow? Come at seven. We'll have ice cream." It's almost but not quite an order.

I thank her, tell her I appreciate that a lot. And I do appreciate it a lot. But at the moment, what I appreciate most is that it's for tomorrow, not today. I need some time to process what I've just been through before I try to process anything else.

"You get some sleep. Nothing's going to happen tonight," she says and then leaves.

I slow myself down. I take my time washing the lettuce, making the salad. I break the eggs in a bowl and scramble them instead of just tossing them in the skillet and stirring them in the hot oil. I butter the toast carefully. I pour a small glass of wine. I sit down. And then I cry, just for a minute.

I eat the salad and the eggs, which are quite good, and sip the wine. I look around at my house. I don't know if this is going to work out or not. But at this exact moment, I don't need to know. I can't know. I ignore everything that has happened since Officer Carl walked in the door.

At Mass the previous morning, way back before any of this unfolded, the priest told us that Herod and Pilate were slaves of fear. They made decisions they didn't believe in, didn't want to make, because they were afraid. The context was different, but I decide that I am not going to be a slave to fear. The deep dark basement isn't much compared to unknowns that worry me right this minute, but it is here and now, and it is conquerable. I go downstairs, I walk all the way around, and I peer into all the dark corners.

"Ha!" I say. "You don't scare me much after all."

Boris waits at the top of the stairs, as always. He doesn't know about stairs, having lived his whole life in a one-story house with no basement. His fear is not the same as mine. Dark holds no terrors for him. He just can't make out how these stairs work.

"Come on, Boris, you can do this," I tell him. He whimpers, lowers his head, and puts a paw on the top step. Then he snuffles and backs up, clearly telling me that he has no particular reason to come down here, that's all.

I sing in the shower to prove that I am not afraid of the basement, and then I go to bed.

CHAPTER 9

The next morning I wake to the sound of voices outside. It's early, but getting light. I can hear the neighbors putting out trash.

I start to put on my black pants again and remember that my laundry is probably dry by now. I put on jeans and t-shirt and drag my own bag of kitchen trash and marijuana plants to the curb. I want to be part of the neighborhood garbage gathering.

A few people wave to me and say "good morning." The sun is coming up. Good day to wash sheets and towels. When I check my weather app, I see sun today, clouds tomorrow, snow on Thursday, sunny and sixty-seven on Friday. Ah, April in Missouri. The snow is unlikely but possible, and the same goes for 0 percent chance of rain today. I'll take my chances.

Microwaving oatmeal, I decide that the morning sun is too delicious to waste and drag my table from the kitchen to the back room, which is bathed in light. I choose a spot where I can keep an eye on the clothesline, telling myself that it's birds pooping that I'm watching out for and not laundry thieves. I want to deny the possibility that anyone would steal sheets off a clothesline. I can also watch out for Josie. I'm feeling protective of her, which is funny because she seems to be protecting me too. I think about baking some cookies to take to her tonight. Maybe I'll do that at lunch time.

It's still early, so I take Boris for a walk. This is a good time to be out and about. I'm not the only one on the streets. Like in most of Kansas City, the streets here are laid out in a grid, and you can walk for blocks and blocks in any direction, turn left or right a block or two, and return on a street parallel to the one you left on. East–west streets are numbered and the north–south ones, which have most of the houses, are named. It's hard to get lost, and there are lots of options for walkers. I wish there were more dog walkers, or walkers of any kind, but at least there are a few people about, since it's trash day. There are a few dogs in yards, but I see only one on a leash.

Back at home, I pour coffee and log into work. Boris finds a sunny spot and naps. I'm quickly immersed in work and forget the clothesline, the birds, and Josie. At 10 a.m., I dial in to an hour-long conference call. There are at least fifteen participants, and I'm not leading the call, so I use my cell phone on mute, plug the earbuds into my ears, and make bar cookies using the recipe on the chocolate chips bag, which is about as easy as it gets. I can pay attention and quickly unmute when I need to talk. I always feel guilty about this sort of multitasking, but I know that in reality most of the people on the call are reading email and not paying attention, which only lengthens the call when they miss questions and key points. I'm at least on top of the conversation.

I am, however, not on top of the laundry situation. When the call ends and I sit back down at my desk, I see that my sheets are gone.

What now? Can you even call the police about stolen sheets?

Boris barks once at the front door. I don't hear anything, but I look out and see the top of an umbrella. Someone is on my front porch, bending down. What are they doing? My porch is absolutely bare.

Boris isn't barking now, he's wagging and whimpering. So

I open the door and there is Josie, leaving a plastic grocery bag with my sheets in it. I smell more than see that it's raining.

"Oh." she says. "I thought you were at work and your sheets were getting wet." She seems embarrassed. "You must think I'm an interfering old biddy. But your car isn't here." Now she's confused.

I explain that I work at home on my computer and that my car is there, it's just pulled in far enough that she didn't notice it. I tell her that I'm parking the car as close as possible to the basement window to be extra sure that no one can break in, which means I have to back in. I don't tell her that I backed in entirely out of habit because my dad always insisted on backing in, so that it's easy to get a jump if you need one. I'm pretty sure he never needed one; he was meticulous about car maintenance, which he took care of himself. I've never backed in since I left home, but I do it here without thinking. I know exactly where to stop, reverse, and slide into the narrow space between the house and the hedge, or rather the phantom hedge, since it's long gone.

"Ooohh," she says, this time indicating understanding. She apologizes and says that she'll see me at seven. I tell her I'll be there and thank her profusely for saving the sheets. She nods and turns to go, then says "You be sure and bring Boris."

So much for me keeping an eye on Josie. I'm thrilled and a little freaked that she's paid such close attention, but decide that I'm going to consider it a good thing.

I hang the sheets in the basement. Now, it's lunch break time, so I'll run out for groceries now and work a little later. No need to be crossing the expressway at five o'clock. I go to Cosentino's, although it's a little farther than Aldi. I want to compare, and besides, Cosentino's is locally owned. I stock up on fruit and vegetables and realize that I need to learn how to plan meals ahead. I'm too used to walking a block to a greengrocer every day.

The rest of the day is uneventful, and I am deep in a document when Cathy messages me that it's six o'clock and I've been logged in since seven thirty this morning. Of course, it's 7:00 p.m. where she is and she's still logged in, but we are both used to this. I tell her I'm logging out and then I do.

Boris and I and the cookies show up at Josie's door at exactly seven. I've been excited about seeing the inside of her house, which is so much like mine and which I remember well. I hear voices inside.

I knock, and Dave from across the street opens the door. While I make small talk with Dave, Boris heads on in and finds Josie in the kitchen. She has a dog treat ready for him. They are friends for life.

Dave and I sit down in the tiny living room. Dave's wife Carol and Josie are talking about a house for rent. They bring their discussion into the living room with bowls of ice cream, and I present the plate of cookies. Josie passes it around and then puts it on a shelf out of Boris's reach. Boris is good, but we should test that only so far.

There is a slightly awkward pause, and then Josie explains that she's invited Dave and Carol because they have lived here a long time too. I'm fine with the extras. In fact I am happy to have more people get to know me and to hear a broader perspective on what's happening in the neighborhood (which I don't let myself call "the 'hood" even to myself). I don't want to feel like Josie's protégé. I tell them the part about being glad they are there and keep the rest to myself.

"First, could I ask a question about garbage collection?" I actually planned this question. I wanted to start off with something banal, and besides, I'm not clear about extra bags and large item collection.

They are happy to oblige and also make it clear that since

each household can put out two bags a week with no extra tagging needed, I can put one in front of their houses any time I see that they have only one bag out.

They may have been planning an ice-breaker question too. They point out that the house on the other side of Josie is for rent and tell me to keep an eye out for a potential tenant.

"Whenever anything comes up for sale or rent, we always try to think of someone we'd like to have as a neighbor," Carol says, adding, "but we're not very successful." She tells me about the neighbor two doors down from her who owns several houses around his, including two on Chestnut that back up to his.

"He's pretty careful about who he rents to, but of course homeowners are usually better than renters. And it's so hard to get rid of renters who turn out to be trouble."

It feels like this has brought us around to the reason for our little gathering, which is the "trouble" with my property, and trouble can surely only mean problems with the people who live there.

Josie takes charge.

"Well, we thought we'd give you a little background and then see if there is anything you can fill in." So they have planned this, which is fine with me. I nod expectantly, but I suddenly feel very alone. Not afraid, exactly, but alone. Boris comes into the living room, sighs deeply, and flops down with his head on Josie's foot. Not much of an emotional support animal for me.

We start by trying to find some common ground between when my family left in 1975 and Josie arrived in 1982. I momentarily lose the thread when I realize that she's lived here longer than my parents did.

"Harry Fortune lived on the other side of us, and Mrs. Logan lived behind us. They were both still here in 1975. The Hughsons lived in your house (nodding to Dave and Carol) but I think they left around the same time. Ernie had Alzheimer's." I tell myself not to wander off into things that have no bearing. "They were all older than my folks, meaning at least in their seventies. The Fortunes had grandkids my age." I guess age is relative. Surely none of them was here much longer than 1975. "The DePeres might still have owned your house in 1975, Josie. They had moved away in the sixties, but they kept it as a rental. The first few tenants were young couples with babies. After she grew up, one of the neighborhood kids lived here for a while with her husband and baby. Then there was a mother and son. . . ." and I tell them the story of Kevin and the break-in. I don't come out well in that story and quickly move on.

"That was kind of a turning point for my mother, and she started thinking about moving away. They couldn't afford the suburbs and looked farther south. I don't know who owned the house in 1975. I was away at college when my folks left."

"Well, Hal and I bought it from the DePeres, Dale and Debbie," Josie says. "Hal was my husband. He died in 2002."

"Dale and Debbie were the kids," I say. "They were older than me, but we did play with Dale some." I remind myself again to stick to what's relevant. "Their mother died a few years after they moved away, so maybe their father died later and that's when they sold it."

"Well, I can tell you it was a bit of a mess in here, but we got it for a good price," Josie says, confirming what we all think we know about tenants.

I know it's off topic, but I say, "Well, it looks great now, and I am really impressed at how good the exterior looks. The DePeres redid the windows and siding in the early 1950s, and it still looks the same." I had never liked the high 50s-style windows they had put in, but they do give you more wall space in a small house and it really was remarkable how unchanged the house was. "I think I have a photo of your house in the mid-50s. Debbie is sitting in a chair in the front yard. She was getting over polio."

I get three puzzled looks. Polio was pretty common. That can't be what's confusing them. Oh. They must wonder how I could have photos if everything I owned was destroyed when my house burned down.

"When we cleared out my mother's house, my husband had all her old photos scanned for me as a Christmas present. My brother had a copy, so I was able to get them back after the fire." They were actually on the computer I had taken to the PC shop when the explosion occurred, but that's too complicated to explain right now. And my brother really does have a copy, or did at one time.

Josie smiles, nods, and gets back to business. "Dave and Carol bought theirs a few years later," she says, "just in time for their baby." I quickly calculate and determine that the baby is out of college by now.

"Did you enclose the front porch then?" I ask and then hope that doesn't sound like I think it's ugly. I really did prefer it the old way, but then again the house was smaller than mine and they would have needed the interior space.

"We *re*-enclosed it, I guess," Carol says. "It was enclosed when we bought it, but it wasn't very well done, and it was all painted bright blue. It leaked pretty badly. We actually tore out the enclosure and made a real room. Plus another room on the back."

I don't know what to say, but I come up with "It looks very nice now. It must have been a huge job."

"Well, we still have some plans for a few more improvements." Carol smiles and looks at Dave.

I take a deep breath. "So what about my house? All I remember is that my parents sold it to a couple. It took quite a while to find a buyer, of course, since by then it was clear that the freeway was coming through. Expressway, I mean. We still thought it was going to be an interstate highway at that point. The buyers were getting an FHA loan, so my dad had to do a lot of work that we thought was silly. Like disabling the switch on the light over the bathroom mirror and wiring it in with the ceiling light switch." I pause, remembering. "He was sick and they were having trouble finding another place to live," I add and then realize how awful it sounds that my parents were trying to get out of a neighborhood that my current neighbors were trying to get into.

"They wanted to move closer to Mother's family south of Springfield," I say in my parents' defense. "And that made it a lot easier for her when my dad died three years later."

They give me a minute to feel sad about something that happened thirty-five years ago.

"Sorry, it was all a long time ago." I say, with a bit of a smile, and I reach for a cookie to encourage us all to get back to "the troubles."

"I don't remember who bought the house, if I ever knew. I must have seen the paperwork when I cleared out the house after Mother died, but even that was a long time ago now. I'm sure they lived here, though, or intended to. I don't think they bought it to rent out." As I say that, I realize that I don't know. Mother had told me about them planning to enlarge the living room by taking out the wall between it and my bedroom, but that didn't prove they were going to live there.

"I think they did live here, but they moved before Hal and I bought next door. It's been rented or vacant most of the time since then. More vacant than rented lately." Josie is quiet now.

"Vacant is usually worse than rented," I say softly, encouraging her to continue.

"Well, sometimes it was not rented but also not vacant," Dave says when it's clear that Josie doesn't want to continue. "There was one tenant who put up chain link fence around the front and kept Dobermans in the yard all the time. That's when the mailbox got moved to the curb, because the postman couldn't get past the dogs. The people weren't friendly at all, and then they disappeared overnight. We didn't even see them go."

"After that, we think someone jimmied the back door and came and went that way for a while. They'd go through the back fence and cross behind the Saunders house next to you and out to the side street that way. Mostly at night, so we weren't really sure."

"We would see lights on sometimes," Carol continued. "We went to city hall and looked up the owner and asked them to shut off the electricity and water, thinking that would stop the vagrants. But that was probably not a good idea. They switched to flashlights and candles, and . . . well, let's just say that there was a waste disposal issue."

Josie recovers herself. "In those days, the police didn't respond much to vagrancy calls. They had too much burglary and robbery to deal with, and some gang problems north of here." She looks directly at me. "Not much gang activity right here, though. We're just not such an attractive target." She shrugs. "Finally, when the expressway construction got this far, the police started paying more attention. Protecting the construction equipment and so on, I guess. Anyway, they finally stopped whatever was going on, and the city made the owners clean up the yard and repair the doors. And I guess clean it up some inside. So then it was rented again, and they took down some of that chain link after someone drove into the gate one night. But no one ever stayed very long. We didn't even meet some of them. If they came in the winter, you know how it is—sometimes you just don't run into them. And by then we'd got so we were a little cautious about just going up and knocking on the door."

Dave is talking now. "And then, no more renters for the last year or so. The owners must come around sometimes because someone noticed the roof leak and put up the blue tarp."

I try to match this up with the timeline I got from Officer Carl on Bud the burglar. It seems to fit. Bud's girlfriend was the last tenant. We don't know for sure why she left and why it wasn't rented after that. Well, aside from having a roof leak.

"There was no For Rent sign?" I ask, thinking of the sign in the front yard down the street.

"They never put a sign out; they always listed it on Craigslist." Dave sort of laughs. "Makes it harder for us to keep track. But we haven't seen it listed since then. After a while, we checked the MLS to see if it was listed for sale, but it never was. That's why we were so surprised when you showed up."

"So we really don't know if there is a mystery here, or if the owners just weren't bothering with it," I say, with a bit of a question in my voice, "and then I call them up out of the blue and take the problem off their hands."

"That's about the size of it," Carol says. "We've been speculating, of course. Like maybe you were a relative of the owners and needed a place to crash."

Josie perks up. "Our favorite theory was that you are in witness protection!" They all are watching me closely while pretending not to. Are they worried or hopeful about this possibility? "The police dog was kind of a clue. For protection, you know." She seems to still like this theory.

"But it's kind of a stretch to believe they didn't give you any furniture or anything," Carol knocks down the theory, or pretends to. "Not even a microwave." I guess one of them saw me struggling to get that inside.

"Plus Carl said that the feds usually let the local cops know," Josie really is disappointed. "Unless the person in protection is a really high risk." She seems to be hopeful again.

"Sorry, I'm not in witness protection," I tell them, "although of course I couldn't tell you if I were."

Dave is laughing at Josie now, and then turns to me with mock seriousness. "To make sure, though, we want to see some childhood photos of you in that house."

"You're on," I tell them. "As soon as I have enough chairs I'll have you all over for a picture party. You can decide for yourself if the feds Photoshopped my first-day-of-school pictures into someone else's snapshots." They laugh, and I have the surreal thought that if my life were a novel, the witness protection idea would be a great story arc.

Everyone laughs again, and then we have one of those moments where everyone is quiet. Sometimes that signals that the party is breaking up, but I don't want to leave things so up in the air. Maybe they just wanted to make sure I was for real, but Officer Carl seemed to have some serious concerns about what happened on Sunday. And if Bud is released, then what? So I break the silence before it becomes uncomfortable.

"Okay, so Carl said you could give me some background on the troubles with my house. You've done that—thank you. But now what? Is there anything else? I admit that I'm a little scared that Bud will be back for whatever he was looking for, unless he was only looking for a place to sleep. It's probably clear to him that he can't do that anymore."

Carol says, "To be honest, what we wanted at first was for you to move in and be comfortable and stay here. You know, change the karma of the place. We don't like having to keep calling the police about something going on there. Now that we've met you, we want you to stay because we like you. And it's cool that you grew up here. It makes some crazy kind of sense. Well, not really, but it seems fitting anyway."

I give her a smile intended to convey that I understand what she's trying to say and that I feel the same way.

Dave is more direct. "Bud is a wild card, but at least no one has any reason to believe he's violent." He's also practical. "I have two thoughts. First, let's secure your house as much as possible." He stops, realizing that he's repeating what he's been hashing out in his head but is probably overstepping by saying out loud and rather forcefully. "I mean, uh."

I let him off the hook. "I agree. I've been thinking about a more secure back door, some lights on timers, maybe motion-activated lights outside. I can talk to my new best friend at Midtown Hardware about that. I can go tomorrow at lunch time." I pause. "You weren't thinking about bars on the windows or anything, were you? I would hate that. I'm not good with alarms, either. Do you all have alarms?"

"No, not at all. No bars or alarms." Dave is reassuring on the alarm and bar fronts. "The lights and doors are the big things, now that the basement window is secure. And I see you've been parking up close to it."

"Yes, and Josie is on duty watching the other side—not that I expect her to do that." Now I feel like I am overstepping. But she nods. She's happy that I want her to do what she's doing anyway.

"I don't know if fencing the back would help, but I do keep thinking about those guys slipping out the back and across that empty lot." Dave again. I think of that empty lot as the Logans' giant vegetable garden, but that's a concept from the previous century.

"I want to fence the back anyway, so I can let Boris out without supervising him. Just the back, though. I would like to get rid of what's left of that chain link in the front. There used to be a gate across the back of the driveway, just in front of the back door—which is on the side, of course, just like Josie's. I'd probably put the gate there again. I might even put the rose arbor back over the gate."

They smile at me, Josie seeming to like the idea and Dave and Carol possibly skeptical.

"Ya know, I think there was a rose arbor over your gate too, back in prehistoric times," I tell Dave and Carol. I don't say more because it occurs to me that they are the ones who paved the space that used to have the rose arbor and picket fence.

"Dave, what was your second thought, after securing the house?"

"Well, now I feel a little weird about suggesting this," he begins, and then pauses.

"Oh, come on, Dave." This from Josie, who clearly plans to like and respect whatever it is that Dave has to say. Maybe she even knows what he's going to say.

"Okay, but feel free to say 'no'—I won't be upset or anything." I can't imagine what Dave is thinking about that he's so reluctant to say, when he clearly thinks it's something that should be done.

"Out with it, Dave," Carol says.

"Well, if he's looking for something, should we try to find it?" Dave is frustrated, so we give him a moment. "I don't know how to say this. I'm more than happy to help look. I think we all are. But it's intrusive to suggest that I or we should go searching through your house. On the other hand, it seems rude of me to tell you to go do it."

The tension breaks, and Carol, Josie, and I laugh.

"It's a great idea," I say, "and I would love the help. You couldn't possibly invade my privacy because I have almost nothing yet." And then, so they don't worry about why I am so slow about furnishing it, I add "A lot of the ceiling plaster fell down in the living room when the roof leaked, and I want to get that repaired and the dust cleared before I buy too much stuff that I'll just have to clean. The plaster guy is coming next week."

That makes sense to them, and we decide to start on Saturday morning. I will make sure I have one more thing to sit on by then.

"And I'll get at least the timers tomorrow." I should probably get another lamp too, so there is something for the timers to turn off and on.

As we are leaving, Carol says, "Just so you know, we always have a block party on Memorial Day. We close the street and have a potluck picnic. It's a lot of fun." There is a slightly hopeful tone in her voice, as though she thinks she'll have to twist my arm to come to that sort of thing.

"What a great idea. Count me in. What can I do?" I had been thinking that I would take the inflatable bed back to my cousins that weekend, but holiday traffic will be bad anyway, so the weekend before or after would be better. I'm not missing the block party.

Carol tells me that she'll invite me to the neighborhood Nextdoor group, which will have all the details for the party. I give her my email address and head home. As I open my front door and send Boris in, I turn and see that all three of them are watching me, making sure I am safely home. I wave and tell them goodnight and lock myself in. Boris is slurping water from his bowl, so I am confident that the house is secure. Sensing security is much more his thing than giving emotional support.

I turn on the ceiling light in my bedroom as a show of occupancy. Then I go down the basement stairs to prove to myself again that I can and also to see if there might be some kind of shop light that I could use upstairs on a timer temporarily. Or even in the basement, for that matter. Crap. Wherever I have lights on I need some sort of curtains, otherwise I'm just making it easier to see that the place is empty.

CHAPTER 10

Rats, I think when I am pouring coffee the next morning and trying not to eat a cookie for breakfast. I didn't get past Josie's living room last night. One of the differences between our houses is that I have a very wide doorway between the living room and kitchen, and hers is just a normal door width. So I didn't even get a look at the kitchen. And I do want to see the rest of her house, to see if it is as unchanged as the outside is. I tell myself to stop being nosy. The time will come. I also tell myself, no cookies for breakfast here at the end of Lent. I self-righteously make oatmeal, which I love, so it's not exactly a Lenten sacrifice.

The dryer hasn't arrived at noon, which normally wouldn't bother me. But for the last six months, it's been harder to let the small things go, and I irrationally wanted to go to the hardware store at noon. I remind myself that this is too small to even be considered the small stuff and make myself some lunch, finishing off with one of yesterday's cookies.

At a quarter past twelve, Boris barks as the dryer delivery truck stops out front. I go out to ask if they want to back into the driveway, which is crazy because the driveway is too narrow for the truck, never mind that it's not even paved, just gravel probably dating back to the 1970s, meaning mostly dirt now. I drag my attention away from debating whether or not to pave the driveway.

The dryer exits the truck on a lift, and I grind my teeth at the mental picture of my dad manually lifting dryers and refrigerators and pool tables out of a truck like this one, every single workday. Back injuries and pain were a constant in the years he delivered for Sears.

The driver and his helper expertly wheel the dryer to my back door, where they stop to meet Boris, and then bump neatly down the basement steps. They level it and go to plug it in, but the outlet doesn't match the plug.

"Hmm, that looks a little out of date," the driver says. "You'll need to get a new outlet put in."

I'm pretty sure I can do that myself, but I'm not sure I will. Maybe I'll ask Jimmy when he comes to do the ceiling. I don't really mind using my solar dryer for a few more days. I thank them, tip them (which I always do because my dad pretty much only got tips for delivery of pool tables to third-floor attics on Christmas Eve), and add "dryer outlet" to the list of hardware store items I need to buy. For good measure, I take a photo of the dryer plug to make sure I get the right one.

Then I take a look at my outdoor clotheslines, because some are missing and they may need some hardware. Matt must have found one of the loose lines when he was mowing and coiled it up, so I take a photo of the eye-bolts and turnbuckles so I can fix it. I probably don't need all six of the originals, but three would be nice.

CHAPTER 11

I wake up early Thursday morning feeling a small sense of normalcy. I don't have to figure out what to do today. I just have to log in and take it as it comes. After years in the corporate world, I know that every day is different and every day is the same, and that whatever drama comes my way is probably just a new version of something I've dealt with before. It's a surprisingly good feeling, in spite of a certain Dilbert quality. This particular day is free of corporate drama, and it's my last work day of this first week back, so I'm also feeling a little Friday effect.

It's also Holy Thursday, which is the day of one of my favorite Catholic services. I am still a little nervous coming home after dark, but I also know that I'll need only about twenty seconds of courage, and then I'll have the door open and Boris will be waiting and I'll be safe. I turn on a basement light and leave Boris in charge of security.

Holy Week services are not on the Catholic Church's list of holy days of obligation, so the people who attend are people who want to be there, plus their kids who mostly don't want to be there, although some clearly are intrigued and paying close attention, especially teenagers.

In April 1968, I was fourteen years old, in eighth grade. The same sisters who had been working with us on social justice issues were involving us in the Holy Week services. All my friends were going to be there—in fact, most of the class would be. My family ordinarily didn't go to Holy Thursday or Holy Saturday services, since they take place at night and my father had a grueling job. This year, though, we all were going.

But it was 1968 and Holy Thursday was on April 11, seven days after Martin Luther King Jr. was assassinated. The funeral was on April 9, and the Kansas City School District did not close schools for the day. So Black students staged a peaceful march to City Hall in protest. Many of those students marched from Southeast High School, heading north on Swope Parkway past my elementary school, and on another fifty blocks to downtown. We had front-row seats at the school windows. There was shouting, of course, but it was fairly peaceful, given that these were teens and feelings were running high. Our school doors were locked just in case, and once the marchers had passed we were sent home for the rest of the day.

What happened next is well-documented Kansas City history: The marching students were met with tear gas, rioting erupted, and the city imposed a curfew. The riots were all anyone talked about that week. For fourteen-year-old kids whose social action club had just won a national award as the top civic club among five thousand Catholic schools, it was terrifying and exciting. We saw the riots as very wrong and very right. At that age, we were just about sophisticated enough to hold those contradictory thoughts at the same time. The fact that it was Holy Week just added another level of significance. We all grew up a lot that week.

There were also practical considerations. The curfew meant that services had to be held earlier and cut short so that everyone could be home before dark.

Holy Thursday was warm and sunny, as though nothing bad

could be happening. I got a ride with a friend whose dad got home from work earlier than mine, in time to drive us to church. Their family station wagon was packed and we had to stop for gas, because gas was rationed and stations were closed at night as part of the curfew. We got to church, and the service was somber and a little hurried, and not at all what we had been planning for the last month. We left hushed and just a little scared and were rushed home, giggling as fourteen-year-old girls do when anything makes them nervous.

Holy Week 1968 is not forgotten here or in any of the other cities where similar events unfolded. I have met former National Guardsmen who were shipped from rural towns to Kansas City and still soundly condemn the riots and the rioters. But I think those of us who lived here, at least those of us who were on the cusp of adulthood and lived at the shifting border of racial discord, were profoundly shaped by that week. Many of us are unable to condemn the marching or the frustrated acting out of kids our own age who faced racial discrimination every day of their lives.

Being back in my old house in my old parish, I can't not remember all of this as I enter the church. The church is not packed this evening, as it was in 1968, but Holy Thursday is the joyful service before the tragedy of Good Friday, and I am caught up once again in the music and the rituals. No curfew, no gas lines, no fear this year.

Oh, and it doesn't snow, either, in spite of what my weather app had predicted.

CHAPTER 12

Since I'm not working Fridays, I don't have to do my usual covert disappearing act to attend Good Friday services, which are normally from noon until 3:00 p.m. I've learned the hard way that any rumor of religiosity can be career limiting.

I don't like the Good Friday ritual as much as the Holy Thursday one, partly because the last church I belonged to always chose hymns that I particularly dislike. One of those is called something like "Were You There," which seems horribly sanctimonious to me and also has a crappy wailing melody that makes me cringe. I'm hopeful that I won't run into that here, or if I do it will be sung with less melodrama. I go late and sit in the back so I can slip out.

Good Friday is also one of the two true fast days still in the church calendar. On other Fridays in Lent, we Catholics just skip meat, which is hardly a burden any more. But on Good Friday, as on Ash Wednesday, we cut back on food intake too. This year on Ash Wednesday, I felt like I was fasting from everything in my life except food, so I ate when I wanted to. I'm getting a life back now, so I think I should at least make an effort.

A few people of my generation, which grew up during Vatican II, still seem sad about losing most of our fast days, hardships that must surely be beneficial to us. A little food-related hardship probably is good for well-fed Americans. But imposing a fast on people anywhere in the world who don't have enough to eat is just wrong. And it sends a message that being hungry is good for them, which it is not.

The well-fed world forgets that Vatican II didn't remove the relatively easy restriction on eating meat on Fridays. The idea wasn't to set us free from a rule, it was to challenge us to freely choose to give up something meaningful to us, like a bad habit, or to do something positive. This is more challenging, and more useful in our quests to become better people. Giving up meat on Fridays during Lent is a reminder of that challenge.

I never miss a meal and get lightheaded when I do. Since I'm driving to church, I have a banana before I go to make sure I don't get woozy and wreck the car.

The service lasts longer than I'm used to, with more music and no melodrama. They do sing "Were You There," but they sing it very softly, a capella, and they've changed the words to "Was I here," which turns it on its head, infuses it with humility and wonder. Instead of "sometimes it makes me tremble," they sing "sometimes it makes me wonder." It makes me tremble. They follow that up with "O Sacred Head Surrounded," whose haunting Bach melody can make me tremble too. When it's all over, I wish I had walked because walking home with Bach in my head seems more appropriate than starting up the VW's engine.

I go home and eat a small bowl of lentils and take Boris for a walk until it starts to get dusky. We get home in time to witness the new lamp timers working as expected, and I turn a few ceiling lights on and off during the evening to further announce my presence.

CHAPTER 13

Saturday starts out sunny, but the house is chilly so I let the furnace run a few cycles. I make more coffee than usual and bake a loaf of banana bread in anticipation of the search party, which starts at ten o'clock. I've just added a wooden stool to my collection of furniture, so I can now seat four people. I assemble my two kitchen chairs, my office chair, and my stool in the back room where the table is. I run around with my hand vac to collect dog hair. Boris has started his spring shedding, so I need to buy a brush. And canine nail clippers. We've been walking a lot, but it's hard to walk enough to keep his nails short. A dog needs only about ten things, compared to the ten thousand things I seem to need, but I still haven't managed to replace his basic necessities.

A couple of minutes before ten in the morning, I start watching for the neighbors. It occurs to me that a ladder or stepstool would be helpful, but I don't have either. When I was at the resale shop looking for a fourth seat, I saw one of those fifties-era metal stools with a big flat seat and two steps that ratchet out and down to the floor. It would be both stool and indoor ladder. But it was missing a step. I couldn't find a good one, so I ended up with a serviceable (and cheap) wooden stool. I didn't go back to the hardware store for a ladder or stepstool, so I want to catch one of the neighbors and send them home for theirs.

Dave and Carol show their faces first, so I run outside and make my request. They go back to their house and return with both items. By then Josie has arrived and is fussing over Boris. I give them a quick tour and we convene in the back room for banana bread on paper towels and coffee using the Garfield mug, the H&R Block mug, my travel mug, and a slightly chipped mug I found in the basement. I've got to review my shopping priorities. We laugh at the cap Dave is wearing, which has a Spiderman logo and battery-powered lights in the brim. "Keeps cobwebs out of my hair and lets the spiders know I'm coming," he says lightly.

I tell them that I've been through all the closets and cupboards except the two I can't see into standing on a chair. We can start with those. The first one yields dirt, another dead mouse, and dusty Christmas wrappings. It all goes in a trash bag and Dave holds the shop vac on his shoulder while I sweep out the cobwebs. I borrow his cap. "Who's laughing about it now?" he says. I mentally add "light-up cap" to my shopping list.

The second one is above a door in the little hallway, so it's a bit of a squeeze. I know my mother left her old handmade formals up there in a dress box. She felt bad about it because I had gushed over them and worn them as costumes, but she had run out of time and energy when they were moving and had just forgotten. I know they won't be there, but the very idea that they might be has been intriguing me since I moved in.

This cupboard is well lit by the hall ceiling light and is empty. Just as well. The dark violet velvet bodice with the moiré striped skirt would be crumbled to shreds by now anyway, or maybe have made a nice home for a family of mice. Dave mans the vacuum again.

He insists on vacuuming the high cupboards in the bathroom while we are there, which takes only a minute. He goes into the small, dark, empty bedroom that had been my brother's and says, "Let's do this one, too." It is easy enough, just a high shelf in the small closet. That's fine with me. I almost never enter this room, but I do intend to get it cleaned up so I can move in here when I buy a bed.

While we are doing cobweb removal, Carol is taking a close look at the window shade. She lowers it and raises it again.

"Look at this. I think it's a blackout shade. I wonder if someone used this as a grow room," she says, pulling it all the way down and standing back.

I turn off the light and we see that no light comes in around the shade. So no light would get out, either. We look at the water stains on the floor and the small hooks screwed into the ceiling. "That could explain the back-door comings and goings," Carol says.

Josie is looking thoughtful. "The last tenants, Bud and his wife with the little girl, I'm sure they used it as a bedroom. I'd look out my kitchen window in the mornings and see them dressing the baby. In the summer, the crib was up against the window and the baby would pull herself up on her little feet and wave at me." Doesn't sound like Bud was growing weed in here.

Next, I show them the big cupboard that has attic access and explain that I wouldn't have thought about it at all except that we found the hatch open when Jimmy went up there to see if the new roof was leaking around the chimney. He hadn't reported seeing anything, but then he wasn't looking for anything but damp patches. It seems like the best hiding place but also the worst.

Dave says that he will go up in the attic. I say that I'm not letting any of them go up. Dave says that this was his crazy idea and he is going no matter what I say about it.

"Besides," he says, grinning, "I have the headgear." I think he knows that I am dreading it, and we all know that we'll feel better knowing that nothing is up there. Worrying about it has probably made all four of us imagine things we won't voice. I had actually pumped myself up to the point that I was ready to do it as long as they were in the house with me, but I quickly cave.

Dave climbs into the cupboard and pulls the stepstool up behind him. I hand up the trouble light and point out the outlet on the ceramic light fixture in the cupboard. Up he goes. None of us moves on to search anywhere else.

"On my way down." Dave's voice is muffled by insulation. His feet dangle through the opening, and then he drops into the cupboard.

"If there's anything up here, it's under the insulation, and that's beyond us for today," he says.

"Or any day," I add. "That's something the FBI or scene-of-crime people do, not us."

"You don't have any reason to think he was going up there last Sunday, do you?" Dave asks.

"No," I say. "I think he would have gotten his feet dirty crawling in the basement window, but there weren't any shoe marks in the cupboard. And my extra keys were hanging right there." I point to them. "Plus, I had left the cupboard door open a few inches and it was still like that afterwards." I tell them about Jimmy's suggestion to make sure it's dry up there before he repairs the plaster.

Now we have to face the basement, which is the most accessible but the biggest unknown, mostly because of the boxes and piles of junk. We grab some trash bags and head downstairs. Boris whimpers, then flops down at the top of the stairs and sighs deeply.

I point out the bags I've already filled and that Officer Carl asked me to keep for another week. "I haven't heard from him since Monday. I wonder if that's good or bad."

We walk around and I show them the few things that are mine. Then we divide up, put on our work gloves, and start in.

"We're not cleaning," I say, "just looking for something of value that Bud might have hidden. It's probably not in plain sight or he would have found it."

There really isn't that much stuff to look through. Over my protests, they pick up everything that is obviously trash and bag it. Dave uses the shop-vac, clearing dirt and cobwebs from the joists above our heads. "This is a good way to look for something he might have wedged up here, or tucked up behind a pipe," he says by way of justification, and we can't argue with that. "Also, I don't have to bend over. I'm leaving that to you-all."

We bag everything we find, setting aside anything that can be used or recycled. I've now got a collection of flower pots and plastic toys, plus a box of baby clothes that the kid has certainly outgrown by now. Josie shook them out to make sure nothing was hidden among the onesies and ruffled t-shirts.

Dave offers to get rid of the old snow tires and the television.

"Well, sure," I say. We put the TV on the washer and plug it in. It comes on, but it's all snow and crackle.

"Oh, but it would need a converter box, wouldn't it?" Dave puts it at the bottom of the stairs.

"Is this a door to something?" Carol is pointing at what does look like a small screen door, about two feet high and four feet wide. It's in the painted plywood paneling that surrounds the stairway.

"It seems to have hinges," I say, taking a closer look. "My dad built the addition over crawlspace instead of digging a whole basement. The crawlspace was completely open to the basement when we lived here. I had noticed that it's closed in now and assumed the screen was just to ventilate the space. I guess it made sense to leave some sort of opening. There isn't any plumbing in the addition, but you still might need to go in there for something."

Actually there are two openings, one on each side.

"There's no need to go in," I say with all the authority I can muster. "We'll shove the light in and just lean in and look around."

Dave eyes me narrowly but concedes, even though I know he's conceding only until we find out if we can see it all from the two openings.

We start with the one that has some small scratches in the paint along one edge, as if it had been teased open before. To our surprise, Josie pulls out a small pocketknife, selects a blade, and gently opens the screen. "A girl needs to be prepared for anything," she says.

I shove the trouble light into the opening and look around. No glowing red eyes look back, so I stick my head in, and then my shoulders. "That's far enough," I hear someone say. I ignore them and slither in a bit further, getting grit in my eyes. A little more and I can turn over and sit up with my feet still sticking out the opening. Now I can see all along the inside of the plywood enclosure. I see a box.

"There's just one cardboard box in here," I report back. "Can you get me that hoe by the back door?"

The box isn't very heavy, and I can hook it with the hoe and drag it to the opening. I slither back out and step away to brush myself off and shake out my hair, leaving the others to wrestle the box out into the light and lift the flaps.

"Well, I'll be darned," I hear Josie say, wonder in her voice. She doesn't continue, but her tone tells me it is not any of the terrible unspoken things we all feared.

"It's presents. Christmas presents."

In the silence that follows, the doorbell rings. The doorbell, still going (sometimes) all these years on, is more of a buzzer, and it's in the stairwell over our heads, so we all jump. Boris barks and we hear his feet on the floor above.

"Maybe it's Matt coming to mow." I head upstairs. Boris isn't barking so he must know who it is, even though he can't see through the door.

It's not Matt, it's Officer Carl—I can hear him talking baby talk to Boris, who is now wagging and whining. I open the door and let him in.

"Good timing, Carl. We may have just found the thing Bud was looking for. Maybe." The others have come upstairs by now, bringing the box. Josie is coming forward, all smiles, and I excuse myself to wash my face. I catch myself in the bathroom mirror, dirt smudged across my face, cobwebs hanging from my t-shirt and hair.

When I return, everyone is in the back room, with the cardboard carton on the table. Carl is putting on latex gloves.

"Is this a crime scene? Are these things evidence?" Josie asks. I think she sort of likes the idea.

"It's a gray area. These aren't exactly related to the B&E charge, but maybe they can help us sort out Bud's story." He looks at me and says, "Technically, these are yours because they are in a house that you legally bought with no contingencies about contents. Whoever hid these abandoned them, which means they forfeited ownership."

He lets that sink in, then looks at me again. "But if you're willing, I can take these and let Bud know that we recovered a box that may belong to him. And if he can tell us what's in it, then we at least know what he was doing in here last Sunday." He pauses and then grins. "Plus I know you're all dying to know what's in these presents."

That lightens the mood. Amazing how he can put on that cop voice and make us all sit up and pay attention, and then break the tension in a snap.

"Of course. Go ahead!" I say. "Unless you want to get the bomb squad in."

My attempt at humor is just real enough that no one laughs. Carl assures us that we are safe, but we can leave the room if we're concerned. No one leaves the room. We don't ask him to explain how he knows he's not dealing with bombs. I guess a box with five or six gift-wrapped and bagged items just doesn't fit the profile.

He opens the bags first, probably so we'll feel safer when he unwraps the boxes. One bag has a long silky scarf and the other has a small stuffed koala bear. Then he takes the ribbons and paper off the larger boxes, which yield a negligee and a wooden basset hound on wheels, with a pink ribbon leash. Finally, he opens a very small box, which reveals a jewelry case, in which we find what has to be an engagement ring.

Carol heaves a big sigh. "This makes me so sad. Those things have probably been here since before last Christmas. I mean the Christmas before this last one."

"Well, we don't know yet that Bud is the one who hid them," Carl says. "I'll have to verify that he was here eighteen months ago and gone by Christmas, unless any of you knows for sure and can make a statement."

The others confer, but can't be sure about dates. I remember the grow house theory and we show Carl the room with the blackout shade, the ceiling hooks, and the water-stained floor. He points out that there aren't any warrants or suspects, and not even a report of a suspected grow house, but he will file a report and attach it to the current case file. I suppose it does connect to the marijuana growing in my back yard and should help reassure the judge about my lack of knowledge or interest in that. It also reassures all of us about that past activity. The growers moved on long ago.

Things seem to be wrapping up when it occurs to me that Carl must have come for his own reasons, since we hadn't called him yet. "Was there anything you needed?" I ask him. "We jumped right in and didn't let you tell us why you stopped by." I realize that I've put him on the spot—he might not have intended to say whatever he had to say to the whole neighborhood. Well, he's a cop. He can cope.

"Oh, I really just wanted to check in, and let you know that Bud is being released tomorrow on his own recognizance. I've been nervous about that. I wasn't convinced he wouldn't come back here. But if he can tell me where the box was and what was in it, then I think it will be okay. He's still facing the B&E charge, and he now knows that you live here and he doesn't; plus, you have a big scary dog."

We all look at the big scary dog, who is leaning on Josie while she scratches his ears. He notices us looking at him and moves to Carl, who continues the ear scratching.

"Okay, I'm fine with that," I say. "I still don't understand why he came up here for a snack before looking for the box, though."

"Once he got into the basement, he probably realized that someone was living here, and either curiosity or hunger got the better of him. His VA counselor says that he's more rational some days than others."

That's not reassuring to me, but Carl goes on: "The counselor has arranged supervised visits with the little girl, so that should redirect his attention."

It's past noon now, and I'm hungry, so I offer to make bacon and eggs for everyone since that's the quickest way I can think of to feed five people. They all ask for rain checks, pleading other matters to attend to.

I see them to the door, and Carl maneuvers himself to the end of the line and then does that cop thing.

"I also wanted to let you know that we resolved the mystery of Bud saying that he knows you." We gave him mug books to look through, and when he couldn't find you there we gave him high school yearbooks. He picked someone out of his own class. So he was just confused. We didn't give him your name, but we were able to convince him that you were not the girl he was remembering."

"That's a relief." I don't ask who the girl was. I've had enough information input for today.

I make myself some lunch, then realize that Dave has left his cap and the two ladders. While I have them, I scrub all my upper cupboards and shelves, and decide that a ladder will be more useful than the stepstool. Besides, I am determined to continue my search for the vintage version. I put on the cap and head across the street with the stepstool. Carol invites me in, but I tell her that I am still filthy and need to clean up and run some errands before dark. She takes the stepstool and cap while I run back for the ladder.

"Thank you so much for all your help, both of you," I say. "I'm so lucky to have great neighbors." Dave has shown up to take the ladder from me and joins Carol in telling me how pleased they are that I've bought the house.

"Even if you don't have a cool hat." Dave says, touching the brim of his lighted cap.

"I got him that to walk the dog at night," Carol says, and I say, "Oh, do you have a dog?"

"No, he's been dead for several years, and we really don't have space for one."

I think about the Hughsons' hound named Sarge, looking out from behind the gate in the white picket fence that is long gone, under the missing rose arbor, over the sidewalk down the side yard that is now Dave and Carol's paved driveway.

"Well, Boris is always available if you need a walking buddy or just want a little canine companionship."

I run my hardware store errands, figuring they've had customers in mid-project who look as bad as I do. The store is busy, and I don't ponder my ladder choices. I just pick the lighter-weight six-foot aluminum one, reminding myself of my dad's admonition to always put a metal ladder on a dry board if you use it outside, even if the ground seems dry. I've remembered my list and find the correct dryer outlet (helpfully labeled "dryer outlet"), along with clothesline hardware and two extension cords, one long and heavy for outside use if necessary. Matt is working at the checkout and doesn't try to sell me more ladders.

"It's been cold this week, so I didn't think you'd want your yard mowed today," he says. I'm pleased that he's thought about that instead of just trying to get his weekly pay.

"Thanks. You're right about that. It's warming up so it might be time again by next week."

"What about the garbage? Need any help with that?" he asks.

A line has formed, so I cut it short. "I'm okay for now, but I'm thinking about doing some fencing, if you want to help with that."

"Sure," he says. "I can set the posts and help you pull it. I can even borrow a come-along if we need one."

"I'll decide on the fencing soon and let you know." And I take my leave.

The Easter Vigil is scheduled for 8:00 p.m., and I'm determined to go, since it's another of my favorite rituals and happens only once a year. By 7:00 p.m. I've had a hot shower, which makes me want to crawl in bed and go to sleep, but soon I'm in my black pants and a sweater I haven't worn to church yet. I tell myself that I've got to buy some slightly dressier clothes or else go to a different church every week. This will be my fourth time at St. Louis in seven days, so people are probably noticing me. I schedule my arrival for 8:00 p.m. on the dot, or maybe 8:02.

No one is outside when I drive by, but there are plenty of cars, so I park and creep up to the door. It's closed, but an usher is standing by. Ah, they light the Easter candle behind the church and process around to the front. I now see why—this is a sell-out crowd and there isn't room on the sidewalk out front. The Lumen Christi has started. An usher hands me a candle, another person lights it from her candle, and we process into the dark church. Someone once told me not to wear a watch to the Easter Vigil. Just forget about time and go with it. It's good advice because it's a long service at any church, and I'm expecting this one to go even longer.

It is a long service, but I clear my mind to listen to all the readings, watch all of the rituals and the turning on of the lights, and listen to the ringing of the bells and the alleluias that have been silenced during Lent. When I leave, it's closing in on midnight. Many of the parishioners are heading for the parish hall for a reception to welcome those who were baptized or accepted into the Catholic faith tonight. But I've had a long day, and I'm not a night person. I head for my car and notice that there are several police cars parked along Swope Parkway among our cars, and uniformed cops are standing around on the sidewalk, calm and watchful. I smile at one as I go by and he nods and says, "Happy Easter, ma'am." Others are speaking to them as though this is an ordinary thing, so I assume that it is.

CHAPTER 14

I sleep in very late on Easter Sunday. The neighborhood is quiet and I just sleep and sleep. I get up and collect the newspaper that I have finally subscribed to, let Boris out for a few minutes, and go back to bed for another hour. I don't really sleep, but I doze and feel luxurious.

Eventually hunger drives me out of bed and into my clothes. I take my toast and coffee to the back of the house since that's where my table and chairs still are. It's unlikely that I'll move them back to the kitchen until I get another table or a desk. I like sitting here looking out at my green back yard. It's raining just a little, and I like that too. "Good for the crops," I say out loud, and wish my tomatoes would somehow plant themselves.

Easter is possibly the feast-iest of the Christian feast days, ending as it does the fasting period of Lent. We are supposed to eat and rejoice. Ham and lamb are traditional in America, probably because spring lambs could be roasted and hams were still hanging in the smokehouse from the prior fall. I'm not that crazy about either one, but I have a thick slice of ham in the refrigerator. Ham won because that's what was available at Cosentino's, with the bonus that it doesn't require cooking. I've never cooked lamb—that was my husband's specialty. I also make scalloped potatoes because they're what Mother generally served with ham, so I didn't have to think about it. I slice potatoes and onions, then am temporarily stymied by the lack of a casserole dish. The cast iron skillet will do. I preheat it on a burner to speed up the cooking, then get the whole thing in the oven. Mother would probably have served canned peas or green beans, but today I'm having fresh asparagus and sugar snap peas. I wonder if it's too late to plant those. Like it matters, since I can't manage to stick six tiny tomato plants in the ground.

I laze around after my ham-and-potatoes feast thinking about the coconut cake a California friend once served for a shared Easter dinner. I text the friend to let her know I'm dreaming of coconut cake and that things are going well. Then I call my brother to wish him a Happy Easter. He's having dinner at his in-laws', so I again put off telling him that I've moved. I just pave the way by saying that I've *decided* to live in Kansas City and I'll keep him posted. A few years ago, he told me that he had driven down our old street one day and had nightmares afterward. So I don't expect support from him and today is not the day to get into a deep discussion. Today is a day for quiet and rest.

The sun comes out just as it is setting, and Boris and I take a ramble around the block. Some houses have lots of cars out front—holiday dinners, I assume. All is quiet and fragrant following the afternoon rain, and I'm amazed at how much greener everything seems than it did when I arrived two weeks ago.

CHAPTER 15

In today's staff conference call, I mention that I've moved to Kansas City, without specifying Missouri or Kansas. Most of them will be certain that it's in Kansas, unaware that the Kansas-side suburb has a population of one hundred fifty thousand compared to Missouri's half million. They know all about it, having flown over Kansas at some point. If they've flown on Southwest, they may have even stopped or changed planes at the airport, firmly believing they were in Kansas. Coastals. What do they know? I ignore that I have spent half of my life so far on one coast or the other.

Cathy knows that I can get sarcastic about this subject, so she steers the topic a bit. "Cool. Now she's in the same time zone as Carrie. They can get together for lunch." Carrie is in Wisconsin. She gets the joke and suggests a wine bar. No one else says anything, probably because they are on mute reading their email.

Mid-morning I get a text from Jimmy asking if he can drop off the drywall at around 6:00 p.m. so it has a few days to acclimate before he comes back on Wednesday. That gives me time for another run to the hardware store for the fan I keep forgetting about, so I agree.

At noon, I raise my head enough to appreciate my backyard view and notice the birds, mostly robins today. I'm hoping for cardinals, which I've missed during the California years, but none appear today. A hummingbird is collecting a few strands of last year's milkweed silk that have survived the winter in the fence-row. We used to yank it out to keep the seeds from spreading everywhere, but I usually managed to find a few and pull out the silks, although I can't remember what I did with them. Maybe nothing in particular, beyond marveling at how cool it was to open a green pod and find white silky threads.

In the afternoon I call HR to make sure my home address has been updated in the corporate database, that my pay is being direct deposited to my new bank, and that they have completed the transfer of my health insurance to a Missouri carrier. The HR clerk corrects my pronunciation of Missour-ee, telling me that it's Missour-a. I thank her and ask her how she knows this. She stumbles around for a while and says something about the movie Fargo. I don't tell her that North Dakota and Missouri are different states hundreds of miles apart, but I do thank her again for the explanation and tell her that I lived here for my first twenty-eight years and Did. Not. Know. That. Then I regret being bitchy to someone who is critical to my health insurance coverage.

At five-fifteen in the evening, I log off and make another trip to Midtown Hardware for the fan, along with plastic sheeting and masking tape to seal the plaster dust out of the rest of the house. The owner recognizes me and introduces himself as Henry. It's not so busy right now and he offers to help me find what I need. I tell him about the fan and he encourages me to get a window-mounted exhaust fan that can be set to blow in or out or can just sit on the floor or table like a normal room fan. It's about the same price, so I take his advice and get his take on hardware to secure the window when the fan is in it. I find the plastic and he educates me about masking tape, recommending the blue tape that will come off without damaging the wall, even if it stays up for a few days. We choose ceiling paint and a dog brush.

"You really are starting at square one, aren't you?" he says. "I'm going to give you the contractor rate on the building materials." I don't know what to say, so he goes on. "You do seem to be acting as your own contractor."

I guess I am, so I say, "Sure, I'm a contractor—with exactly one client," and tell him that I've talked to Matt about fencing the back yard but I still haven't decided what I want.

"Plenty of time for that," he says, and lets himself be distracted by the next customer. I hurry home and turn my new fan on in the living room, where it whirs quietly, alone in its space. A fan is not usually where one would start to furnish a living room, but nothing is usual about my life right now.

Jimmy arrives on time and leans the Sheetrock against the wall. I am momentarily puzzled that there are only four sheets, but then realize that they are long sheets and it's a very small room. He's anticipated my lack of everything and brought a pair of sawhorses for a makeshift worktable. He carries in tools and a bucket of drywall mud, and we set a time for Wednesday at 8:00 a.m. I immediately see that there could be a problem, since he'll be running an electric screw gun while I'm working, and there are no doors between his workspace and mine. The plastic sheet isn't going to block much sound. I wonder where the nearest free Wi-Fi is and then decide not to worry about it. I can probably sit in the car if I have to be on a conference call.

CHAPTER 16

I'm now into my third week, which means time is running out to get my car licensed in Missouri, which means I first have to get it insured in Missouri. I decide that this coming Friday will be dedicated to car stuff. I spend some time online and discover the obvious: I need to download and print forms, and I haven't gotten around to buying a printer.

I hate comparison shopping for electronics, so I set aside my "shop local" principles for the day and go printer shopping virtually. I make a list, then a chart, then finally pick one and pay for two-day shipping so I can be ready to go on Friday. That is, if I can make the printer work. I miss my husband every day, but usually that grief is qualified by his last miserable months, when he was angry and confused and I had to keep telling myself "It's not him talking. It's the Parkinson's." I did most of my grieving long before he died. But he always bought the computer equipment and kept it all working. He made the hardware work and I made the software work. It was a good combo.

Panicking a little, I transfer my AAA membership online and buy AAA insurance too, so I'll be that much ahead on Friday. I should do comparison shopping—I should talk to my neighbors. I don't know if there is an upcharge for living in this neighborhood, and if there is, if that is even legal. But I need to keep my stress level in check, so I go ahead and buy it. I tell myself I can always change carriers next year. I don't know for sure that I'll be here next year, but it's easier to act as though I will be.

CHAPTER 17

I set an alarm and get up early on Wednesday. I want to have breakfast cleared away and my lunch ready in the refrigerator before Jimmy arrives. I wonder if I should offer him lunch and mentally inventory potential sandwich supplies. I still have ham, so that is covered. I also want to get in an hour or two of work before he comes, so that I can take some time off while he's here if I need to. I'm excited about getting the ceiling done so I can move on to paint and furniture, but I'm also anxious about his being here all day. It has nothing to do with him; I'm just always unsure about these situations. Do I offer him coffee, leave a pitcher of water for him, tell him he's free to use the bathroom, offer to help him lift the drywall into place? I focus on my laptop and am surprised when I hear the doorbell. Boris is not surprised; he's already waiting. I let Jimmy in and offer him coffee. He's got his own go cup.

"Looks like you've been through this before," he says, nodding toward the plastic sheet hanging in the kitchen doorway. "I'll seal that up before I start anything messy." I've taped it only at the top so we can go back and forth for the time being.

He tells me he'll start by taking down the crown molding (*crown molding? I hadn't even noticed. Who would put up crown molding instead of putting a shower in the bathroom?*). He'll save it and put it back up if he can but warns me that it might split and be unusable. I'm fine with that, and he says that he'll finish the corners so they don't need the molding at all, and I agree. This is hardly a crown molding sort of house. Next he'll take down the remaining plaster and bag it—he's brought heavy paper construction waste bags. He says that he'll be finished with that by lunchtime and he'll take the bags away for disposal. So that absolves me of lunch duties. "If there aren't any surprises, I'll start with the Sheetrock this afternoon," he says. I point out the bathroom as though it weren't clearly visible, tell him to let me know if he needs anything, and go back to work. I've moved my chair so that he can see me if he wants something.

Once he's pulled the nails out of the molding, the noise is reduced to muffled thuds, and the morning passes smoothly for both of us. Around eleven thirty that morning he calls through to let me know that he's leaving and has left the fan in the window to clear the dust.

I eat my lunch and go out the back door, around the house, and in through the front door to see how it's going. I'm pleased to see that he's put down drop clothes. The floor isn't in great shape, but I'm glad he's not making it any worse. The plaster ceiling is down and gone and he's even swept up. I think about hauling the shop vac upstairs but realize there will be more dust when he sands the drywall joints.

When Jimmy gets back, he brings in a large T-brace, so he probably won't need my help lifting. I'm quick to offer it, though, now that I'm pretty sure he won't need it. He thanks me and says that he's got it covered. By four o'clock he's got the drywall up and tells me that he can stay another hour and get the first coat of mud up if that's okay with me. I'm all for it and decide that I'll install the new dryer outlet while there is someone else in the house. I'm confident, but still. I tell him where I'll be and he gives me a skeptical look.

"I've done this before," I assure him. Which is sort of true. I have changed outlets, just not a 220 outlet, and always with my husband nearby and watching. "I've already turned off the breaker, and I'm just swapping out an old one for this new one. I bought a new dryer and it didn't match the old outlet."

Either I sound convincing or he decides it's not his place to object. I realize that I'll have to eat crow if I run into trouble, but I don't mind too much. I double-check the breaker labeled "dryer," and for good measure I turn off the only other 220 breaker, which I assume is for the big rusty air conditioner installed through the back wall. The basement doesn't have finished walls, so the outlet is in a metal box screwed to a board that is securely fastened to the foundation wall. I open the box and take a picture to be sure I get all the wires connected properly. I don't see anything slipshod about the old installation, so I forge ahead. I do have an anxious moment before I plug in the dryer, wishing I had a multimeter to test the outlet, but I don't and even if I did I would have to spend some time watching YouTube videos before I was confident that I knew how to use it.

The plug fits the outlet just fine, but the dryer won't turn on. I'm ready to go upstairs and admit defeat when I remember that the breaker is off. Idiot! Uber-cautious now, I unplug the dryer again, flip the breaker, and inspect the outlet and the breaker for . . . what? I'm hedging my bets and delaying the moment of truth. I plug the dryer in. Nothing happens. No sparks, no smoke—all good. I press the start button. Nothing happens. Not so good. Oh, I need to set it. I should have read the instructions for running this thing, but I can't remember where I put them. In fact, I can't remember even seeing them. I peer at the controls and set it for timed drying, five minutes. I press the button again, and yes, it starts. With a lot of clattering. Ah, now I know where the manual is. I turn it to off and remove the manual and warranty and wonder once again where I'm going to keep this stuff.

Jimmy probably thinks I'm a total idiot, it's taking me so long. But he doesn't let on when I go upstairs. He has taken the fan out of the window and is carrying out the T brace.

"That all go okay?" He's being casual.

"Yep, all good. It's nice to have a dryer again."

"I guess so—it's been raining a lot," he says. "I took the fan out of the window, but you might want to leave it running tonight. I should be able to do the second coat tomorrow afternoon."

We agree on three o'clock and he takes off. I loosen the tape and go through to admire his work, making Boris stay in the kitchen. This feels like a big step, a good step. I secure the front door and check the window locks. Boris and I go out the back door for an evening stroll.

CHAPTER 18

I'm up early again, with nothing pressing before my first conference call at eight o'clock. The day is uneventful except for the big event of drying laundry in the new dryer. I run downstairs more than once to stare at the outlet and make sure it's not sparking. When Jimmy arrives at three, he knocks instead of ringing the doorbell. When I let him in, he asks if the bell is on the fritz again.

"I forgot about it. I guess it's been working." I go out and press it and nothing happens.

I remember that he offered to look at it the first time he was here, but now that I've pretended to have electrician skills I feel funny about asking him. It's likely that it's just a loose wire, but I don't have any idea which breaker is involved or how to test it. I've pretty much exhausted my knowledge of home repair in the electrical department. I decide to come clean.

"Maybe you could take a look at it? Changing outlets is pretty much the beginning and the end of my ability."

He laughs and asks where it is and I show him the stairway. "Your dad did all this, huh?" He's saying this mostly to himself, so I just mutter a "yup" and let it go.

The printer arrives by FedEx and is surprisingly easy to set up. As long as everything is in the same room, it even works over

Wi-Fi so I don't have to have another cable gathering dog hair. Until I have more table space, I put the printer on a shelf in the closet. At noon, I go out for printer paper and an extension cord. Two extension cords: this won't be the last time I need one. I print my DMV forms and my proof of insurance.

Jimmy says that he'll be back Friday after three and rings the doorbell on his way out.

CHAPTER 19

Looking online, I am pretty sure I don't have to take a written test or driving test to transfer my driver's license, but I definitely have to go into the DMV for a sign-recognition test and a vision test, and to surrender my California license. I look through the sign information and am pretty confident about both that and my vision. I can also get my car registered and get new plates.

I choose an office in Raytown, which might not be the closest but it will be a nice drive through Swope Park. I pack a sandwich and iced coffee, in case the lines are really long and I need sustenance so I won't be crabby with the staff. If I get done quickly, I can eat in the picnic area at the lagoon boathouse in the park.

The office opens at eight and I'm on the road at seven forty-five with the morning commuters. The route along Gregory, down the long slope over the Blue River and around the Lake of the Woods was always our route to points east. It is still familiar and pleasant in spite of the morning fog. Traffic is lighter than I expected, but then 63rd Street to the north is now a major trafficway, so maybe that's taken some of the commuter load.

East of the park the route is not so familiar, but my phone's navigation app gets me there easily, shortly after eight. I'm finished and on my way out the door by eight thirty. I've had two moments of reality check: the first when I arrived to find only three people ahead of me in line, which is clear proof that I'm not in California anymore. The second was when I had to hand over my California license and plates. I am officially a Missourian again. Somehow this is sobering.

I've brought tools, so I attach my new plates and ponder my next move. I've got more Friday than I expected. It's too early to try any local used furniture shops, so I head back to the park to enjoy my peanut butter on toast. Rounding the lake, I signal a right turn toward the lagoon. And keep rounding the lake. There is no right turn and no sign that there ever was a right turn. I know there was a right turn here, it's how we got to the lagoon and to the swimming pool. I sigh. It's not the first time my memory has been wrong. I think about heading south toward the picnic shelters and hiking up Dead Man's Trail but decide that it's probably not where I think it is, either, so I drive through the park to Elmwood, which is exactly where it belongs, and make my way to the Plaza. I want my own pillows.

The Country Club Plaza was the first shopping center in the world designed to accommodate shoppers arriving by automobile. It's not a mall by any stretch. It's a village, with Spanish-style architecture and lots of fountains. It's beautiful and always full of shoppers and tourists, and it's where my friends and I used to hang out once we got our drivers' licenses.

Topsy's popcorn was a hot spot, so I park and sally forth to see if it still exists. It does, and they still sell my favorite cinnamon flavor, which is red, as in Red-Hots, rather than brown. I'm all grown up so I can eat sugary popcorn before noon if I like, and I do. I can't shop with sticky fingers, so I meander, reveling in familiarity. I find my favorite little fountain, a bronze sculpture of a nude boy with a frog spraying water up at him, a Midwest version of Manneken Pis. I surreptitiously rinse the popcorn sugar from my hands.

This is the neighborhood where I would probably live if someone had told me a few years ago that I was required to move to Kansas City. It's everything I like: in town, not the suburbs, perfectly walkable, tree-lined, gracious. I also know the back story, which is that when J.C. Nichols developed the lovely residential district around the Plaza itself, he imposed racially based covenants on all properties. Although these were made illegal in the mid-century, the homeowners found ways to continue the practice throughout the 1900s. The Country Club District is still predominantly white, and it is among the wealthiest neighborhoods in the United States. I know this and am somewhat ashamed that I still enjoy my day here.

I move on to pillow shopping. My mother's favorite store was Emery Bird Thayer, which is long gone, so I look for Macy's and can't find it. I end up at Scandia, where I enjoy testing the $300 pillows, but this is too much of a splurge. I enjoy the stroll, but the boutiques here now seem out of my league. I pick up another bag of popcorn for later and drive to Surplus Sales to buy a bed and get back home in time to let Jimmy in. The bed I want will take about two weeks to arrive, which is perfect for me. I've got that decision out of the way, and I have time to get ready. While Jimmy works, I order pillows and other bedding from Vermont Country Store, and then check the Eddie Bauer and J. Jill websites to order some lighter-weight summer clothes, and something a little dressier than my current meagre collection. Being tall has some advantages—I can reach the top shelves, for example. But it certainly restricts my choice of clothing vendors. Today, I'm good with that. I don't think I could stand facing the entire world of clothing options.

I make a note to get more hangers. So far, everything still fits in the little closet in what I'm trying not to think of as the grow room. I've decided to sleep there when the bed arrives. I'll need a dresser too, although it will have to be small to fit. For now, I'm getting away with storing underwear in a bathroom drawer.

Jimmy packs up and tells me he'll be back Monday morning to paint the ceiling and asks if I have any other projects in mind. I give him the short version of the grow room story and ask him what he thinks about sanding the floor and painting it to hide the water stains. He likes the idea and gives me a price for sanding the floor and painting the whole room, top to bottom. I had planned to do that myself, but I'm feeling overwhelmed by all the things I can do in theory but can't seem to get to. I like the price and we agree that he'll start the bedroom as soon as the living room ceiling is finished. I'm feeling good about progress because I know that the dilapidated and empty state of my house is causing a lot of subtle but persistent stress. Just knowing that things will be better in two weeks lifts my spirits and I have a glass of wine to celebrate.

CHAPTER 20

I decide to walk to the library while Matt is mowing, even though it means walking alone, without Boris. The public library has moved, so it's a little more than a mile now. We used to ride our bikes there in the summer. We shoved them behind the shrubbery and never imagined that anyone would steal them.

As I stroll along Meyer Boulevard, a police cruiser passes me and parks about a block farther along but the officer doesn't get out. As I walk by, he is busy with his cell phone. Another block, and he passes me again. At the next intersection, I cross Meyer. I need to be on the other side anyway, but now I'm curious about the cop. I don't recognize him, but then I can't really see him behind his tinted windows. Am I so conspicuous here, a middle-aged white woman strolling down the boulevard? I make up stories about him watching me. I might be under cover. A purse snatcher. A truly bizarre hooker. I'm heading for the middle school to kidnap my grandson from his soccer game. I wish my childhood pal Angie were here to make up more stories and laugh with me. Finally I decide he is just making sure I'm not a runaway from the Swope Ridge nursing home. Maybe I should color my hair.

By now I've passed Southeast High School, which I would have attended if I hadn't gone to Bishop Hogan High. I round the corner onto Swope Parkway and pass what was Southeast

Junior High, on the same campus as the high school but a much newer building, with the entrance around the corner. I got my polio vaccine there in 1962, through a program called Sabin on Sunday. I can't believe that information is still in my head. I'm not sure what the building is now.

The library is next door, in a new building that is open and airy. I sort of miss the old branch, which was all wood with windows high up near the ceiling, above the bookshelves. It was in the high school building, with its own outside entrance. I loved that library, although I would have loved any library. This new library is more suitable to the twenty-first century and I'm happy to use it, even if I wish it were closer to home. I get a card with no trouble but leave without checking out any books. This is just a morning walk and I'm not ready to focus on reading.

I return home the way I came, greeting people and feeling some déjà vu as I pass familiar houses that seem to be in the same condition they were when I last walked or bicycled home this way. One of the very last times I biked down this street, I was about fourteen and had biked to visit a friend who lived near my old grade school. It was dusk as I pedaled home, which is probably why I started feeling creeped out. Not long before, a high school classmate's older brother had been shot and left bleeding on the street. No one passing by would help him, and he died. Around the same time, another classmate's younger brother was shot and killed on his front porch, just two blocks from my grade school. I had a vision of being shot on my bicycle. That was probably the last time I went down these two streets alone and not in a car. I try not to think about that now, and the walk home is uneventful.

I want to keep Sunday clear. I'm thinking of taking Boris and a picnic lunch to Holmes Park and going for a long walk. So I spend the rest of Saturday vacuuming and wiping down the living room to be ready for painting on Monday. The walls have some water stains, so it's back to the hardware store for Bin primer to cover them, plus spackle to patch holes and minor cracks. I need a toolbox for my growing collection, but I decide to wait. Maybe there's a used one out there for me. There were a couple of big holes in one wall where someone must have hung a shelf, or even a television. It looks like that didn't work out so well. Jimmy has patched those holes with drywall mud. I have to make sure I pay him for the extra work he's done.

CHAPTER 21

At 5:00 a.m. on Sunday, I'm standing at my kitchen counter with a hot towel pressed to my head, nursing a horrible sinus headache. My own fault, I should have worn a dust mask yesterday. I know better.

It's still dark and I don't want to sit at my table in the back room with three windows and no curtains, but I'm not up to moving furniture. Instead, I carry my stool into the kitchen and sit at the pullout bread board, still holding the hot towel to my forehead. When the towel cools, I reheat it in the microwave. I take tiny sips of coffee and feel sorry for myself. I feel exposed and wish I had curtains. I wish I had a hot water bottle. I wish I had a comfortable sofa to curl up on. I wish I had someone to make me toast and rub my neck. I wish I had my old house and my old stuff and my old life. I let tears stream down my face.

The phone rings, the real phone, not my mobile. I'm jolted by the sound, I don't think it's ever rung before. I've only used it to dial into conference calls for work. It rings again and I get up to answer it. I can't think who would be calling. Even telemarketers usually give us a break on Sundays at 5:00 a.m.

"Hello?" I clear my throat and try it a little louder. "Hello!"

I hear Josie on the other end of the line. "I'm on the kitchen floor; I tripped," she says. Her voice quavers. "I saw your light on. I don't know what to do."

My first thought is that I don't have any lights on, just the light from the open microwave. My head hurts too much for light.

My second thought is to get to her as fast as I can.

"I'm on my way. Can you get to the door to unlock it?"

She tells me where her hidden key is, and I hang up and head for the door, only to realize that I'm dressed in an oversized t-shirt that basically hides nothing. Josie's house is not on fire, so I take thirty seconds to put yesterday's clothes back on and grab my phone and purse.

I find the key, acting all casual in case crooks are casing the street, and let myself in the back door, calling to her as I enter. Josie is still on the floor, although she's managed to prop herself up against the kitchen cabinets. She tries to smile and tells me that I don't look so good. I laugh. My head still hurts, but not as much as it did. Adrenaline must be an effective pain reliever.

I don't know much about first aid, other than that moving an accident victim is best left to professionals. I ask what hurts and ask what she can and can't move. I also ask if she was dizzy before she fell. She's adamant that she was not, that she slipped on the rug in front of the sink. I can see the rug, bane of my mother's generation and their hips, now bunched up in front of the stove. She thinks she can get up if I help her, so I finally agree and we get her into a kitchen chair. She still looks shocky to me and I offer her water.

"If we were British, I'd pour you a brandy and make some tea," I tell her in a weak attempt to cheer her up.

"And I'd drink them both," she says, "but I'll settle for coffee."

I get coffee started and let her get her thoughts together, assess her pain. I get her walker but I can see that she's not ready to stand up.

"Should we call your daughter?" I ask, hoping to foist off responsibility.

"She's in Columbia." Right. So that won't work. Columbia

is two hours away, and that's after you're up and dressed and caffeinated.

"Then I think we should call 911 and let the EMTs take a look."

She doesn't want this but agrees, since we are out of other options. She too, has a landline, so I use it to call, since that will pinpoint the address precisely. Not that I don't know this house number as well as my own. I stress that she's conscious and not bleeding, but has fallen and can't stand. I don't know if she's hit her head. While we wait, we sip coffee and I get her a sweater from the closet in the room that is a close replica of my grow room. I'm delighted to see the built-in bed is still there. When the DePeres added on, they put the basement stairs in a slightly different spot than we did, and the bed is built over that stairway. When I was six, I thought that was genius.

Sunday morning must be a good time for calling 911; they pull up by the time I am back with the sweater. I open the front door and stand back to let them take over. Josie has regained her calm demeanor and doesn't need an interpreter. I pour myself coffee and roll my shoulders, easing the pain in my neck and head. Looking out her kitchen window, I see why she said that she saw my lights on. As part of my random-lights-on security plan, I had flipped on the overhead switch in the grow room the night before, leaving the shade up so the light could be seen from outside, but closing the door so I didn't have to look at the squalor. I'd forgotten to turn it off. At this moment, I am glad I did.

The EMTs check her out and Josie agrees to go to the hospital for X-rays. I make sure she has her purse and keys and cell phone and make her promise to call her daughter. I tell her I'll feed Boris and then meet her there. I'm relieved that they are taking her to Research Hospital, which is only blocks away.

By now, the ambulance has drawn some attention. Dave and Carol are out in their bathrobes, and they introduce me to Benny and Joyce, who live directly across from me. I probably met them on the day of my break-in, but that was a blur so I'm glad to meet them properly, even though we're having another emergency situation. Dave and Carol offer to go to the hospital, but I've already promised Josie that I'd go, so I tell them that I'll call when I know something and we'll take it from there. I know she's in good hands and didn't seem at all nervous about the ambulance ride, so I take time to eat a bowl of cereal as I stand in the backyard while Boris sniffs and pees. I clean myself up a bit and put on fresh clothes before leaving for the hospital.

Research Hospital was built, at 63rd and Prospect, when I was very young. When I drove down Prospect in my first week back, I was a little surprised that it had grown rather than relocating to the outlying Missouri suburbs or "the Kansas side." It must be a boon to this part of the city, which doesn't even have a supermarket nearby. Downhill from the hospital and on its much-expanded campus is a large new CVS, exactly where Milgram's, the largest grocery store in the area, once stood.

It takes me a while to locate parking for the emergency room, but it's still fairly early on Sunday morning, so the lot isn't full. I find Josie sitting up on a bed in a cubicle in the ER. She's got a few monitors on, but just blood pressure and oxygen. She's talking to her daughter on her cell phone. The nurse asks if I'm family and I say "no" just as Josie says "yes." She knows the drill better than I do. The nurse hedges and says that Josie can fill me in and the doctor will be back soon. Josie is subdued but relieved that it's not worse than it could be. She tells me they think she sprained her ankle and that her newly replaced hip was not damaged. Her daughter and son-in-law are on their way.

A case manager arrives and talks to Josie without making

me leave. He says that they can release her to rehab and she will need to be there for at least two weeks. Josie asks if she could go home if her daughter stays with her and they arrange for a home health physical therapist. The case manager says "maybe," but she'll get more therapy and get better faster at rehab. They talk about which rehab facility she might go to, and Josie agrees to go once she is almost-promised that she can go to the one she wants. I'm getting a great education here. I feel like I should take notes. I'm only about twenty years younger than Josie. She's got it all figured out.

"My daughter would stay if she had to, but I don't want her to talk about assisted living for two weeks solid, so I'm going to rehab," she confides when the case manager has left. She tells me more about the neighbors while we wait for paperwork and Sue. I find out that Josie is seventy-six, still plenty young enough to live on her own. I'm firmly in the no-assisted-living camp when it comes to Josie. I realize that she's a bit of a lifeline for me, which makes me glad I could be there for her.

I remember Dave and Carol and have Josie call them, since they'll be more relieved hearing from her directly. They appear twenty minutes later, and I gratefully take my leave. They are old friends and they know her daughter, and I'll feel like an intruder when the family arrives. I tell Josie I'll see her soon and leave it at that.

At home, I take a hot shower to finish off the headache, then go back to bed. It's well past noon when I wake up, and it looks like it could rain any minute. This seems like a good time to finally plant those tomatoes. I spade up most of the old garden area and plant them, then tuck them in with the grass clippings Matt has left behind the outdoor fireplace. I am wondering if I should get out the hose to water them in or just use an empty milk carton when I hear voices next door. I look up and see Sue and Joel getting out of their car. They wave and I go over to ask about the patient. I don't want to seem too involved in their business, so I open with a low-key "How is Josie?" and let them take it whichever way they will.

They tell me she is fine and that they have taken her to the rehab center. They are just picking up some things for her and will be staying at her house overnight. If she does well, they'll head back to Columbia early since they both work. I tell them that sounds good and that I'll miss Josie while she's away.

It's starting to drizzle, so I tell them goodbye and they thank me for coming to Josie's aid.

"No problem. Let me know if I can do anything," I say, hoping for casual but helpful.

CHAPTER 22

I don't see Josie's daughter that night, and I hear the car leaving shortly before six o'clock the next morning. I feel like I've lost my bodyguard. I'm reminded of when my ninety-five-year-old aunt was in her last year of life. I'd stay with her occasionally for a week or so, especially if she was sick. I had no problem sleeping alone upstairs in her big house because she was sleeping downstairs. A sick ancient aunt stood between me and whatever. But if she was in the hospital and I was alone in the house, I cowered upstairs listening for burglars. I guess I subconsciously knew that no one had ever broken in while she was there alone, but there were no data on people breaking in when I was there alone. In my new house, I somehow feel safer knowing that Josie is a stone's throw away, only now she isn't there.

"Suck it up," I tell myself.

Jimmy arrives Monday morning and paints the living room ceiling. While the first coat dries, he starts getting set up in the bedroom. As I move my clothes out of the closet, we talk about dust control. I ask him if he would consider sanding the living room and the hall floors while he's at it, and he says that he might as well do the front bedroom too and get it all over with.

"Once you get furniture in here, you'll never get back to it."

He's right, and I decide that I can use the fan to ventilate the work areas during the day and set it up to blow fresh air in on me at night. I deflate the borrowed bed and move it to the back room.

"Crap," I mutter to myself. No curtains. I set up the bed as far into the corner as it will go so that only one window is really critical. I check the time. I've still got hours until dark. I'll make something work.

Jimmy doesn't ask about painting the other room. I know I can do it, but not before he does the floors. I'm thinking there is a good chance that I'll add that to his list in the end.

When Jimmy is finished for the day, curtains become important. I know I won't sleep if I feel visible and vulnerable, dog or no dog. But I've come up with a plan that doesn't involve newspaper and masking tape, although I'll go that route as Plan B or C.

My first stop is my favorite resale shop, where I rummage for tablecloths. I'll loop them over tension rods and secure them with safety pins, and then sew on buttons to cover the pins. If I can find tension rods, safety pins, buttons, needle, and thread before dark. Or even straight pins and forget the buttons. Blue tape as a fallback, but I don't trust tape on cloth.

I find an Indonesian print tablecloth and am considering how ridiculous it will look in a room with pale gray paneling. A clerk offers to help and I tell her what I'm doing. I feel like I'm babbling and giving her my whole life story. I mentally roll my eyes and tell myself I've got to get a social life. She is, or acts like she is, interested in my story and gets into the hunt. She finds a turquoise-blue chenille bedspread with ball fringe that looks new and is big enough for at least two windows.

"You could piece together enough for the third window if you have a sewing machine," she says. My eyes open wide. I *do* have a sewing machine. The friend I visited as I was leaving California is an avid quilter and is a sort of sewing machine magnet. She says that people just give them to her, and she finds homes for them. I stayed with her for two nights, and she talked me into taking one. At the time, I was still feeling like I didn't want to be responsible for anything, but she insisted that I would be glad later. I agreed, on the condition that it could be squeezed behind the passenger seat, on the floor of the car. And that's where it still is, hidden under the rug that is spread across the back seat for Boris. I have never taken it out of the car.

I picture the Indonesian print, which I really like, in the grow room instead, with the soon-to-be green walls.

"Sold," I say. "I'll take both."

She rings up the sale and puts them in a plastic bag. The California girl in me starts to refuse the bag, but I remember that I'm a Missouri girl now who has found a lot of valid uses for plastic bags. And although I'm not at all worried about bedbugs, I do intend to dump these directly into the washing machine and then dry them on hot. So I take the bag and tell her about the sewing machine.

She asks if she can see it and walks me out to the car. "Do you need scissors and thread? Sometimes they have a compartment with stuff in it. Otherwise, I can see what we have."

I heave the machine into the back of the station wagon and we open the case. Lots of sewing machine needles and several spools of thread. I've got scissors at home that will probably cut cloth, and if not I still have time to get to the hardware store.

I have to go to the hardware store anyway for curtain rods. But I stop at home to put the future curtains in the washer, which gives me a chance to test the scissors. I can chew through the cloth, but I'll need better scissors anyway, so they go on the list. I also measure the windows to get the exact inside dimensions. I'll buy tension rods because they don't require much installation, don't damage anything, and can be used at other windows if I decide on something more permanent for these windows. Since the addition is paneled, the marks are still there from my mother's curtain rods, and it looks like at least one more set has been installed and removed, leaving its own scars. I can probably minimize them, or maybe I'll hide them behind real curtain rods later. Today, it's tension rods or duct tape.

The floor is the biggest surface I have for cutting, so I clean it and spread out the chenille bedspread. I put Boris in a down-stay to keep him from walking on the fabric and licking my face. In his opinion I should keep my face a lot closer to the floor.

Then I clear my table and put it in the middle of the room and set up the sewing machine. I should have taken the time to buy thread in the right color, but it's too late to do anything about that. I use a sort of grayish thread to make casings using a long stitch that I can easily pull out later. I leave the edges unhemmed. Hems can wait until I have blue thread.

I feel a little exposed sleeping in the big room, and it bothers me a little that the two high windows on the north side are curtain free. I finally shift the bed so that my head is directly under those windows and I feel better. I also feel ridiculous that it even matters.

In the morning, I see why chenille is not normally used for curtains. It lets in too much light. But the ball fringe amuses me and the blue curtains did keep me safe all night.

CHAPTER 23

For the rest of the week, I work in the back and Jimmy paints, sands, and paints again in the grow room. I've chosen a dark olive green for the floor, with light sage green for the walls and the same ceiling white as in the living room. He finishes the painting and starts the floor sanding. When the floors are sanded, we agree that paint is still the best option for the grow room but that the oak in the other rooms isn't too badly damaged and can just be varnished. He tells me about a low-odor varnish and says that he'll pick it up and bring the receipt. By now he's fully aware of my aversion to dust and odors, although I haven't confessed to the nasty headaches they give me.

I figure out that I'm spending my entire take-home pay this week, and am rather proud of the fact that it doesn't bother me very much.

Our first eighty-degree day is predicted, so I make sure I'm up and out early with the dog. I haven't gone south past Gregory and I want to take a look, to see if anything is left of Fairyland, the old amusement park on 75th Street.

You bought Fairyland tickets at a ticket booth and spent them on rides: maybe one ticket for a kiddie ride and two for the teeter-dip and three for the roller coaster. We went there to ride the rides exactly once a year, on Suburban Bank day in August.

When Suburban Bank day started, a bank customer could get free tickets every time he or she did business at the bank during the several weeks prior to the big day. Mother would go as often as possible and collect enough tickets for my brother and me to ride as much, or almost as much, as we wanted. In later years, you just had to show up at the bank once and get a sticker. As long as you had the sticker on your shirt, you could ride anything. By then we were tall enough to ride everything and made sure we did. We loved it all indiscriminately: the Caterpillar, the Whip, the bumper cars, the funhouses, everything. We even rode the kiddie rides late in the day when there weren't any lines in Kiddieland. I can still picture the place, with its gravel surface and shade trees and shooting galleries.

The rest of the summer, we went there to swim. The park had an Olympic-size swimming pool, with a ten-foot deep end and diving boards at its far end. Mother signed us up for swimming lessons as soon as we were old enough. After the early-morning lesson, we could stay there for the rest of the day without paying. It was much closer than the nearest public pool in Swope Park, which was important since our dad took our only car to work, and pool admission was only fifty cents. From the time I was eight, Mother let me go there pretty much as often as I liked. I would walk to Angie's house on Montgall, and we'd walk to the pool together, with whichever of her eight brothers and sisters wanted to go that day.

I can't get there on Montgall now, since it is buried under the expressway, so Boris and I walk up the hill on Chestnut. I rarely walked on Chestnut south of Gregory, so I don't expect to recognize much. And that's just as well, because Chestnut ends at 73rd Street now, and I have to go east to Bellefontaine before I can go on south to 75th. The expressway has curved east and become a freeway. I walk under it along 75th as far as Prospect and find what looks like a corporate campus, where I think the entrance to Fairyland was. A sign in the middle of an expansive green lawn says that it's the headquarters of Alphapointe, which I've never heard of. Satchel Paige School campus has taken over the space where I imagine the roller coaster and the pool were. There is no historic marker, let alone a leftover neon sign to remind us what was once here.

It's all pretty unattractive and I turn back to the north, not surprised but a little sorry. I spent a lot of time at that park, but it was changing even then. My earliest lesson in racial discrimination involved Fairyland. When I was six, which is about the time I would have started swimming lessons, there was a story in the newspaper about a lie-in at Fairyland. We didn't have a working television in 1961, so I had to have learned this from the paper, or from hearing my parents talk about the article in the paper. I could not wrap my six-year-old head around the idea of lying down in the park. My parents had to explain that Black people were not allowed in the park and that they were protesting this. I had no context for a policy like that, since the places I went—mostly church and school and local stores—had both Black and white members and patrons. I don't remember being outraged about the park rule, just puzzled, partly about the rule but mostly about lying on the ground.

By 1964, segregation at Fairyland Park ended. The swimming pool, however, was converted to a private club. We paid fifty cents to join the club at the beginning of the summer and then had to remember to take our membership cards each time we went swimming. I was aware that the club was formed to keep Black swimmers out, but we still swam there. I don't know what my parents thought about it. We wanted to swim, and there was no other swimming pool within walking distance. I'm having a hard time imagining how the screening even worked. Did the teenager who granted me my fifty-cent membership card tell Black kids no? Or did the Black kids just know better and stay away? Fifty years on, it's hard to imagine, but then again it isn't hard to imagine at all.

Within a few years, though, the pool began to deteriorate. The ladders rusted and the blue-painted surfaces turned green with algae. We were older and bigger and had bicycles, so we started going to the pool in Swope Park.

The Swope Park pool was closed one day a week, Monday I think, and scrubbed. It gleamed. Black and white kids swam there together without much trouble. But it was a long uphill bike ride home after a day of swimming, and twice our bicycle tires were slashed in the parking lot, which meant we had to push the bikes home. With no other place to swim, we gradually lost interest in swimming.

Boris and I walk home and I read old online newspaper stories about Fairyland. The amusement park held on until 1977 when a tornado damaged the Ferris wheel beyond repair. My parents had moved to southern Missouri by then, but someone sent Mother a newspaper clipping and she sent it on to me in St. Louis. The Ferris wheel was folded like a taco.

Attendance was pretty low by then; the newer-style Worlds of Fun had opened up north with bigger and better rides, although with no pool and no dance hall. By the time construction of the expressway got under way, the abandoned park was an easy target for the land needed for the transition from expressway to freeway. I don't know how I feel about it, its long history and its probable role in the residential development around it, its place in the struggle for civil rights in Kansas City, and even my place in that history. But I do sort of wish I could walk through the park once more and ride the Ferris wheel. Or maybe ram my brother a few times in the bumper cars.

CHAPTER 24

On Wednesday, my bedding order arrives and I revel in the extra pillows and lie in bed reading after dinner. I'm reading *The New Jim Crow,* or trying to.

I've been a voracious reader since I was old enough to hang over the side of my dad's chair and look at the words as he read stories to us. I've got the black-and-white photo to prove it. I can't remember not being able to read.

After the fire last year, my shell-shocked brain couldn't even focus on a newspaper. I read the comics, which didn't register, and some days I did the Sudoku or the crossword. Eventually I got my hands on Jane Austen, my go-to reading in times of trouble, and was just moving on to Anthony Trollope when I started getting ready to drive east.

Before I left, however, I went to a local library book sale and got a paper grocery bag full of books for five dollars. I made a beeline for the table labeled Literary and scooped up P.G. Wodehouse and Trollope, then went to the Mystery table and added a few lightweight murder mysteries for good measure. Trollope novels have all the human drama and joy and failure that modern novels have, but they are safely removed to another century. *The New Jim Crow* got in the bag too. It's fascinating, yes, but it's tearing me apart. I peek into it for a bit, but I always go back to

Wodehouse before I turn out the light. The problem is that it's not like *The Fire Next Time,* which is rending but in the past. The new Jim Crow is now, and it's here, and it's my problem as much as anyone's, no matter where I live. And I can't think of one true thing to do about it.

That's part of my whole worry about what I've done, coming back to the house where I grew up during a dramatic demographic shift of the 1960s and 1970s. Was I part of the problem, and now I want to be part of the solution? Is a white woman moving into a mostly Black neighborhood any kind of benefit? Does the neighborhood need or want my presence? Am I providing stability by taking one problem property and making it something more like normal? What is normal, or what should be normal? Am I Pontius Pilate asking "What is truth?" It is not my neighborhood anymore, not for me to say.

I'm glad I'm not being questioned in court under oath about how I made this decision and why. Because the truth is different every day. I need to talk this out, and there is only one person I can talk to. My childhood best friend, Angie.

Angie lived on Montgall, the street that has now disappeared from 50th Street south. In my mind Montgall has completely disappeared, but the expressway slips slightly west at 50th and Montgall remains where it always was from 50th north to 30th, and then appears sporadically from 30th to the river.

Angie and I went to the same public kindergarten and then the same Catholic grade school and high school. Our families were denizens of the far southwest corner of our parish, so all of our grade school friends lived north and east of us. The school bus picked up her family and then mine, so we almost always sat together. We bonded, however, during a playground discussion of birthdays. We were both born on January 20, and that was enough to cement a friendship between two six-year-olds that lasted through high school and beyond. I've been friends with her longer than I've been friends with anyone else. That longevity, the shared experiences of our youth, and the embarrassing, sentimental, and ordinary things we know about each other mean that I know that I can trust her totally. I know that she will support this move I have made. I know she will. I know that fact about her better than I know anything about myself.

So I text her and I tell her I'm in town and ask if she has any free time in the next week or two. Months go by when we don't contact each other, and she doesn't know I've moved here. She will assume nothing. She will just answer the question I have asked and let me know when she is available. I know this.

She lives on "the Kansas side" now, but very close to 70th Street, so the bizarre fact is that I can take Gregory due west until it loses its name and goes back to being 71st Street at the state line, and then keep going practically to her front door. Once again, we can almost see each other from our front porches, if it weren't for all the houses (and one expressway) in between.

In response to my text, she calls and we don't waste much time with small talk. She asks me where I'm staying and I give her my address, which she knows as well as her own. She is gleeful. I knew she would be. She's a teacher in a low-income school district and the rest of the spring semester will be grueling for her, as she does everything she can to make sure her students all do as well as they possibly can. We make plans to get together in June, after school is over for the summer.

"I'll go to your house," she says. "I can't wait to see it again. I drive around there sometimes, looking for some remnant of my yard, where it backed up to Prospect. But there is nothing."

"Yeah, I did that too. I thought maybe the wall along your mom's garden would still be there."

"Going to your house will be almost as good."

She'll never see her childhood home again, even from the outside, but she can see mine. We talk until we are hoarse and I hang up restored and exhausted.

CHAPTER 25

Jimmy has the grow room—now I can call it the green room—finished and I'm giving it some time to itself. I've gone back for a second window fan and have it ventilating the room full time during the days to get ready for the arrival of the new bed. He moves on to varnishing the rest of the sanded floors, making a little block-and-board bridge so I can get from the kitchen to the bathroom without stepping on the varnish. He's taped a sheet of newspaper to a sawhorse to keep Boris on the kitchen side of the bridge. He'll be finished soon and I'll miss him a little, but I can't wait to get my house back and finally start furnishing it. So far he hasn't asked about future projects, so I bring it up.

"Jimmy, I'm so pleased with all this," I tell him. "I'm going to have to take a break for a couple of months at least, but I do want to figure out a shower in the bathroom before winter. I'm happy to have a shower stall and no tub, but the window is a problem. I don't want to just put a curtain over it. Can I call you when I'm ready?" and then add, "I really want to make the back door stronger too. Is that something you could help me with?"

He says, "Yes, of course," and tells me to call any time. I almost feel guilty, like I'm laying him off, but he tells me that he's got a job next week on Bellefontaine, so he'll be nearby if

I have anything that needs attention. He also advises me to get a plunger. "Not that I think there's anything wrong with the plumbing here, but I haven't seen a house yet that didn't need a plunger sooner or later."

I'm due for another trip to the hardware store anyway, so I add "plunger" to the list.

CHAPTER 26

I've discovered pallets.

I start Friday with a run to the hardware store and come back with pepper plants and bean seeds. It's too late for peas but it's not too early for beans now. I also get hooks and loppers and a straw hat that won't look too ridiculous walking the dog.

But the main things I bring home are three pallets. I saw them behind the store and asked Henry if they were for sale. He said they were free and then sold me a saw and drill so I could take them apart and make other things from them. I'm going to start with a simple rustic table for the laundry area so I don't have to keep detergent and bleach on the floor. In my head I see a larger table so that I can sort the laundry too. But my first one will be one pallet perched on four legs cut from a second pallet.

The best thing Henry did was advise me not to try to pry out the nails if they were put together with a lot of large nails. "Those aren't worth it. Just cut off the part with all the nails and use what's left. Or don't even take home the ones with tons of nails. There will always be another pallet. Try the supermarkets if you want more choice."

I spend the rest of the morning lopping tall elm sprouts and using them to build a tomato and bean trellis. I think these are Siberian elm saplings. After the American elms lining the area streets died from Dutch Elm disease, many people planted non-native elms. The neighbors across the street planted three on their double lot. They grew quickly and looked beautiful, but lost branches readily in storms. One uprooted and the others were removed when the absentee landlord moved a house onto the open side yard. These may be their descendants. They are everywhere, and it will be a long time before I remove mine, so at least maybe I'll get some use out of them.

By noon it's hot in the sun and I go down to the basement with my pallets. "It's a lot cooler down here," I tell Boris, but he lies down at the top of the stairs and sleeps.

In the afternoon the wind comes up and I return to Midtown for metal fence posts to reinforce my makeshift vegetable trellis. I've blistered my hands using a screwdriver to construct my new laundry table, so I talk to Henry about a screw gun. Expensive, but I know I'll use it a lot. I've got shelves and curtain rods and all kinds of other projects in my future. "Screw the cost," I joke lamely. I'm getting my contractor's discount, after all.

Henry asks if I've decided what to do about reinforcing my back door. I haven't because I'm in denial that I need to take on something that big. I know I can't do it myself. Plus, the doors I've been looking at online are in the five-hundred-dollar range.

"Have you thought about ReStore?" he asks. "They get all kinds of things."

"Oh!" I say, mind racing with ideas. "Is there one nearby?"

"Not really. There are several of them, but none around here. You might be able to call and see what they have before you go. They can be a bit overwhelming."

I know about Habitat for Humanity's cleverly named ReStore resale shops, mostly because we donated things to them in California. We always thought it was a great idea, but the store closest to us was extremely picky about what it would take. No doors more than seven years old. No brass light fixtures. No flooring, even new in the box, unless there was enough to do a ten-by-ten-foot room. So we usually just left things on the curb with a Free sign and they disappeared quickly. In a climate with no rain for seven months of the year, it's considered curbside recycling.

I thank Henry for the idea, and he gives me some pointers about measuring my opening (gotta find the studs) and about buying only a prehung door with a reinforced frame.

"No point in putting a steel door in a flimsy frame."

Well, that's obvious, but I've been known to miss the obvious.

I look at shelf brackets and am pondering how to attach them to the stone foundation in the basement, when Henry gently butts in again. He knows I'm working in the basement and he knows I'm trying to build storage.

"In the basement, sometimes it's easier to suspend shelves from the joists overhead," he suggests. Some contractor I am. I buy hanging hardware and scrounge one more pallet.

CHAPTER 27

My hands and shoulders hurt, but I need to keep moving on multiple fronts, so I go back to the garden to install my trellis reinforcements. I'm dreaming of planting bulbs in the fall and adding grape vines and a chicken coop next year when I hear car doors closing nearby. I look up and see Sue and Joel in Josie's driveway.

They shout their hellos and wave, but go on in the house, so I go back to pounding and pruning and dreaming. I still look out back sometimes and expect to see the shed and the maple tree. I'm keeping an eye out for a transplantable maple and wondering what it will take to replace the shed. I pretend I'm really going to do that and shove sticks in the ground to mark the corners. I'm pondering whether it really has to be exactly where it was in the 1900s when I hear Sue calling to me.

"I was wondering if you'd like to have dinner with us," she says.

Dinner? I haven't had dinner with anyone since I left my cousin's house a month ago. Of course I'll have dinner. I hope I remember how to eat with other people at the table. Is that a skill you can lose in a month?

I'm thinking all that while I'm saying "Yes, that would be great." and I want to ask "When? Where? Now?" but instead I wait for further information.

"Nothing fancy, we thought we'd get pizza and eat here, bring Mom over. She's doing really well and can probably come home in two weeks," she says. "Mom says ONE week, but we'll see." She seems relaxed and not worried. "About five thirty? Mom's gotten used to eating early over there."

I offer a salad but Sue says that they'll get that with the pizza. They want this to be a little thank-you for helping Josie.

I decide to go to Saturday evening mass. Every service has its own vibe, brought about by the music and the priest and mostly something subtle about the people who choose that service as their regular one. I want to see what the evening service is like at St. Louis. It's on the early side, 4:00 p.m., so even if it runs long I can be back in time for dinner. I know full well that I'll have to slip out at 5:10, but I'm still in stealth mode there anyway. The dinner just gives me an excuse to leave early, not that anyone but me will hear that excuse.

I misjudged completely. At the Saturday service, they have about a half hour of singing before they even get started. I'm forced to leave immediately after communion and then still have to push it a little to avoid being late. I wonder what Boris will think about hearing the car park and then hearing me walk away.

I needn't have worried about him. The inside door is open and when Josie sees me through the screen her first words are "Where's Boris? You go right back and get him." So I do, and he must have heard Josie because he is panting with anticipation when I open my front door.

Dinner is casual and relaxed and I feel welcome and at ease. We sit at the table in the kitchen, although I can see that Josie has a larger table in the back room. In her house, the addition is bigger than mine, two distinct rooms with a regular door between, so the half behind the kitchen makes a nice dining room.

The kitchen table is an old one with a Formica top and I

wonder if they would be amused if I told them that it reminded me of the chrome table with the yellow Formica top that the DePeres had in this room. Then I wish I could just carry on a conversation without analyzing everything I say before I say it. Filters are good, but mine seems to get clogged.

"Were you in this house a lot when you were a kid?" Sue asks as if she heard what I was thinking.

"Quite a bit when I was little. Not so much later. The girl who lived here was probably ten years older than me, so we didn't play much. And after they got a second car and the mom went to work . . . well, you know. Everyone gets busy and you don't see your neighbors so much. I missed that, even as a little kid."

Everyone seems to be mulling that over.

"You work at home, though, right? Are you self-employed?" Sue asks, and then frowns. "Sorry, it's none of my business, but it is nice for Mom to know you are around a lot."

Josie gives her a look that says that she doesn't need a babysitter, but she adds, "She's right. It's been a long time since anyone was home over there, and it does feel neighborly."

I explain that I'm not self-employed, I have a regular job but I telecommute. So I spend the whole day logged into my computer, connected to my office. Plus a lot of time on the phone. "That's why I got a landline." That sounds like a non sequitur, but now it's out there so I hurry on. "I work for a large tech company based in California. They actually like having certain kinds of employees work at home so they don't have to have office space for everyone. Keeps overhead costs down." I hope that's enough information because what I actually do is too obscure to explain without boring people silly or confusing them to the point that they figure either they are too stupid to understand or I'm too stupid to explain. Or that I'm making it up because I actually work for the CIA.

They nod in a way that I take to mean I've talked enough on that subject, so I give them a chance to talk.

"Have you lived in Columbia very long?" seems like a wide-enough opening. They explain that they both went to Mizzou and they met there and got jobs there after they graduated and got married. I start to say that I had planned to go to Mizzou until I got the scholarship to Wash U, but that sounds like boasting, so I think I'll mention that lots of my friends went to Mizzou, but I can't remember who actually went in the end. By now they've moved the conversation on and are saying that they have one kid in college and a younger one staying with his other grandmother for the weekend. So I can ask about the college kid instead. It turns out that he is at Wash U, so we bond over that and finish off the pizza.

Over the ice cream, which I now know is a given at Josie's house, I tell them that I'm thinking about fencing the back yard, although I'm still thinking about what kind of fence it should be.

"You'll have to look at it, Josie, so what kind would you like?" I ask her.

"Don't like chain link" was her instant response. "Makes it look like you've got something to either keep in or keep out."

I reassure her that I'm not a fan either, and she says "Long as you put that gate back in, I'll be happy with anything you want." So she does know that there was a gate between her carport and my yard.

"Pinkie swear, there will be a gate," I tell her.

Joel asks Josie if she would like her yard fenced too. He looks out the kitchen window, pondering exactly where you would put the fence so that the back door is inside the fenced area. He turns to me and asks if that yard ever had been fenced.

"Not when I was here," I say. "It was fenced across the back, and of course there's the retaining wall and fence on my side, but

I think that was all. We used to go out the back corner of Josie's yard and run down the driveway to go play on the next street." I think about the dog that lived here. "They had a little dog, but they let him run loose. Prince was his name, I think. He chased cars until he got hit by one. When he finally recovered, he didn't chase cars ever again."

"Funny how dogs used to chase cars all the time. Never see that now, with the leash laws," Joel says.

And so we stray from the fence topic and the party winds down. Boris and I go home and they take Josie back for another week of rehab.

CHAPTER 28

Sunday I have a lie-in and then go to the library. My bag of sale books isn't depleted, but I want to get back to my normal reading, whatever that was. I can't remember what I used to read. I'll have to find a new normal.

The staff picks and the new acquisitions shelves have plenty to offer. There seem to be a lot of zombie and vampire books, which I'll leave for the next patron. I'm not up to following the plot twists of John Grisham or Stieg Larsson and don't want anything with pictures of automatic weapons or explosions on the cover. I pick up *Little Bee* and read the back cover and decide to save that for later. Finally I pick up *Half-Broke Horse* and *Cutting for Stone* and check them out with my new library card, reminding me once again that I. Live. Here. Now.

On my way out, I stop to peruse a bulletin board with various community notices about book clubs and classes and lectures at the library. I see one about voter registration and mentally add that to my to-do list. If I live here, I have to vote here.

CHAPTER 29

While Boris is doing his Monday morning yard inspection and meet-and-greet, I check on my new tomato and pepper plants. They are gone. I immediately suspect retaliation by the marijuana growers and am both scared and angry. On closer inspection I can see that they've been nibbled. Now I suspect rabbits, and now I'm just angry.

I'm sure I never saw a rabbit here when my dad was growing tomatoes, but there are fewer houses and no dogs running loose, and a lot more weedy vegetation in a lot of yards. Most of my seedlings were planted with a collar made of milk cartons or yogurt containers, so the bottom tier of leaves is still there, and they will probably be okay. And it's now May, so they should really take off in the warmer weather. But I need to protect them or the rabbits will keep nibbling off the tops. I make some stick teepees and admonish Boris to keep an eye out. At lunchtime, I go out and get fifty feet of twenty-four-inch chicken wire and put a quick-and-dirty barrier around the whole vegetable plot. I planned to buy eighteen-inch wire mesh, which I know will work because I've seen the movie *Rabbit-Proof Fence* and remember that it was eighteen inches high. At the last minute I decide that my memory isn't that good and that I'd better be safe than sorry.

The next three days I work all day on my computer and work in the evenings on the living room walls and ceiling. I've repurposed the plastic door seal as a drop cloth and have edged and rolled the ceiling. I'm stumped about wall color, so I move on to my old bedroom and paint that ceiling, which takes a little longer because I have to take the light fixture down to paint the ceiling properly. Someone has slopped paint on the fixture during the last thirty years, so I self-righteously clean it off, knowing that I'm just as likely to do the same thing they did, just not on this particular project.

CHAPTER 30

Today I'm going to ReStore. I've been thinking about it all week and have looked at the website and called all four stores, even the one north of the river that I know I won't go to. None of them has the door I'm looking for, but one of the employees I talk to says that his store does get them fairly often and he will call me if one comes in. He's at the closest store and suggests that I come take a look at what they do have. I'm looking for any excuse to go because the list of what they accept has me expecting all kinds of things that I'm looking for, including lamps, tables, curtain rods, building materials, and tools.

I park and walk past the donations area, where a man with a pickup truck is talking to an employee. He's got a big roll of used woven wire fence, the kind with round tops. It looks like it's about four feet high. The clerk is hesitating, saying that there isn't much interest in used wire fence. I butt in and say that I'm interested and ask how much he has. "About a hundred feet," he says. I know I need forty feet across the back of my lot and at least sixty feet on the Josie side. It might not be enough, but it's perfect for my yard. I forget all about cedar pickets. I take a closer look and see that it does have closer-together wire at the bottom to foil rabbits.

I look at the clerk. "I'll take it." His eyebrows go up—this isn't the way it usually works. "Well, uh, how much is it?" I guess I need to know that before I commit. I look from one guy to the other. They aren't sure what to do. "It's not really in inventory yet."

Maybe I look pathetic; I am wearing my only old clothes, the ones from the day of the fire, and they are getting pretty worn since I can't bring myself to paint or garden or haul trash in my new clothes. Whatever the reason, the guy who was trying to donate the fence finally said to the clerk, "If it's all the same to you, I'll just give it to her. I really just want to get rid of it without throwing it away."

The clerk looks relieved; two more pickups have arrived. "Sure, that's fine. I don't think we can take it anyway."

The roll of fence looks huge when it's out of his big truck and on the pavement next to my station wagon. I fold my back seats down and he gives me the worn tarp he had used to protect his truck bed. We lift and shove and smash the roll into my car.

"You want the gate too?" he nods toward the truck.

"A gate is exactly what I want, but I don't know where I'd put it." My car is as full as it can possibly be.

"Roof?" he asks.

"Hmm, maybe."

The clerk is back to see how it's going, and he brings out a roll of twine. We secure the gate to my roof racks and I decide to plot a low-speed route home.

"Don't worry about driving on the expressway. That gate's not going anywhere." I guess my poker face needs work.

As I pull away, I realize that I didn't even get inside the store. I consider going back so I at least know what it's like, but I'm hungry and decide to leave it for another day.

Backed into my driveway, I have no trouble getting the gate off the top of the wagon, but I can't budge the fencing, so I leave it for Matt. I can't do any shopping with nowhere to put anything, so I work on painting for a few hours and then take Boris for a long walk in the late afternoon. When I look for something to eat for supper, I realize that I've been here long enough that I need to clean out my refrigerator.

CHAPTER 31

When Matt is finished mowing, we inch the fencing out of my car and unroll it. It's in three separate lengths, which turns out to be a good thing, even if the lengths don't match up with the dimensions of my yard. We lay them out and measure them and find that I need about twenty more feet. I've promised Josie a gate between our yards, so I need another gate to put at the end of my driveway to separate the back yard from the unfenced front. I don't want to have to go through the house, or around through Josie's driveway, to get between my back and front yards. I'm still picturing the long-gone white-picket gate with rose trellis above, but I'm starting to think of more practical options too.

Matt agrees to work on the fence the next weekend, which gives me time to get posts and decide where to put them. I need to read up on spacing and post depth and I don't know what else.

"I've seen this kind of fence around here," he says. "Keep an eye out and maybe you can find that last bit that you need. Someone else might be glad to get rid of some."

It's none of my business, but I wonder if he lives in the neighborhood, so I take the opportunity to ask oh-so-casually, "Oh, do you live around here?"

"Not too far," he says, and I think I'll have to make do with that, but he goes on. "On the Paseo."

"Ah, nice," I say. "I used to walk home from school on the Paseo. Part of the way, anyway."

He thinks about that. "You mean you went to Hogan? I went to Hogan."

I'm trying to calculate what years he would have been there, since the school has gone through several incarnations since I graduated.

"It's a public charter school now, right?" I ask.

"Yes, but my mom went there when it was Catholic. The Catholic high schools are pretty expensive now, so they decided on the charter school. I think she liked us being in the same building where she went. We moved over there so we could walk to school."

"Well, as I remember it's a great neighborhood."

"Not bad. It's east of Troost though, so. . . ." and he trails off.

Talk of neighborhoods makes me think about Nextdoor, so after he leaves I log in to see if anyone happens to be giving away a gate. I am distracted by the block party announcement and I sign up to bake cookies. I read up on local church events and school advice and babysitting. Eventually I get back to task and post a picture of my fence, asking if anyone has any like it that they don't need. I'm not specific about whether I'm buying it or hauling off someone's discards; we can figure that out if anyone responds. Next I read up on installing fence and start to worry about how to use a come-along and top rails. I seek out Henry's advice.

Matt has already told him about my fence find, so Henry is prepared. "You'll be okay with metal posts pounded in at least eighteen inches. You probably don't have to worry about water or gas lines if you're installing it where the old fence was. But for gates and corners, you'll want to set the posts in concrete and let them cure. You can use Quikrete and they say that it sets hard in less than an hour. It works pretty well, but if you're going to put a lot of tension on a pole, you might as well give it overnight." I pay for the Quikrete and he says that he'll have Matt deliver it.

Talk of concrete makes me think about paving the driveway, pouring a bit of patio around the back door, and pouring a slab for a future garden shed. I really want the garden tools out of my back room. And the mud puddle around the back door has gotten so big I've resorted to laying out a little walkway using pallets. Boris doesn't like walking on them, but he hates puddles more and he can't get to his buddies any other way, so he does it.

I ask Henry if he knows a guy, since by now I know that he always knows a guy, although I'm always curious if someday he'll know a gal instead. In this case, the guy is a nephew.

"His name is Sean and he's just starting out on his own, but he's done a lot of concrete work for other guys. The work he did at his own place looks pretty good and survived last winter, which is the key thing."

CHAPTER 32

Sean comes out a few days later and we talk about the driveway, the patio, and the shed. I show him Josie's carport, which she really uses as a covered patio, and we talk about whether that would work for my property, which is not as flat as Josie's. He says that he'll give me separate prices for the three projects in case I don't want to do all of them at once, and a price for all three together. "I can mix enough myself to do a little patio, but the driveway and the slab will need a truck load, and it's gonna be cheaper to just get them out here one time. Same with the bobcat to do the digging." By late afternoon, I get his estimates in email. I'm pleased to see a lot of detail.

That night, I pour a glass of wine and look up my bank statements. I still have a solid balance left from the insurance payout. I can pay for the concrete work and still continue to buy furnishings. I have a comfortable amount left for emergencies, like replacing appliances, if necessary. Plus, I have an income again so I can start saving for a bigger emergency, like replacing the furnace.

I'd really like to get all the concrete work done at once. It's quite a bit cheaper to do it all together, and my dislike of dust and noise is enough to make me do it all. And I don't want to pour the driveway and patio and then have them damaged when they bring in heavy equipment to do the shed later. I try to work out my priorities. Patio is top, because of the muddy mess. I waver about the driveway or the shed being second. I give up and decide to call my brother. It's time to tell him what I've done. And even if he is appalled, he'll talk to me about concrete.

I sip my wine and admit to myself that my quandary isn't really about concrete at all. My quandary is what the neighbors will think. Put that way, I have to laugh at myself. It sounds like something from a fifties sitcom. "Don't go outside in that outfit—what will the neighbors think?" "We will NOT put flamingoes in the front yard—what will the neighbors think?"

My situation is not that exactly. I am liking my neighborhood more and more. I don't quite have friends here yet, but I know that takes time. Everyone is friendly, and that is enough. But I don't know what they think of me and my unexpected presence here. Do they think I'm harmless if slightly crazy for moving back to my childhood home? I can live with that. Am I thinking that I can gentrify the neighborhood? Am I a police plant watching for drugs or gang activity? I'm sure my lack of furniture puzzles them, in spite of my explanation.

I guess my worry about the concrete is that it will look like I've got a lot of money to spend on what is probably the worst house on a block that is desirable only because prices are low. The obvious explanation, I think, is that I'm here to flip the house. I'm paving the only gravel driveway on the block, filling in the eyesore of a mud hole, and building what might look like a garage on one of the few lots that doesn't have one.

And if I am a flipper, is that good or bad? Surely it's not bad to spruce up the eyesore and make it possible to have people living here again. On the other hand, it's tricky to upgrade too many houses without increasing property taxes. And it's sort of rude to act like you are part of the neighborhood and love it here when in reality you can't wait to get out.

I really do analyze way too much. I finish my wine and call my brother, who did not inherit the same analyzer gene.

He moved out of Kansas City when he retired in his mid-fifties and now lives at the Lake of the Ozarks. I catch him as he's getting off his boat and we chat as he walks back to his cabin. I tell him I've moved as planned, and he is glad to hear that. We've never been estranged, but we're also not particularly close. But it will be nice to get together more often than every few years at a cousin reunion.

"Where are you staying?" he asks, and I tell him I've bought a house.

"That was quick." He wasn't expecting me to have looked for a house, found a house, bought it, closed, and moved in since I texted him at Easter. Of course he wasn't, but he recovers and asks me where it is.

I start to say "near Swope Park" and kick myself for trying to be coy. My brother is a straight-forward guy. "I bought our old house."

I can hear gears turn in his head. I can't mean "our" as in "our family" and there isn't any other "our" since I never lived within two hundred miles of here as an adult. "You mean. . . ?"

"Yep, I do mean it. Crazy, huh?" I might as well give him permission to say what I know he's thinking.

"Wow. That is crazy."

"Come by and see it. It's better than you think. You can even stay over, I've got a queen-size guest bed." No need to mention that it's inflatable.

He finally says that he'll be there Saturday around noon but he won't be able to stay overnight. I tell him that's great and that I want his advice on paving the driveway. He's got several days to cope with this new reality.

I spend Thursday evening cleaning and on Friday I go back to ReStore. This time I make it all the way inside.

It's both of the things I was prepared for—the amount of stuff is overwhelming but not necessarily what I want. I get out the notebook I brought to help keep my thoughts together.

I don't need anything for the bathroom but I start there anyway, just to see. I make a note that they have several shower stalls that might be suitable for my bathroom. In another area I see glass block, which I think might make for secure basement windows, although of course they won't vent. I make a note and shift my attention. A lot of people have donated bookcases, and I've been thinking that would be a good idea along the north wall of the living room. I've brought measurements. I find the perfect size and style, but the finish is bad. I picture it painted in semigloss enamel, maybe ivory, and buy it, along with a lamp to put on top. I finish up with a goofy kitchen clock that will probably not work for long, but it will amuse me while it does. I pay and get a clerk to help me load the book case.

I tuck the car up close to the house, leaving room for my brother to park in front of me in case he's still worried about the neighborhood. I take my lamp and clock inside. He will have to help me move the bookcase inside tomorrow.

CHAPTER 33

I'm a little nervous about my brother's visit and wish I had more furniture so my situation doesn't seem so pathetic. But the inside of the house itself doesn't look neglected anymore; the new floors and paint have made a huge difference. Those rooms won't look very familiar, but they also won't make him sad. I've forgotten that Matt was going to start the fence work today, but when he arrives he tells me he's got finals the next week and would I mind waiting a little longer. He says that he can work on weekdays too, after finals.

When my brother drives up, I'm out talking to the neighbors across the street. I think that makes the whole neighborhood seem friendly and warmer than he expected. We go inside and he reacts as I did, as I knew he would: "It's so small!" He puts his hands on the walls and ceiling as if he can't believe they have closed in so much. He remembers the lantern light fixture in his old room and I tell him he can have it if I can find something to replace it with and if he comes back and installs the switch himself.

"It's not like you'll even need a ladder." At 6-foot-5, he does fill up the room. It's a stretch to remind ourselves that he lived here for a few months after the Army, when both he and the room were the same size they are now.

He helps me carry in the bookcase and I offer to take him out for lunch, but he wants to eat in. "It feels funny in here, but it also feels good." I make grilled cheese and feed him cookies and he reminds me that Mother's pet name for him was "Cookie Pusher."

After he's explored the basement and the backyard—"Well, this is different, but I see you planted tomatoes in the same place"—I tell him what I'm thinking about the concrete work I'm so conflicted over. I don't tell him that I'm worried about what the neighbors will think.

"If you can afford it, you should just do it all. Mother always hated how muddy it was around the door. Dad got some bricks and put them around this area, but I don't see them." I'd forgotten that. We look at the concrete work our father did out front—the walkway from the public sidewalk to the house, the porch step. It's all still solid. We're both thinking about how hard he worked, but we don't say anything.

Finally, my brother says, "The neighbors will like it if you do all this. It will make them feel like they didn't waste money on their places."

This feels like an odd sort of logic, but I see what he means. And he's not acting like I'm a nutcase and should sell the place and get out before sunset. If he thought that, he would definitely say that. It's always been his job to tell me I'm crazy.

"When I was here before, the screens were flapping in the breeze and the yard hadn't been mowed in ages," he tells me. "And the Hughsons' house was bright blue. It was just awful."

I don't tell him that I had Jimmy back a few days ago to fix the screens. "Yeah, the people in the Hughsons' house are Dave and Carol. They repainted when they bought the place." I'm feeling like my house and I have gotten a passing grade on a difficult test.

He heads back to the lake and promises to visit again in the summer. I make a note that I'll have to do something about air conditioning before he does. As he pulls away, Josie's daughter arrives. She greets me like a friend that I hope I am and tells me that Josie will be back home in another week. "I'm taking some time off work and I'll stay here with her for at least the first few days. She doesn't want me to; she thinks it's a waste of my vacation time. But I get plenty of vacation. I think she doesn't like the idea that she might need help. And I probably am worrying too much. They've got her cooking and washing dishes in her room at the rehab."

CHAPTER 34

Sunday night my phone rings.

"Hey, I was in Versailles today. I had a flat tire this morning." This is my brother. I know he's not calling about the flat tire, but I also know I'll just have to wait it out. He'll get to the point sooner or later. And the story may be interesting. I'm glad he didn't get the flat in my driveway. I might not have passed my test.

"There's a tire store in Versailles. It's run by Mennonites. They don't use electricity at home but they do at the tire store. I bought tires there last year for my truck. My old one, before I got the one you saw me in yesterday. Anyway, what happened is I ran over a spark plug and it was stuck in the treads. They fixed the tire and they asked if they could keep the spark plug. It turns out they have a whole collection of things they've pulled out of tires. This was the first spark plug though."

"So they have like a little museum?"

"Well, more like a big jar. But they took a picture too, so maybe they have a photo collection."

It sounds like the back story has about run its course, so I wait for the next installment.

"Anyway, I was driving by this antique store in Versailles, well really it's crafts and antiques. Actually, I stopped at Sonic to get something to eat and I saw the antique store and I thought it might have a light fixture like the one in my room. Well, I guess it's your room." Now I see where the story is going.

"Anyway," he says again. I can picture him waving his hand as he gets back to the antiques. "Remember those green and white dishes that Mother had. She only had a few, some of them had a clock?"

Bam, I remember exactly. I think she had service for two. They might have been a wedding present. I haven't seen anything like them since the sixties. I think all that, and I say, "Yes, I had forgotten all about those."

"Well, they had those and I remembered that you didn't have very many dishes." That's a kind way for him to say that he noticed that he got his coffee in a plastic mug with H&R Block on it. "So I got them for you. They said they would take them back if you didn't want them."

I'm irrationally pleased by this. "I would *love* them," I say. "They would be perfect."

And they will be perfect. I've dithered and dithered about dishes, resisting picking up odd pieces here and there. These are old and solid like my house and totally unpretentious, also like my house. Possibly chipped like my house, and that is okay too.

"I'm so pleased," I say, and I can tell that he's pleased that I'm pleased.

"Okay, well. I can bring them up to your house next weekend if you want." Next weekend is the block party, but maybe that's okay. He seems anxious to give me this gift, and I'm definitely in a hurry to get it.

I tell him about the block party and that although I've met quite a few neighbors I'll be happy to have a plus one along. He is not the introvert that I am so that probably makes no sense to him, but he's agreeable and says that he'll spend the night. I log into Nextdoor and say that I'll bring sausage balls in addition to the cookies.

The mere idea of these dishes makes me cheerful all evening, both the dishes and the thought that my brother found them and bought them for me. I look up pictures of them online and relish the details in the pattern. They will be familiar, but they aren't the dishes we used every day, so I won't feel like I'm trying to replicate my childhood. I had a great childhood, but once is enough.

Which reminds me that I need to get serious about a living room sofa. I'm set up to paint the bookcase, but it's going to be lonely in there with just its lamp for company. I know what I want now, and it's nothing like what my parents had.

When I was little, the living room had two sectional couches and a big comfortable chair for my dad. Everyone sat in that chair when it was available, but when he got home from work, we were shooed away and he settled in to smoke and read the paper. Those three pieces and three side tables filled the space pretty completely. Later, the sectionals were replaced with a small sofa, and my mother got her own comfy chair.

I'm not interested in having any of that. I want to fill the long south wall and short west wall with a single sofa, where I can snuggle into the corner. I want it long and wide enough to sleep on in a pinch. That and a wooden armchair at the end of the bookcase should do it. I'll need reading lamps too, which may have to hang on the wall or ceiling. Maybe a coffee table, maybe not. I want people to feel like they can walk right in without mincing around furniture. Something just big enough for a couple of wineglasses maybe, and solid enough that Boris won't knock it over with his tail.

After Mass on Sunday, I figure that since I'm most of the way to Surplus Sales, I should go the rest of the way and find the sofa I'm looking for. I find something that's close enough. It's not the mossy green I've been picturing, but I don't want to spend three times as much and wait three months to have the perfect piece of furniture made. I don't have that kind of life now.

CHAPTER 35

By Saturday, the sofa and the bookcase with its lamp are in place and I can start to imagine a table and reading lamps. I've put my bag of books on the shelves, but the shiny paperbacks remind me of a college apartment, so I put them back in the bag, leaving only the hardbacks. I've set up the inflatable bed in the far reaches of the back room.

The bathroom door is a pocket door, which I love. My dad installed it because the original swinging door took up most of the bathroom when you opened it. I thought he was a magician when he installed the pocket door, when I was five or so. By then I knew about studs, and I couldn't figure out how he could get a door in the wall with the studs in there. Magic!

But lately it's been sticking. This hasn't been a problem since I'm alone in the house, but I suddenly realize that it will be a problem later today. I jiggle it but it won't fully close. I picture a dead mouse stuck in there.

My brother arrives and is amused by the inflatable bed. He bounces on it, expecting the frame to collapse, but it doesn't. I offer him the sofa if he'd rather, but he seems to like camping out in what was once our parents' bedroom. Matt is working on the fence and the two of them kibitz. The next time I look out, my brother is taking a turn pounding fence posts.

I drag him in and ask him to see if he can get the bathroom door to close, otherwise I'm going to have to rig up a curtain. He's wise to the ways of pocket doors and locates the problem. "Screw fell out." Maybe I can stop thinking that every mystery involves dead mice.

At four o'clock we go to the block party, which is a lively affair with a bounce house and music and a Sno-Cone machine. Tables are set up on the blocked-off street, along with grills and coolers. Some kids are playing corn hole, and the younger ones are running around screaming and blowing soap bubbles. Lights have been strung across the street and as the sun goes down there is dancing. My offerings look pretty white bread next to what everyone else has brought, but I don't fret about it. We introduce ourselves and eat too much. I lose track of my brother, and later find him talking about trucks and boats.

Neither of us is a night owl, so we leave long before the party winds down.

"Well, that was fun," I say, hoping he's had a good time.

"Yeah, they think I live here." He says that like he's flattered. "And some guy who lives on Chestnut has a friend who has a place on my side of the lake. We're going to meet up and go fishing."

He made friends in the first five minutes? And what about the nightmares the last time he drove past our house?

I sleep like a log with someone else in the house, even though I know that nothing would wake my brother unless maybe a gun went off next to his skull. Boris sleeps in the back room, where my brother is staying. What the heck?

CHAPTER 36

My brother leaves early Sunday morning and I go to Mass at St. Therese. I tell myself that I want to do a little comparison shopping before I commit. The St. Therese website lists a traditional service at 8:00 a.m. and Gospel Mass at 9:15. I opt for traditional and think I might stay long enough to see what the Gospel one is like. It's a lovely church with a diverse assembly and a good priest. I can see fitting in here. I hang around for coffee afterward and make small talk with the other coffee drinkers. Like most Catholics, they are welcoming but not smothering. At 9:16, I creep into the vestibule and peek into the church. The music is robust, and this group is at least half Black. Clearly the music speaks to a lot of different people. I end up staying for the entire service and leave humming the closing hymn.

I go home and wash all my new dishes and put them in my cupboard. I open the cupboard door every time I walk through the kitchen, just because it now looks like someone lives here.

I missed Josie's homecoming on Saturday, so I go over on Sunday afternoon to welcome her back. I take a plate of chocolate cookies—they were supposed to be cut-out but I don't have cookie cutters, of course. So I used a glass, whose rounded edge didn't cut the dough that well. I ended up cutting them in squares with the side of a metal spatula and pretending they are supposed to be rectangles. Josie doesn't comment, either to spare my feelings or because my ruse is successful. She seems to be in top condition and her daughter is staying only one more night. When I leave, Sue tells Josie she's going to stretch her legs and walks me out. Behind her back, Josie rolls her eyes.

We stand on the sidewalk and talk a bit, as I knew we would. She says that she had been all set to talk Josie into moving to assisted living. But her doctors think she is at no special risk and Josie has promised not to replace the trip-hazard throw rugs that Sue took home with her last weekend.

"But mostly, I feel safe because you are next door," she tells me. "I mean, there are a lot of good neighbors here who watch out for her. And I know you're not here all the time and you can't keep her from falling or come running if she does fall. It's not that at all." She pauses. "It's just that it feels a little bit more like a real neighborhood now. The dark spot outside her kitchen window is gone."

"I know what you mean," I say. "She's the bright spot outside my bedroom windows."

CHAPTER 37

June arrives and I put the coffee maker on the top shelf and start making cold brew instead. Angie calls to set a date for us to get together. I sign a contract with Sean for the concrete work, and we choose a day to start at the end of the month. I insist on a contract because he is young and new at this and needs to protect himself. Jimmy is an old pro and can take care of himself.

Matt comes over one evening to finish the fence posts—"Too hot to dig during the day"—and returns the next Saturday when I can help him stretch the fence. I spend an evening sweating in long pants and long sleeves installing chicken wire along the ground at the base of the chain link fence. Bunnies can get through chain link, it turns out. A woman named Fern who lives on Bellefontaine responds to my Nextdoor post and I get enough fencing to finish off the yard. It doesn't exactly match, but we put it in a back corner where the fireplace and lilacs hide it from view. Fern says that she has a double gate too, but it's behind the garage and she wants to wait for her nephew to move some bikes and lumber before she can give it to me. It's all under a tarp, and I can't see what's involved, so I don't offer to shift it myself. Meanwhile, we've stretched chicken wire across the end of the driveway. It won't keep Boris in, not that he's shown any interest in jumping over it, but it will keep the rabbits out. The tomatoes are growing like crazy. After years of coddling tomato plants in cool, dry California, it's a joy to watch the jungle-like growth fueled by heat and humidity.

I still haven't met the neighbors behind me. I've trekked around the block and rung the doorbell a couple of times to talk about the fence, but no one answers. The house is fairly neat and tidy, though, and there are flowers blooming in a basket on the porch, so someone must live there. I decide not to worry about the fence between our yards. I remove the excess vegetation from my side but leave what's on the other side, so the new fence shouldn't bother them anyway.

One evening a few days before Sean is due to start work, he rings the doorbell.

"I just want to go over the job before we start, see if anything has changed," he says, "I'm going to get the permit tomorrow or the day after."

We go outside and survey the terrain. He says that we should go ahead and get the permit for the shed, even if all we do is pour the concrete right now. "We don't need much in the way of drawings for a shed, unless you wanted plumbing in it."

This makes sense to me, and I don't want plumbing, so I draw up a simple sketch. I tell him I want this shed to be basic, to last forever, and to be vandal-proof, so we agree on concrete block with small windows and a metal door.

"You think a metal door is overkill?" I ask.

"It won't be if a wooden door gets kicked in just once." He gives me a wry smile.

"You want me to go ahead and get that old fireplace out of here while I'm at it?"

I don't, because it's the only thing left of the original yard. On the other hand, it wasn't very useful then and it's completely useless now. It's not even attractive.

He lets me think about it, and then he says, “I could knock it down and use the stone for the front of the shed. It won’t save you any money because it will take me longer, but it would look nice and those are pretty cobblestones.”

We agree on that and turn to the patio area.

“I guess you couldn’t wait.” He’s laughing at my pallet patio. “I’ll haul these out of here for you. Looks like it actually worked pretty well.”

I tell him I might want to brick the patio later and ask if that will be any problem.

“Probably not, but what I could do is one of these stamped flagstone finishes right in the concrete. I did one last summer. Went back last week to make sure it got through the winter since we had a lot of freezing and thawing this year.” He shows me pictures, and I am on board.

“I’ve got the equipment, so it will cost you just a few more hours of labor.” He looks at me over his glasses. “Maybe just one more hour—I’ll be faster this time around.”

The driveway itself is straightforward, and we agree on where the posts will go for the future canopy and for the gate I don’t have yet.

He gets stakes and spray paint and marks everything, then has me check it all.

“You know what would be nice? I could put down a gravel path from the patio to the shed. Put a little curve in it.” He swoops his arm, turning toward the shed. “No need to pave it, and I’ve got to bring in a load of gravel anyway. I’ll put down a couple inches and roll it.”

“Or not,” he says. “I’m getting carried away.”

“This whole place has been neglected for a long time,” I rationalize out loud. “Let’s go ahead and do the path too.”

CHAPTER 38

Angie is coming on a Friday, and I am up early sweeping dog hair and wishing I had make a bigger effort to get a living room rug and another table. I've come up with a sturdy little table that I'm using as a sewing table, but the other table is still doing double duty for dining and desk. I put my computer away and move the table and the two chairs that go with it into the kitchen, hoping that looks a little more normal. I wish I had flowers or something to put on it, but I can't come up with anything. I think about the constant kitchen clutter of my former life and sigh. Finally I move the salt and pepper shakers from the counter to the table, roll my eyes, and answer the doorbell. Boris rushes out to meet her on the porch. She tries to pet the dog, hug me, hand me a potted plant, and exclaim all at once.

"I can't believe this," she says, "I just can't believe I'm back in this house. When I pulled up I thought I had the wrong street or something. The porch looks so different. But I saw the front door and I knew this was it. Isn't that nuts? I even recognize the doorbell button." She takes a breath. "I know I'm babbling but this is just so . . . so . . . I don't know what it is, but I'm so excited."

I'm in tears at this point, although I don't know why. "Sorry," I say. "I don't know why I'm crying."

"Because we haven't seen each other in forever and you're all stressed out and this is not an easy thing that you've done."

She always did see things clearly. She wasn't a social work major for nothing. Her eyes are teary now too.

"Come in. Look around. See if anything else is familiar."

"Are you kidding? I remember every detail. The kitchen! This is the same!" she says, and it is, or close enough. We go through the house and she marvels at what she remembers from so many years ago.

"Can I see the backyard? We spent so much time out there."

We go out and she stops cold. "This isn't right. What happened to the tree? We spent so many hours up in that tree. And wasn't there a shed? And the swing set?" She's walking around as if these things could be hiding somewhere.

I tell her that the tree died when we were in college and the rest vanished after my parents left.

"It has been a long time, but I gotta say, I still look out the window and expect to see that tree and shed. I guess that's why I'm having the shed rebuilt," I say, pointing to the stakes and paint marks. "That, and I'm tired of storing the garden tools in the house."

We go back inside and talk about the house, and then talk about her childhood house and how we'll never see it again. We mentally walk through her house, pointing out the corner cupboard where the Christmas crèche was set up out of the reach of the babies, and the room she shared with three younger sisters.

"I loved coming here," she says, looking around again. "It was always so calm."

"I loved your house," I shoot back. "It was a lot more fun. And you guys ran all over your mom, but you were always nice about it. She was the perfect mother for nine kids, or the nine of you, anyway."

"Remember how we had to eat on TV trays when you spent the night?" Their table was already at capacity. "Oh, that reminds me—I have something in the car."

We troop out to her car, which is an SUV. She puts her hand on the hatch and says, "You won't believe this, but I was driving down my street and I saw this on the curb with a Free sign on it, and I thought you could use this on your porch or your patio or wherever—I wasn't thinking that there aren't patios over here." She opens the hatch and reveals a metal patio table with a glass top. It is upside down with three chairs squeezed in on top.

I squeal like a teenager.

"I can't tell you how much I need this table. I've been looking everywhere for the right one."

This is a table I would have walked right by at ReStore or any of the resale shops I've been frequenting. Glass and metal have not been on my radar. I don't have a patio yet and my porch is too small for one. But here in my driveway, I can picture it in my house and it looks perfect.

"I'll move my car and we can take it in the back," I say, thinking of fewer steps, fewer turns, and no new paint to nick.

We put it in the back room, where it looks good with the silly blue curtains and the gray paneling. But I can't see working at it somehow. I put my laptop on it and pull up the desk chair.

"You know, I think I want this in the kitchen." So we move everything around and bring in the chairs and put her plant in the middle.

"This is so perfect. It really is."

"Only three chairs, though."

"That's okay. This way the table can be right up against the wall and you can get through here. Wasn't it wider when we were kids?"

"No, we were narrower," she says, which is true, but still.

Then we have to talk about where everyone sat at the table, always the same place. She had her own spot at the table and her own plate (mine was yellow, hers was white) when she ate dinner with us.

We leash Boris and walk around the neighborhood a little, covering the ground where we knew every crack in the sidewalk, every house where they would buy Girl Scout cookies, every house that would buy the Catholic Christmas cards we sold every fall in grade school. They were a hard sell in this far edge of the parish. The blocks close to the church were far more Catholic, and those kids had an easier time of it.

We stand on Chestnut looking at the expressway without saying much and then we take Boris home. We talk about the diner at the corner of Gregory and Prospect, where we used to go to celebrate our joint birthday. Now we would need to get in the car to eat at a restaurant with table service, so we go back to my house and marvel at it again and eat at my perfect new table using my green and white dishes.

One of the lovely things about talking with Angie is that she remembers my father, who died in 1978. My father could do anything, and anything he couldn't do, my mother could. I was lucky in the parents department. They were older when my brother and I were born, which put them in a different generation than my friends' parents. I didn't appreciate this for a long time, of course. But they had come of age in the Depression, which deprived them of the buoyancy and limitless possibility that come with early adulthood for most of us. And they were just that much too old to be completely idealistic about World War II. World War I had been real to them, and to have to repeat it had to have been a terrible burden.

Not that they ever said any of that. They never said much of anything about any of those events, but the stories they did tell about their early years informed me anyway, although only when I was much older. My dad was drafted at age twenty-nine. By the time he mustered out and started what he must have considered his real life, he was thirty-four years old. He was still strong and fit. But with little education and a quiet demeanor he was not poised to take the post-war world by storm. In a different era, he would have been an engineer instead of a truck driver.

We were frugal, but we were comfortable. The house was paid for, and they bought everything with cash. My brother and I have compared notes and are reasonably sure they never had any kind of debt. So that explains the little house with no garage. That and the fact that they thought they were too old to conceive children, so the four tiny rooms and full basement were fine for them.

Then we kids showed up. We certainly knew families where boys and girls shared bedrooms, but I think my parents saw early on that I was going to need my own space. Beyond that, the kitchen was so small that the table had to be pushed up against the wall. It was pretty tight for four of us, never mind squeezing in any visitors. So in the summer of 1959 my dad used all his vacation time, plus many nights and weekends, to build the addition.

He spent months planning it, down to working out how to extend a not-perfectly-square house: should he square up the addition, or continue the lines as they were? (He chose the second option.)

CHAPTER 39

After talking with Matt about Hogan and spending a day with Angie, I am curious about the area west of Prospect and take a long walk with Boris retracing my route to high school. I can't take the exact route because of the expressway, but I can get close. My dad usually drove us to school, so I start out on the driving route, north to Meyer and west across the expressway. Then we have a long curving walk that skirts the south side of the hospital campus and swoops on downhill north and west along Dunn Park to where Meyer comes together with the Paseo and 63rd Street, with Troost standing off a long block away. I cross the park to the Paseo and walk on down the hill and then curve around to the left past a convent. It used to house a cloistered order but is now home to the Franciscan Sisters of Christ the King. On around the bend is Hogan on the left, most of the way up a grassy hill, and a mall called The Landing on the flat ground to the right. We went there a lot after school, mostly to try on clothes we didn't need, since we wore uniforms, and to eat ice cream and occasionally buy records at Record Rendezvous. I'm glad to see The Landing still there, even though I'm 99 percent confident that it's had 100 percent turnover.

I head up the hill through the Hogan parking lot and on to 65th Street. I'm a little disoriented; it seems that the convent that was associated with the high school has been separated from it, with a new street added. But I finally find myself on the walk home along the Paseo. I get disoriented again and have to get out my phone and head toward Gregory and the expressway. Paseo still looks pretty good, but as I go east I begin to see the same signs of stress that I see on my own block.

The Paseo is still within reach of Troost and its shops and services. Farther east, people would be just as likely to patronize businesses on Prospect. But Prospect is hard up against the expressway, and everyone east of that is effectively blocked from the Prospect businesses. Prospect lost half its customer base, struggled, declined. Its customers to the west may have quite rationally looked more often toward Troost, which was not affected by the construction. I wonder why they didn't run the expressway, which is called both Bruce Watkins Drive and US 71, right down Prospect, since Prospect was already called 71 Highway. Maybe it is more difficult and more expensive to acquire commercial property than to condemn single-family homes. If that's the case, why didn't they run it down the west side of Prospect, leaving the east-of-Prospect residents with its stores and services and leaving Prospect businesses with the larger customer base to the east. I don't have the energy to try to tease out the thinking behind a project that took forty years to complete. People in committee rooms make decisions for all kinds of reasons, one common one being that the first and loudest guy to speak often carries the day. Who knows who that was and where he might have lived or owned property?

CHAPTER 40

As the weather heats up and I'm faced with the forgotten reality of summer in Kansas City, I finally admit that I need an air conditioner. I've worked in the basement on really hot days, but I'm miserable there. It's not all that cool, it's humid, and it's still a dank, unfinished basement. The air conditioner mounted through the wall of the back room looks like it could be the one my dad installed there sometime before 1975. It doesn't work. Not a creak. It's rusted inside and out. Controls are missing and the plastic vent covers are broken.

I measure the nonworking air conditioner carefully and shop for one until I find one that fits. I confer with Jimmy and hire him to go to the store, measure it again to be sure, and install it on a Saturday morning when Matt is here to help him lift it. Unlike when I hooked up the dryer, I don't need to replace the 220 outlet, and coolness soon flows into my workspace. The room is still sparsely furnished, but I like it that way. I almost break one of my rules about buying temporary things and buy a twin-size inflatable bed so I can sleep in the air-conditioned space if we are hit with a particularly bad heat wave. But then I discover the genius of the exact alignment of the air conditioner in the back wall of the house. My dad had installed the original so that it's a straight shot through the doorway into the kitchen and from there to the living room. Once the sun goes down, the air conditioner cools the living room down to the point where I can sleep there on the sofa in a pinch. I'm glad I fretted about buying the inflatable long enough to figure this out.

I haven't heard anything from Fern about the gates. I message her through Nextdoor and get no reply. One day I drive by her house. It looks a little more bedraggled, and the tarp-covered pile is untouched. I decided to let it go and look elsewhere for a gate. The bit of chicken wire annoys me, but it's keeping the rabbits out. Boris respects it unless I call him to jump over it. So it's doing its job. And something will turn up.

I walk Boris early on hot days, and sometimes again late in the evening, although always before dark. I finally meet the next-door neighbors to the south, a young couple named Patrick and Liz Saunders, who seem to work long hours. They are friendly enough, but not around very much. She is pregnant, however, and hoping to take some time off when the baby is born, so I may see more of them in the future. I've been careful not to remove all the volunteer vegetation in the chain-link fence between us, but it turns out they are motivated by my efforts to do some yardwork themselves. "We just sort of turned our backs on that house while it was empty," she tells me. "The less we saw, the better."

I discover the reason for the tall wooden fence and No-Trespassing sign along the side street of the corner house—they have a boat, which was repeatedly vandalized. They hope to eventually store it in their garage and change to a friendlier fence. "We'll always have a sturdy fence along the side street, though."

The concrete work is finished and I have permission from Sean to park on my new driveway. Neighbors are complimentary and tell me how nice the property is looking. I have to think this is said mostly to encourage me, since I haven't done a whole lot to increase curb appeal. Maybe removing the remnants of chain link and getting a nicer mailbox attached properly to the house contributed to the overall look. Maybe it's the screens that don't flap in the breeze anymore. Maybe it's just seeing a car in the drive and a person coming and going at normal times. I don't know, but I am inordinately pleased when they tell me that it's looking good. I still worry that I might look like a house flipper and they might be keeping an eye out for the For Sale sign, but I worry less and less about it as I begin to feel at home.

The garden is growing and eventually I have enough tomatoes to share with neighbors. I eat green beans dripping in butter. I look across the back fence and wonder if there are any remnants of the peach trees in the next yard and decide that they are irretrievably gone.

One evening as it's cooling off I take Boris out, and on the way back I run into Josie, who is out for a walk too. She seems to be completely recovered and goes out every day with only a trekking pole, which she uses to point to things if she happens to find someone to talk to. Today she is standing in front of a house partway up the next block, talking to a man about my age.

"There she is now." Josie says, pointing. And then to me: "You two know each other."

Maybe we met during the aftermath of my break-in, but my memories of that are muddled and I can't be sure, so I just stick out my hand and say, "Hello."

The man seems to know who I am, but then Josie has been talking about me, so of course he does. He sees that I don't know him and says, "I'm Flynn. Flynn Barry."

I make a show of trying to place the name, which does sound familiar. All I can think of is Tim Barry, and then I can't get past that.

"We moved here when I was a little kid. Maybe you remember my big sister, Marilyn. She was more your age."

Now I remember. The Barry family moved in sometime in the early sixties. They were the family we all looked down on. I strain to push that memory aside and come up with the other kids' names. Why can I remember Bonnie and Francie Alewine, who were gone before I was eight, but can't remember the kids who were here for longer, when I was older?

"I do remember Marilyn," I say at last. "She was a couple of years younger than me, in the same grade as Darlene across the street, I think."

"Yep, that's right," he confirms, and I'm glad I've come up with something. "And I'm still here. The others all got married and moved away, but I like it here."

I nod, me too. "It's great to see you again!" I put more enthusiasm into this than I feel. "And your house is looking good," I add, because it is, or anyway it looks better than it did in the 1970s. The family let it get pretty run down and they became a sore subject on the block. And this was before race became an issue—the Barrys are white.

"Nice bars," I say, which sounds stupid but I'm hoping he'll tell me why his is the only house around that does have bars on the windows.

"Yep, things were pretty bad in the 1980s and my dad put 'em up. I just never took 'em down. Seemed like if I did, that would be right when someone would decide to break in."

"Ah, makes sense," I say, and I suppose it does.

"Yep," he says again. "I really liked your dad. He used to call me Pete and sometimes he'd give me a dollar to pull weeds." Definitely my dad. He called lots of kids Pete. Little kids seem to be tickled when an adult they like gives them a nickname.

Flynn spins around, points toward his house. "He gave me that lawn chair when they moved."

I look at the chair in the front yard. It's a fifties classic and we certainly had one like it. I'm sure there is a black-and-white picture of me sitting in it in our back yard.

"Do you want it back?" He's hesitant but sincere.

Of course I want it, but even more I like knowing that my dad gave it to him and that he still remembers my dad. Taking the chair back would wreck that somehow.

"I'm so glad that you took care of it all these years," I tell him. "It's yours now."

"I keep it painted." And he does. It's survived the decades well.

Josie jumps into the conversation, saying that she needs to get on back. I tell Flynn goodbye and walk home with Josie. I don't want to tell her any of my memories about Flynn's family, although that's mostly because it will make me look bad.

I, again, go to ReStore on a busy Saturday morning and find someone trying to donate a water-damaged butcher-block countertop that the clerk doesn't think can be sold. He is pointing out water stains and warping and mildew. Again I butt in, and take it home to make a top for my basement workbench. I tell the clerk that they should have a free pile outside in a shed for stuff like this. The sign can say JUNK JUNKIES—GET YOUR FIX HERE. I'm looking for old metal pipes that aren't good enough for plumbing but would make good tomato stakes. My trellis collapsed long ago and my tomato patch is a wreck, although still producing like crazy.

The clerk laughs, shrugs, and sells me two very small metal-framed windows and a scratched metal door for my garden shed. Sean is anxious to get the walls up and will be happy to see these.

My latest finds make me think of posting about ReStore on Nextdoor with pictures of what I've brought home. I get lots of questions and patiently look up the answers on the ReStore website, assuming these are young people with smartphones who can't be bothered looking it up. I'm probably wrong about that and apologize to them in my head. I notice that the questions start out "Do they have this or that?" and later turn into "Will they take this or that?" I respond to some of these with "Maybe someone around here wants that and could save you hauling it to the store. Any takers?" This is purely selfish. If someone is replacing water pipes, I want the old ones.

I don't see much of the Saunderses, but I do notice that they've been clearing the fencerow between our yards. I can see that their deck is missing some boards and wonder how long they have owned the place.

Sean stops by to take photos of my patio and look at the shed door and windows I've found. He notices the Saunders's disaster of a deck too, and I suggest that he take his card and go talk to them. He can send them over to look at the work he did for me. He texts me later that they said they are thinking of moving after the baby is born. This makes me sad. They do ring my doorbell, though, and ask to see what Sean did at my house. They are complimentary but noncommittal and don't mention moving. They ask about the obviously used doors and windows lying on the patio waiting for Sean, and I tell them about ReStore.

CHAPTER 41

In the middle of July I get together with Angie for lunch. After some catching up, she says, "You know, last time we got together, we started reminiscing and I never got around to asking you how you decided on this house. I just keep thinking about how you just up and moved back here and not just back to Kansas City but back to this house. I love that you did, but. . . ." the question is there but unspoken: *had you gone a little crazy, or is there a plan here?*

I've wondered the same thing, and I have several elevator speeches about it, one of which starts, "I was probably not thinking clearly." Another begins with, "I didn't know what else to do." But the truth is that I don't know why. I was at a dead end, and then I saw a path and took it.

"I guess it was incremental," I tell her, the one person I expect to truly understand. "I was staying with friends, and that can go on for only so long. Once I got the insurance money, I worked out that it would be gone within fourteen months if I tried to stay in the area, and then I'd be renting a room in an apartment with three other people. So the first, obvious decision was: leave the Bay Area." Angie nods. Part one was pretty straightforward.

"I never really considered staying, but I was not in any kind of mental state to pick an entirely new place—say, Montana—even though part of me did want to disappear into the unknown. I would have spent months agonizing and grinding away the enamel on my teeth." Angie is sitting back, watching, and saying nothing.

"Consciously or unconsciously, I wanted a bolt hole, someplace known and safe." I pause after "safe" because we both know I missed that by a mile. Or several miles.

"Well, you know what I mean—safe emotionally, if not physically." She smiles. She does know.

Every other place I've lived since leaving here . . . I have friends in those places. . . ." I'm figuring this out as I am speaking. "But I didn't want to show up and say, 'Hey, I'm back and my life is a train wreck.' If that makes any sense. The ties in all those places were more work related anyway." I sigh.

"You know I'm not that close to my brother, but he is family. And from Kansas City I can drive to lots of my cousins. I can see them without moving in next door and creating the expectation that they'll take me into their social circle." I look up to see if this is making any sense, and Angie nods and smiles. She's from a very large family. She has siblings and cousins from here to the moon and back.

"I spent a lot of time on the internet. I looked for houses I could afford that were not way out in the burbs. I didn't look in Northland since it's a foreign country to me." I look up again. "Did we *ever* go north of the river at all?"

"Not that I remember, except when we went to St. Joe for that retreat in what? Eighth grade?"

"After that, we have to blame Google Street View. I 'drove' around the Plaza area—too expensive but I had to look, right? I drove down this block out of curiosity. I looked up the owners out of curiosity. They lived way out somewhere, and there was a phone number. Click, click, click."

"You just called them out of the blue?"

"Remember, I wasn't really being rational in those days. I was a wreck. I don't think they knew what to make of me. But they had lived here for a while when their kids were little, which may be why they held on to it. That, and it was hard to sell. Or even rent, once the roof leaked. After I talked to them for a while they got kind of excited about the whole thing—getting it off their hands and also helping me out. I paid for the appraisal, which came in so low that I offered them more but insisted on the new roof and assurance that the plumbing and electrical be in working order." I give her a goofy grin and wave my arms around the room.

"And here I am. Want a glass of wine?"

She does, and I ask her about crime and the general perception of this part of the city, questions I am uncomfortable asking my neighbors.

"For a long time, there was a lot of news about crime over here. I got the impression that they wanted to make it seem like this was a bad area so that other parts of town would seem safer," she says, choosing words carefully. "I'm trying not to blame the police or the news media or anyone in particular, but it did seem that way. I would go to work and people would talk about some shooting and say, 'Didn't you used to live right there?' all googly eyed, like I was either a drug pusher or the child of drug pushers." This makes me a little edgy, but I realize it's on her behalf and not mine.

"Then one day I realized that they would say that even if whatever happened was at, say, 35th and Troost, or even in Swope Park, where everyone goes from all over the place. One time it was a drug bust in Raytown. They didn't pay attention; as long the problem was east of Troost and they were not east of Troost, they were safe." I refill our glasses.

"I don't hear that so much now. I mean I still hear the term 'east of Troost'," she says, "but I think the perception is that it's not as bad as it was."

"Maybe because once the expressway was built people drove through and no one shot at them?"

We laugh and she says, "Most likely. And you know how people are—we get tired of one topic and move on to something else."

"Okay, so I need to ask you a question." I've been wanting to ask her for a long time, but until now I've been a little afraid of the answer. "I'm not going to ask if you think I'm crazy to move here, because we both know I am. But, I do feel a little bit like a fish out of water. Or not out of water, but maybe in the wrong pond. Like I'm trying to prove something, or maybe improve something, come in here and save the old 'hood. You know, do-gooder crap."

"So what was the question in there?" Always the straightforward one.

"Should I even be here?"

She thinks about that.

"Well, you are here. You aren't doing harm. And you are doing good—and also doing well." Ever the grammarian. "I think maybe you are asking a question that doesn't need a direct answer. Didn't Winnie the Pooh say something like, 'A Thing which seems very Thingish inside you is quite different when it gets out into the open and has other people looking at it'? Stop worrying about unanswerable stuff. You've got other things to worry about, things that might have actual answers."

CHAPTER 42

I gradually get used to planning meals ahead since it's a bit of a drive to buy groceries, especially fruits and vegetables. I do most of my grocery shopping at Cosentino's and John the produce guy now knows me by name. One Friday morning, I'm wandering around his section and he asks if I need help finding something.

"I was hoping for arugula, but it doesn't look so good."

He gives me an exaggerated eye-roll. "And I suppose it has to be local, fresh, and organic?" By now, this is an old joke between us.

"Well of course."

"Tell you what, you just make do with romaine for now and go over to the garden section and buy yourself a pack of arugula seeds. You grow it and I'll buy it from you and then sell it back to you at a profit."

The romaine looks great, so I do buy it and I decide to call his bluff and buy the seeds too. They are on a rack that with a banner that says "Time to Plant for Fall Harvest." I get sugar snap pea seeds too. I've never been successful with fall gardening, but I'm willing to risk a dollar and a half.

When I get home, it's too hot to think about doing any gardening more strenuous than picking a tomato for lunch, so I do that and leave the arugula seeds on the kitchen counter where

I hope I won't forget them. I call Josie and ask if she wants tomatoes.

"Sure, and why don't you bring them over here around six and we'll have a nice cool salad for supper."

Josie has central air conditioning, so I say, "I would love that." I try to think of something more I can contribute and come up with cornbread.

"I've been wanting some crispy cornbread. How about if I make some to go with the salad?"

"Okay, you heat up your kitchen baking it and then bring it over here to eat it where it's cool."

After we eat, we sip iced tea and Josie tells me about the Tai chi class she's been taking.

"The rehab people said it would be good for balance and I figured it would help keep Sue happy."

The class is in the Brookside area, a little north and a mile or two to the west.

"How do you get there?" I ask, wondering if there is an OATS bus or something, and also wondering if I could offer to drive her there and how that would go over.

"Well, I drive, of course!" and she laughs. "You thought I was an old lady who couldn't drive?"

I guess I did, and I'm embarrassed about that, but I say, "Well, there isn't a car parked out there, is there?" pointing to her driveway.

"Ha! Fooled ya. I keep it in the garage back there." She points to the house behind her. "He's got one of those big-ass SUVs that won't fit in there, anyway. We worked out a deal: my car over there and his dogs over here. I like to keep it out of the sun in the summer. Sometimes I keep it here in the winter, when it gets icy back there. I'll show you."

I can't believe I just heard her say "big-ass," but I let it go. We go out into the heat, which has eased a little, and the air smells of freshly cut grass. Someone nearby has braved the muggy weather to get the mowing done before the mosquitoes come out.

Josie has worn a path in her yard, but I assumed it went just to the dog pen. Now I see it goes around and through the gap at the corner that we used as kids.

"I was wondering if your guy (I have a guy?) would be interested in fixing a real path through here, and maybe a step or two through there," she says, pointing to the gap.

"Maybe even a gate," I suggest, which gets a noncommittal "Mmm." She's got her eye on something in my yard.

"Are those lilac bushes? I never noticed those."

"You probably couldn't see them with all the brush that had grown up. But yes, those are lilacs and they were wonderful back in the spring. I've pruned them back so next year they'll bloom a little lower, where I can reach them. I love lilacs." I notice that I haven't found it necessary to tell her about how nice they were "back then" and am pleased with myself.

"I love them too," she sighs.

I tell her I'll send Sean over to discuss the path and thank her for dinner. I go up the step from her carport to my backyard and through the gate. Boris looks at the step, which is high and narrow, and leaps all the way up. "Coward," I say to him.

I have no idea what Josie's financial state is, but I wonder why she doesn't have lilacs if she likes them so much. Then I recall that I didn't buy a maple tree for my back yard, I relocated a promising-looking sprout. So I look up propagating lilacs and find that it's possible to root cuttings. I decide to give it a try. I picture myself clandestinely planting lilacs all up and down the nearby blocks so I can smell them when I'm walking Boris next spring.

CHAPTER 43

Taking the bus to shop downtown with my mother was a childhood thrill that happened several times a year before shopping malls were built and we got a second car. Mother was big on shoes that fit well, and we always bought them downtown, in August, just before school started.

A local bus still runs all the way down Prospect, although there is also an express bus on the new expressway. I have a distant cousin who works downtown and extolls the virtues of twenty-first century downtown KC. I am intrigued and I want to see it, both old and new. I am particularly intrigued by the new public library, which has moved to a classic old bank building and built a parking garage with a façade that makes it look like a row of three-story-high books. I want to see the cathedral, which I had hardly ever been in, and I want to see if it is still possible to take an elevator to the open-air viewing deck on top of city hall. I want to see if anything is recognizable. And I want to ride that bus again. I make a lunch date with my cousin. I don't tell her that I am taking the bus.

I leave home plenty early and take the Prospect bus; I even walk an extra block to get around the expressway and board at my old stop. I remember finally turning five and getting to put my own nickel in the farebox. It costs me a bit more today, but far, far less than parking and driving.

North of 63rd Street I'm out of what I would consider my own neighborhood, then and now. It's familiar and it's not. I didn't pass through this area often enough to recognize much of it anyway, and now the expressway is marching along beside Prospect. On the other hand, the buildings are quintessential Kansas City, at least in my out-of-date view. Some of Prospect is residential and the homes are larger than in my area. These are mostly two stories, solid-looking, with wide front porches, the classic local "shirtwaist" architectural style that I have always loved. Some are boarded up or have bars on the windows, but most look well cared for and could be anywhere in the older part of town, east or west of Troost. The residential sections have large street trees, lots of sycamores.

The Prospect bus is the slow way downtown, with lots of stops. It's after rush hour, and the bus is never full, but someone gets on or off at most of the stops. Occasionally someone sits next to me and we say "hello" and return to our phones or newspapers, or in my case to gazing out the window.

I know that the 1968 riots took place around 31st and Prospect, and I admit that I'm curious about what it looks like now. My only memories are black-and-white footage from the evening news and photos from the morning and evening newspapers. I mostly remember the fires and looting and death of unarmed Black protesters. Since then, some rebuilding has definitely gone on. A few blocks are more strip-mall like, with off-street parking in front of new stand-alone commercial buildings. Not attractive, but I guess the lovely old brick buildings I prefer lost their charm when they were boarded up and tagged and abandoned too. This part of Prospect does seem busier than my part, maybe because the expressway has moved west and no longer cuts off a wide swath of potential customers.

At Truman Road, the bus turns west and I look for one

landmark I remember, a large store on the corner with The Store Without a Name emblazoned across the sides facing both streets. The building is there, I think, but no sign.

By this point in the trip I was always a little carsick from diesel fumes and eager to get there. The bus makes a right turn on Troost, left on 11th. I've arrived. I get off at a random stop and navigate on foot to the art deco city hall, where I go through a metal detector and take the elevator to the observation deck. It's breezy up there, but not so windy that they've closed it to tourists, so I peer this way and that looking for landmarks. Mother always pointed out the West Bottoms, where our dad started and ended his work day. It was always a mystery to me, the West Bottoms, an odd name and I had no idea where it was. I only saw it from the top of city hall.

I meet my cousin for lunch. She says that she had forgotten about the observation deck and is sorry she missed it. We talk about the defunct Forum Cafeteria and wish we could have gone there and found a table on the mezzanine. I tell her I would have had the fried whiting because that's what I always had, every time we had lunch there, which was every time we took the bus downtown. I was not a very adventurous child, I guess, or else I just loved that crispy fried fish.

My cousin goes back to work, and I go looking for the library, feeling slightly guilty, as if I'm playing hooky. I don't go past the foyer, but I do spend some time admiring the façade of the parking garage, which is covered in signboard Mylar displaying a row of twenty-two books, each twenty-five feet high and nine feet wide. Plato stands between *Fahrenheit 451* and *The Adventures of Huckleberry Finn.* I make a note to read *Their Eyes Were Watching God,* which stands next to *One Hundred Years of Solitude.* I wonder who lined up the final selections.

As I'm standing there, tourists are taking selfies, and three young women ask me to take a picture of them with *Invisible Man* in the background. It's a bit of a challenge getting the angle right, and while I'm lining it up I make small talk.

"I wonder who got to choose which books would be represented," I say, although I'm actually wondering why this group chose *Invisible Man* and if they have read it.

"We picked them!" They are almost squealing, delighted with the question.

"Seriously?" I ask, hoping they'll elaborate.

"Well, kinda," one of them says. "We were in high school and they asked for suggestions and our English teacher had us all pick a book and write why we thought it should be included."

"Sounds like you had a pretty cool English teacher," I tell them. "Did you all pick *Invisible Man*?" I'm pretty sure they didn't, but I'm really curious now.

"Nah, I don't even remember what I picked, probably something stupid."

"I picked whatever we were reading in class. I was hoping she'd give me an *A* for that. She didn't, though."

"So why *Invisible Man*?" I ask them.

"It's just the most amazing book. It literally changed my life," one of them says. "And it's so ironic," says another, "I mean here we are totally visible, standing in front of someone invisible."

"He's not actually invisible, girl," the third one says. "He *feels* invisible."

They start arguing about invisibility and I realize that this isn't the H.G. Wells story I thought it was. The author's name is right there on the spine: Ralph Ellison. I don't actually know this book at all. I hand back the iPhone, say goodbye, and then take my own selfie. Mine is with *Catch-22.*

I think about looking for a shoe store because I know I'll need something nicer than sneakers and flip-flops by fall, but I'm not really in the mood and I'm not sure downtown is the place for shoes anymore. I look up bus stops and try to find one for the express bus on the expressway, assuming it will stop at Gregory or at least at Meyer. It does not. It's an express from the distant suburbs to downtown, with no stops. Troost has more options, regular and express, and I can transfer at Gregory, so I take that. I'll go right down the great divide.

But I only go as far as 39th, where I see St. James Church. My parents were married there and I have never been inside. Theirs was a good marriage, so I go in and I light a candle in their memory. As I am leaving, I see the 39th Street bus pulling up and hop on it. I'll take it east to Prospect instead of continuing on Troost.

There are no surprises on 39th. I see the now-familiar mix of well-kept and unkempt, with some board-ups and graffiti, and quite a few vacant lots where houses used to be. When I get off to change at Prospect, the corner seems especially bedraggled. A new Aldi occupies most of the block on one corner, though, and the bus shelter is on that corner. While I wait, I can see vacant lots in all directions, and several boarded-up buildings. A young man leans out of a car as it passes me on Prospect and calls, "Hoooo, mama." I don't make eye contact. I'm aware that everyone I know would tell me I was insane for being on this corner, even in broad daylight. They have a valid point. It's not likely that I'll do this again, though, and I know the bus is less than ten minutes away. Maybe fifteen; I'm no longer sure about the Prospect schedule. I am relieved when a woman with two kids crosses the Aldi parking lot and walks up to the stop just as the bus arrives. They all are carrying shopping bags, and the kids seem tired and whiney, asking about dinner and a TV program they are eager to see when they get home.

We all board and I sit in the first row of forward-facing seats. The mom and kids crowd together on a sideways seat behind the driver. The older girl is reading a book. She snuggles her back against her mother and leans her head sideways, resting on the back of the seat, and twirls a braid with her free hand. The little girl is jostling the grocery bags, reaching up to touch her mother's face and enquire earnestly about the possibility of having hot dogs for supper. *They live here, or go to school here. They take the bus to the grocery. I'm here on a lark, really. They are not afraid. They can't afford to be afraid.*

The three of them leave the bus at 51st Street, an intersection that has absolutely nothing to recommend it. While the bus waits for the light to change, the mom and kids walk across Prospect and start up the hill to the overpass that crosses the Watkins expressway. A long-forgotten song plays in my head: "My mother forbade me to walk down these streets. Where does their mother forbid them to go?"

I arrive home without incident, feed Boris, pour a glass of wine, and think about Diane Reel. She's the one who wrote the song that popped into my head. She was a few years ahead of me in school and led the guitar mass group at St. Louis. I wonder whatever happened to her.

I text Angie, who knows that Diane joined a cloistered order of nuns but doesn't know anything else. Even Google can't penetrate the cloister, unless, maybe, if she has died. And of course she may have left. I try more web searching and come up with no likely results among the noncloistered Diane Reels, and no obituaries. I hope she's still in her order and at the same time hope the song is out in the secular world. I Google what I remember of the lyrics but don't find what I'm hoping for. It's too bad. The words and melody are going to haunt me. An awful lot of people spend their days on streets that my friends and family, and yes, I myself, are afraid to even walk down.

It's all a matter of degree, of course. I'm now living in a place where many of my friends and relatives will not visit me, although Angie and my brother have breached the divide. But I am unlikely to retrace the trip I made today.

CHAPTER 44

I've been shifting my dog walking to suit the weather, sometimes early in the morning and sometimes in the evening. As the days get a bit shorter, I've sometimes been out in the twilight. My mother's "Be home when the streetlights come on" seems baked into my subconscious, and I feel a little vulnerable if I'm out past that curfew.

But shifting the times has given me a peek into the neighborhood, seeing different people out at different times. In the evenings, people are more likely to have a minute or two to say hello, pet Boris. Some people sit out on the porches or take lawn chairs into their yards. Dave and Carol may have converted their wide front porch into a room, but they have built a little patio in front of it, where the afternoon shade makes it comfortable enough to sit out on cooler days. One evening when they are out, they wave me over and offer me a glass of iced tea and make small talk until the mosquitos come out. The neighborhood feels completely, perfectly safe.

Then we hear sirens, close by. My gut reaction is that my house is on fire, which it quite obviously is not. While Boris howls, we get up and look around to see that the flashing blue lights have stopped at the far end of the next block and that it's the EMT van.

"Well, thank goodness," Carol says, and then realizes how that must sound. "I mean. . . ."

"Oh, it's okay," I rush to say. "I had the same thought. It doesn't mean anything."

None of us knows who lives at the house, but the mood has shifted and I thank them and cross the street.

Two nights later as Boris and I are walking up the street, Dave and Carol are out front again, and Josie is with them.

"Did you hear what happened?" Carol asks, a question so vague that I am instantly on alert. Whatever it is must be so serious that if I had heard, I would know what she was talking about.

"No . . . what is it?" I want to know, and I don't want to know.

"Break-in at 69th and Chestnut, a house or two from the corner. They took a big-screen TV and a computer." Now I know, and I'm not happy, even though I don't have a big-screen TV, or any kind of televison.

"A neighbor saw two guys coming out with the TV," Dave adds. "They shoved it in the back of a pickup truck and hopped on the expressway."

First I think, *two guys, so my intruder isn't back. Or maybe he's got a buddy.* And then I tell myself to focus and say, "I thought that access onto the expressway was pretty convenient, but maybe it's not such a great idea."

And then I go back to thinking of myself and ask, "How did they get in?"

"Kicked in the back door." I cringe when I hear that. "It was an old half-glass door, probably the original." I cringe again because that's the kind of door that was on Josie's house back when I was in college and watched a burglar break in through it.

We say the usual things, feeling bad for the victim and secretly glad that it wasn't any of us this time.

I go home and remind Boris that he's got guard duty tomorrow because I will be out buying a door. I don't sleep well, reliving the scene from thirty years ago and listening for someone to kick in my door. I think of a concept from a college sociology class: urban tax. It's the nonmonetary cost of living next to a freeway, or at the edge of a gated community, or any other place where the city environment intrudes on you just a little more than on those in the next house or the next block. The people who suffered the break-in this time can get to the northbound expressway lanes conveniently, but they have to put up with a little more traffic on their own street and in this case more risk because a burglar may feel more daring if he can disappear quickly into the anonymity of the expressway.

The next morning I start early, calling all four ReStore locations and asking about doors. I find a good candidate at the store north of the river and ask them if they can hold it for me until one o'clock. The woman on the other end is a little amused by that and assures me that it will be there.

Jimmy has given me a lesson in doors and written down the minimum and maximum widths and heights, and reminded me to pay attention to which side the hinges are on. I have that information with me, along with the mental image of a beautiful-but-strong door that has made me reject every door I have found so far. I also have pictures and prices of new doors for comparison purposes. I plan to go at noon so I am not too obviously taking time away from the project I have promised to finish for Cathy by Wednesday. Not that Cathy would begrudge me ninety minutes away from my desk. I just don't want to tell her that I am buying a security door from a resale shop. So I plan to leave at noon, but at ten I give up and leave, rationalizing that ten is the sweet spot for missing traffic and that I will be able to concentrate better if I finally have a door in my possession.

I buy the door at ReStore. Two days prior, I would have rejected it as too ugly. Today, it's perfect. A clerk I haven't met before helps me load it up, and I call Jimmy from the parking lot. He says that he will be over around five thirty to look at it.

When the doorbell rings I look up in surprise. Once I got back from ReStore, I had calmed down and gotten lost in my work. Boris is at the door wagging his tail, and I think it's Jimmy until I walk through the kitchen and the goofy clock shows that it's only 3:25 p.m..

It's not Jimmy at all. It's Officer Carl. He is friendly but somber, so of course I'm worried and wonder what the burglary on Chestnut has to do with me. This time he's in a regular police car with "Community Relations" on the side—all reassurance, no intimidation.

"I just wanted to check in with you." His opening isn't giving me any clues. I assure him that all is well and invite him to have a seat. He looks around, appreciating the improvements. It's pretty bare still, but he hasn't been here to see the new paint and furniture.

"Yeah, I can actually say, 'Have a seat' and mean it now." I sit on the far end of the sofa so he can sit on the ell and face me.

It was a pretty weak joke, but he smiles and then gets serious again and small talk is over.

"I assume you heard about the break-in on Chestnut," he says, and when I nod he seems reassured, either because now he doesn't have to be the one to tell me or because if I know it means I'm in touch with the neighbors.

"We don't have that guy yet, but there's still a chance we'll get him." I can't tell if he believes that or just hopes.

"But it was definitely not Bud Forsythe, so I thought I would let you know that. He seems to have settled down and I'm not really worried about him right now." That's good, but who is he worried about now?

"Last night there was a mugging, and you probably haven't heard about that?" It's a question.

"No, where was it?"

"On Meyer, near Walrond." I can convince myself that there's a little buffer between the mugging and myself.

"What happened?"

"It was just before midnight, and the mugger came up from behind and pulled the victim's stocking cap down over his eyes, then punched him in the gut and took his wallet."

I don't have a stocking cap or carry a wallet when I'm walking, but I do have a gut and it's not liking this story.

"Did he have a dog? The victim, I mean?"

Carl laughs. He knows what I'm thinking.

"No dog, and he was out very late on a street where the neighbors across the street can't see anything across the parkway AND where there is a lot more traffic than, say, this street."

I relax one iota and laugh myself, and say, "Really? A stocking cap in August?"

"It's kind of a look."

"Okay, since you're here, can we just talk about crime in the neighborhood? Before I left, I knew two families with kids who had been shot, not right here but close enough. And there were burglaries. We even put a lock on our toolshed, and the gate—there was a gate then. And there were burnouts. So I get it. But what's the deal now? Is it gang stuff, is it racial, is it random? Am I reasonably safe walking the dog? No one else walks dogs around here."

"No one walks dogs because they are either too old to walk up and down these hills or they are too busy driving out of this neighborhood to shop and work and take the kids here and there. You probably walked to Blenheim, for example. You know it's closed now, don't you?" He sounds a little bitter.

"Kindergarten. After that I went to Saint Louis, on Swope Parkway. It was so jammed packed that they had to drop kindergarten in the late 1950s." Not relevant. "But yeah, I wondered about Blenheim. Running the expressway right by the front door took out a lot of houses with school-age kids who used to walk to school there."

"Some developer wants to convert the building to apartments now," he says.

"Maybe that will be good, increase the population around here," I say. "And at least they aren't going to level the building. It's a cool building."

"True. And back to your questions, you are going to be pretty safe if you keep your doors and windows locked, keep your car locked with nothing visible inside, and don't go walking after dark. Although I really don't think anyone will mess with you as long as you have Boris. Can you teach him to bark on command?"

"Boris, speak," I say, and he woofs.

"Come up with a different command, maybe a hand signal. You want the other person to think he's barking because he perceives a threat, not because you told him to."

"Ah, right. I can do that. He's good at learning new things." Then I look at Boris. "Tell Officer Carl what the firetruck says." Boris howls like he means it, and Carl laughs.

"He is good! And he's your best protection, so take care of him. And don't worry too much. Murders in Kansas City now are almost all gang related or domestic violence, with a few late-night store robberies. Street hold-ups are more random but you can avoid those by not being out alone at night, especially on the boulevards."

This sounds like a lecture or a public service announcement, and he sounds like he's said it a thousand times before, but I still find it reassuring.

"So that leaves break-ins, and, again, the dog and your neighbors are your best line of defense. That and good doors, provided they are locked. I can't tell you how many robberies aren't true B&E crimes. They've left a door or window open." I'm only a little reassured by this, because if that many people are forgetting to lock up I probably will forget too.

"And I really shouldn't say this, but break-ins here are no worse than in most of the city. People don't want to believe that. They want to think all crime is somewhere they are not. There are some much nicer targets in other neighborhoods. But you didn't hear that from me."

"So why would you trust me with that?" I ask.

"I want you to be trustworthy, I guess."

Carl gets up to go, and I walk him out, thanking him for keeping an eye out.

I go back to my computer, but keep mulling over what Carl said and why he said it.

Jimmy arrives, spends some time looking and measuring. He removes the trim from around the inside of my back door.

"Your dad did this in the 1960s?" he asks.

"Summer of 1959. I was about to start kindergarten."

"He did good work, and this door is pretty safe. It's not the prehung kind that some people just sort of tack in with a nail or two. He built the whole frame right into the house. But the new one will be better. It will take four, five hours. I can do it in the morning if you like. I told my other client I might need tomorrow off, so I'm going to go back there now and finish up some things so I don't get behind with her."

"Yes, that's fine." I want him to do it instantly so I don't have to stay awake listening for burglars again tonight, but I know that is irrational on several levels. "I'm thrilled that you can do it so quickly."

"I know about the break-in on Chestnut and I know you'd like to have it tonight," he says. "But it's not a good idea to rip out a door after the hardware stores are closed. It's a long drive to the nearest Home Depot if something breaks or a part is missing."

"My father-in-law used to say, 'Never plumb on Sunday'."

"Wise man. See you tomorrow."

I don't sleep all that well, partly because I'm listening for burglars at my house and at Josie's, partly because I sat at my computer too late, catching up on the work I wasn't doing when I was buying the door and talking to Carl and Jimmy, and also because I didn't take a walk. I'm letting an unknown burglar wreak havoc on my personal life.

The door installation goes smoothly with only one trip to the hardware store.

"A couple of screws are missing, so I'm going to go talk to Henry," he tells me. By now I know that "talk to Henry" is code for "go to Midtown Hardware."

"Want me to have the locksmith come out later today?"

Crap. I completely forgot about that. I would have been the doofus who left her house unlocked for burglars.

Jimmy finishes the door and tells me that the locksmith will be there before five. "If he's not, call me and we'll rig up something." Then he asks about the old door. "I could replace the basement door with this one. It's the same size and the jamb is deep enough." He's not saying that the exterior door will be sturdier than the hollow-core door that's there, but I hear him.

"Not that I think you need it, but it might make you feel a little better." By "better" he means "safer." So we agree to that and he says that he'll call next week when he has a couple of hours.

When I open the refrigerator looking for dinner inspiration, I discover that the lettuce is icy. I adjust the control and put jars of water in the crisper, the main compartment, and the freezer. A thermometer would be more accurate, but this will give me the big picture, and now that I have jars I don't have to risk my H&R Block mug. I never use it but I've developed a fondness for it, probably because it's ugly and almost useless. When I check back later, the jar in the crisper has a skim of ice.

I Google "crisper freezing" and read various blog posts. I find the model number so I can look up how old it is. It's fourteen years old, so I know that if I call someone to repair it, they will charge me for the call and then tell me to buy a new one. I've been there before. I find one suggestion that seems to be worth trying when the refrigerator compartment is fine but the crisper is too cold: leave the crisper open a bit. This seems to be worth a try, although I see no reason to ruin the food that's in there, so I take the food out but leave the jar of water in. Apparently this can be a problem in really hot weather, which is what we've been having.

CHAPTER 45

The next day is Friday, and I make myself a large iced coffee and sit down to take stock. First of my finances and then of my life. I plan to bail on taking stock of my life if it gets too hot or I think of something else I need to do or if I just can't face it.

The refrigerator and the checks I've been writing to Sean and Henry and Jimmy and ReStore are starting to worry me. It's still hot and I have put off thinking about what I can or should do about winterizing, but winter is coming no matter what. I make "Winter" a separate page under "Finances".

I calculate what is left of my insurance payout once all the checks clear. I have about 25 percent left. I calculate my monthly income and subtract the standard bills and average household costs for gas and groceries and the like. I subtract for property taxes and homeowner's insurance, both substantially less than I am used to. I'm relieved to see that I have extra each month even though I'm putting as much as I can into my 401(k).

Next I consider what I still have to do, what I would like to do, and what I might have to do if I have an emergency like a broken refrigerator and washer. The dryer and air conditioner are still under warranty and the stove is not the sort that breaks, having no electronics or compressors, so I don't put them in the potential emergency list.

I decide to err on the side of caution and keep what's left of the payout for emergencies. Who knows when a water line will break or a sewer line will freeze or I will wake up to a cold house and a silent furnace? And in the back of my mind, I know I need an escape fund. Two years ago, we had an escape fund in case of catastrophic earthquake, so that we could get out of the Bay Area and live somewhere else until the dust settled and we could rebuild or relocate for good. Now I need an escape fund in case something happens that means I just can't live here after all.

I am confident that I have enough disposable income each month to let me continue furnishing the house and doing minor upgrades. Cathy has asked me about going back to forty hours, and I'm not ready for that but I told her I might do that in the winter. That would let me put more money away for retirement, something that two years ago was considered secure.

Finances settled, I work for a while on a to-do list, which includes putting in a new kitchen floor and doing some work in the bathroom. I put "shower" on the list but I still haven't figured that out. "Gate" is on the list and I waste some time on Craigslist.

I top up my iced coffee and decide I'm done with analysis for the day.

I walk outside and see Josie getting out of the driver's seat of a red SUV in her driveway. She waves and starts unloading groceries.

"Is this the car you keep back there?" I wave toward the neighbor's garage.

She grins one of her gotcha smiles. "Yep. This is a small-ass SUV."

Once Jimmy has the doors switched, I realize that I have something to donate to ReStore. I check the website, though, and discover that they won't take it since it's not prehung. So I post it on Nextdoor and get a message later the same day from someone named Charles who is interested. We set a time and I haul it outside, taking Boris with me, and lock the doors. Nextdoor is not Craigslist, but why take chances? I leave the dog watching from behind the chicken wire, prop the door up on the front of the house in full view of the street, and move my car out of the way.

Charles arrives and looks it over carefully and quietly. He asks if it's hollow-core and I say "I think so." I have the strike plate and hinges in a bag ready. He asks how much I want and I tell him he can have it if he wants it, I just didn't want to throw it away. He changes from serious to talkative and tells me all about his house, which he and his wife have just moved into. I make sure he knows about ReStore, and he's already been there.

He looks at Boris, who is standing and watching, alert but not alarmed. Boris barks twice and Charles asks if he can pet him. I say "sure," then look at Boris and say, "Boris, friend," as if that were something he had been taught. Boris wags his tail then and whimpers, so I say, "Boris, come," all serious, like he's a trained guard dog or something. I don't know why I'm being this way, but I'm pleased with Boris and it makes me feel safe.

Boris elevates himself over the chicken wire and trots to me, then noses Charles, who pets him.

"Not much of a gate back there," Charles says. "He stepped right over it."

"No. It keeps the rabbits out of my garden, though. Boris is inside a lot and the rabbits are pretty bold. I thought I had found a gate through Nextdoor to match the fence on that side." I nod toward Josie's house and see her peeping out the window. "But it didn't work out, so I'm still looking. I cross my fingers every time I go to ReStore."

Charles loads up the door and thanks me several more times, before heading off down the street.

The following Friday I am cleaning the kitchen counter and come across the arugula and pea seeds. I also notice that the sun has moved south just enough to paint a strip of sunlight across the back of the kitchen counter. It's late August, now or never for fall planting, even if it feels too hot.

I stick the packets in my pocket and go out to the garden to reconnoiter.

"Boris, it's a jungle out here," I tell him, and he sniffs for bunnies, then whines at the side gate. The fence has made it harder for him to check in with his buddies. I know he could jump the fence if he had to, but he's happy to wait for his staff to open the gate.

The tomatoes have taken over, sprawling into the grass and weeds around the spaded area. The peppers have struggled to hold their ground, but now their own heavy fruit is weighing them down. I prop some of them up—I'm hoping to leave them until they turn red—and pick a few others. I can make stuffed peppers tonight. I make a mental note to plant eggplant next year, or something else to stuff peppers with. I rely too much on meat and rice now that I'm so far from a green grocer. The beans that shot up above the jungle of tomatoes are still producing. I've neglected them and some have gone shelly, the pods brown and the beans inside large and starchy. I think about shelly-stuffed peppers and pick a few, stuffing them in my pockets.

Nowhere do I see space for peas or arugula. I'd have to spade up new ground. I picture arugula seedlings in mud and look around at the front of my new garden shed, which is more of a fortress than a shed. Maybe the stones and concrete block were overkill. It looks like I'm hiding something in there. It needs climbing roses or something to make it look friendly. Peas aren't roses, but maybe they will do.

I measure and decide that eight cinder blocks will make a nice raised bed in front of the shed. Maybe the block wall will keep it all warm enough to extend pea-and-arugula season into November. Ugh, more cinder block. It will just look like a prison garden. Maybe railroad ties. Ick, creosote. Who cares? It's only peas. I can buy peas if I need to. I go back inside.

It's hot and going to be hotter in the afternoon when the sun moves around to the west. That shrubby thing out front gives me some shade late in the day, but I need a big shade tree. I go back out and look for a maple sprout. I'm sweaty and the buzzing insects annoy me, so I go back inside. A maple will heave the sidewalk, a trip hazard for Josie. Gum balls are a worse trip hazard. Sycamores shed bark. Pines make too much shade in the winter. I Google "street trees" and come up with Bradford pears. Ubiquitous and not a real shade tree. Then I see the Heartland Tree Alliance. They will plant street trees for free, but they have to be ten feet from the street—not the parkway planting I was imagining, which means I probably can't legally plant a real tree in the parkway anyway. I close the browser and put my head down on the table. I don't even bother to turn on the air conditioner.

After a while I get up to make another iced coffee and find that I'm out of coffee and milk. I scrape up enough energy to get in the car. The cool air makes me feel a little better, and I treat myself to iced coffee before I start shopping. I haven't really planned this trip, so I toss things into my cart randomly. John the produce guy waves but doesn't tease me about arugula, which is good because I am not in the mood.

When I open my back door, it's so hot I can smell the heat. I have left the curtains open and sun is pouring in. The windows are closed and the AC is not on. Boris is not there to greet me. I call him, put down the groceries in the kitchen, run from room to room. I feel guilty because I've let him die in the heat, let him get stolen, missed some vital sign of illness. I hear a bark, but I can't find him. I call him again and he whimpers from the back of the house. The basement door is open—I've been leaving it open so the exhaust fans can pull cool air up the stairs. And there is Boris, at the bottom of the stairs, tail waving, front paws on the second step.

"Oh, so it got hot enough that you went down to lie on the cool concrete? Now you have to figure out how to get back up because I can't lift ninety pounds of squirmy dog."

He woofs softly, and I say, "Come on, Boo, you can do this." He is not convinced. I go down and get behind him, moving his paws and pushing while he whines and complains. When we get about two-thirds of the way up, he sees the light and bounds the rest of the way, then turns around and woofs at me as though I am the one needing encouragement. I sit on the step covered with dog hair and laugh.

Early Saturday morning, I decide that I have to plant those seeds, for my own mental health. I've fretted about them for too long. So I get in the car and drive to ReStore, which is somehow not nearly as far away as it was last spring. I start to leave the AC on for Boris but decide the stairs practice will be good for him. Since it's Saturday, my usual clerk is there. Today he's wearing a nametag, so I say, "Fred, I want to make a small raised bed out of something that is not cinder block and not soaked in creosote."

He says that they don't take anything with creosote anyway and that I should think outside the blocks. I groan and he tells me he needs to unload donations, but that I should take a look around back. He grins slyly.

There is a new, open shed out back with a sign over the entrance that says FReStore and then in smaller print ReStore's shabby stepsister. Inside are rejects from the donation checkpoint, including old galvanized pipe. A worker is talking to customers checking out the goods.

"We thought about calling it 'Junker's Joint' but the board thought that might be misinterpreted," I hear him say. Fred appears beside me.

"The board was pretty skeptical altogether, but my boss let me present the idea to them," he says. "I told them about you taking things I was about to reject. So they agreed to try it for the rest of the summer, and it has to be things we can scrap if no one takes them. So it's mostly metal."

I call dibs on the galvanized pipe, and he says that he'll help me load it.

"Oh, and we couldn't agree on a name. They were just going to put a Free sign on a sawhorse. This one guy kept talking about standards, 'ReStore this' and 'ReStore that'. I saw my chance and said, '"FReStore"? Did you say "FReStore"? That's a great name.' So he thought it was his idea, and here we are."

"You should be in management. Or politics," I tell him, and he goes off again. I load the pipe myself and then try to think outside the blocks. I find some bent and peeling fireplace screens that don't match and could never be made flat enough to use inside. But they will hold back the dirt in my raised bed just fine. I pick up the rest of the pipe to use as stakes and go inside to look for a pipe cutter and make a donation. I wonder if a hacksaw would be better and decide to take my problem to Henry. I wave to Fred on my way out. I don't feel like building the raised bed today, but maybe lunch will help.

I skip Henry's and go home. Boris is wagging his tail like he's done something noteworthy, but I can't tell if he's been down the steps again. I leave the AC off while I eat lunch, and sure enough he goes downstairs. I hear his nails slip a little, but no crashing. I tell him he's a good dog and he races back up. I close the door and turn on the AC and he goes to sleep.

In the sweet spot of the day when the sun is about to set but the mosquitos aren't out yet, I stand up the fireplace screens, making what looks like a little pen against the front of the shed. I decide I don't need to cut the poles, I can just use the shortest ones and pretend they are supposed to be taller than the screens. I fasten the corners with twine, but I know that won't work. I'll have to get cable ties or some wire that is heavy enough to last until spring but light enough that I can bend it.

I slap the first mosquito and go inside.

On Sunday I tell myself it's a day of rest and that I'm not going to do any gardening. My hands could use a day of rest, for sure. I'm a knowledge worker, after all.

When I'm honest with myself, which is mostly only on Sunday mornings, I know that my increasing indecision, my lack of energy, and the knot in the pit of my stomach are things I need to deal with. Even though it's summer, I am aware every day that winter is coming. And while I make lists and plan to do something or other about winterizing, the thing that presses down on me is the knowledge that dark, cold days are coming. I'll be more afraid of noises in the dark when the dark lasts for fourteen hours a day and the neighbors, like me, will be inside most of the time. I will also have to face the holidays and the first anniversaries of loss, and do it alone. I know this and I know that I should be preparing for it, but I don't have the energy.

Monday at lunchtime I go to Henry's for cable ties and to ask about winterizing. He sells me a spool of wire instead. I make sure I can bend it without hurting my hands too much. He also tells me that I should use potting soil in raised beds; ordinary dirt somehow makes itself too hard for seeds to sprout. He doesn't carry potting soil this late in the season, though. He does sell me wire cutters and tells me that I can thank him later.

I put off the winterizing discussion and decide to try dirt and compost anyway. But when I leave, I turn left instead of right and drive a few blocks farther south on Prospect to Van Liews Home and Garden.

I don't remember Van Liew's being here when I was growing up, which is odd because they claim they've been in business for more than seventy-five years. Maybe they weren't on Prospect in the 1960s, or maybe I just didn't notice. I might get just a little potting soil for the peas.

I'm puzzled by what I see at the store: fountains, statues, outdoor furniture. Upscale stuff, not the sort of thing I see as I walk around this area. Then I notice the parking lot. It's full of contractor trucks and Kansas license plates. Now it makes sense. Locals don't shop here; people from the wealthier suburbs come here to look and the contractors come to pick up what their customers have chosen. The store owners are taking advantage of low rents on Prospect. Or maybe they *have* been here for decades and own the property. I'm pleased on behalf of my neighborhood that they are here and making money so far east of Troost. Maybe they are hiring locals too.

I look around a little more, but I'm soon impatient to leave. This is not my world anymore. I don't mind that, but I don't know what my world *is* anymore. I'm not unhappy in this place, but I'm not happy, either. I have a nagging suspicion that this isn't going to work out. But I can't think of any place else to go, or imagine having the energy to make another move.

CHAPTER 46

Labor Day approaches and the heat continues, although the nights are comfortable now. But I am still feeling anxious. I find myself having to check what day it is and getting teary over stories I hear on *All Things Considered.* One day I miss a conference call, even though it's on my calendar and I get the electronic reminder fifteen minutes before it starts. A few days later at the library I see a poster on the bulletin board that says "Sensory Sensitivity is a Symptom of Autism." I think of how I don't like bright lights indoors and I avoid loud restaurants, or did back when I went to restaurants. On business trips, I often made excuses to avoid the inevitable post-meeting drink at the bar. I would always say, "I've got a lot of email," or "I have a report due in the morning." Anything to retreat to my hotel room and shut the door. *That's not just being an introvert. Maybe I'm autistic.*

That evening, when I'm tired and feeling sorry for myself, I say to myself, "Here I am alone and I've got Alzheimer's and autism. And arthritis." I've been noticing that my ring fingers and little fingers are numb and have diagnosed myself with Reynaud's syndrome based entirely on the evidence that my mother had it. "The three As," I tell Boris, who is completely disinterested. "At least I don't have alcoholism," I add, "although I might have a glass of wine later." He doesn't care about that either.

"And now I'm talking out loud to my dog. I wonder if that's another A condition." I think about it. "Anthropomorphism, Boris. I also have anthropomorphism. It's incurable." He finally gets up and comes over for petting, which cheers me up enough to Google "numbness in little finger." It turns out to be a thing, and I read a couple of articles. Sure enough, Reynaud's is listed as a cause. I read on and learn about cubital tunnel syndrome, which you can get by repeatedly leaning on your elbow, especially on a hard surface. I take my chin off my hand and my elbow off the table. Another cause is bending your elbow for sustained periods, such as while sleeping with your hand crooked under your pillow. I picture myself curled up in bed, hands tucked safely under my pillow. Great, now I have something else to worry about when I can't sleep.

"Okay, Boris, maybe I don't have arthritis yet, and anthropomorphism isn't really a thing. Let's have dinner.

CHAPTER 47

The first week of September is a little cooler and almost crisp, which makes me feel a bit more energetic. I get a burst of back-to-school inspiration. I plant the peas and arugula and string twine for the peas to climb. I go to Cosentino's and tell John I'm competing with him now.

Angie and I talk on the phone every few weeks and get together one Sunday for a trip to the zoo. I tell her I want to see if we still recognize anything. When we meet at the entrance, we compare notes and realize that although the zoo was so close and always seemed like part of our lives, we hardly ever went there as kids. I think my frugal parents saw it as a special treat to pay to see animals, and her family of nine kids was pretty hard to corral. We both remember our eighth-grade picnic there, when I was feeding peanuts to an enormous gorilla, who reached out and took hold of my hand. Nothing happened—he got the peanut and let go. The next time we went to the zoo, the railings had been moved back, and the gorillas were out of reach.

The Great Ape house was new at that time, but it's gone now. In fact, nothing is recognizable. We could be in Tupelo or Denver for all I can tell. Plus, it's enormous. I can't get my bearings, and I finally stop trying. I think it's a good sign that the whole Kansas City area supports the zoo in a part of town they would otherwise avoid. But it would be nice to find something I remember, maybe the life-size whale whose mouth you could walk into.

Finally, we are in an ape exhibit. It is the same shape as the main zoo building, just a lot smaller. Then I see the historic marker. This is the old main zoo building, and it seems to be the size of my house. It used to house lions, tigers, and monkeys in cages along the sides, hippos in a big pool in the center, and African elephants at the far end. I can picture it, I can smell it. Now it has a single species. It seems impossible. How awful that must have been for those animals.

We have lunch and talk about how our memories deceive us. I tell her about having autism, Alzheimer's, and arthritis. I add "anthropomorphism" to keep it from sounding too heavy. She tells me what I already know, that forgetting things is part of grieving, that autism is a spectrum and if I'm on it I'm pretty close to the edge, and that talking to my dog is therapeutic as long as I don't think he's talking back. "And you know all that. So give yourself a break. And call hospice. You also know you can get grief counseling there for free."

"I know, I know. I'll call."

"Promise?"

"Promise."

We spend a little more time at the zoo and I discover why I couldn't find the lagoon all those months ago when I was driving home from the DMV. The zoo expanded and took over that part of the park. Now you get to the lagoon by boat or tram. I am thrilled that Kansas City has managed this, and it's all east of Troost and people come here by the busload anyway.

A few days later Angie calls and asks if I have called hospice yet. I hedge, say I'm going to soon. She tells me to put my cell phone down and pick up the landline and call while she waits. She has never been like this before, so I do it. I get a recording and leave a message and my phone number.

Angie says, "See? How hard was that?"

I get a call back within the hour and give the counselor the short version of my recent past and current state of mind. She asks the routine suicide-prevention questions and then asks if I'd like to join a group or have some one-on-one counseling. I say "group," mostly because I somehow feel like a fraud using their free service when I could use my company-provided employee assistance program. But I trust hospice and I don't trust the confidentiality of the employee program, even if it is run by a third party. We discuss the various types of groups and the time-and-place options and settle on one. It sounds like a good fit and it's not too far away, but it's in the evening and I'm concerned that I won't go if I'm tired and it's getting dark outside. She says that I can try it for a few weeks and we can always find a different group.

Just talking to her makes me feel optimistic enough that I decide to take on the winterization task, even though all I'm going to do is keep the cold out, not the darkness and not the bad guys.

At the first griever group meeting, I tell them about putting leftover salmon in a glass container and then putting it back on the cupboard shelf instead of in the refrigerator. A few days later I couldn't figure out what the bad smell in the kitchen was, and I was afraid it was a dead mouse, and then I finally took the container down to use it for something else and found the decaying salmon. They nod knowingly and watch to see if I'm smiling or crying before they decide it's okay to laugh. They tell a few similar stories, and I relax a little. I don't have to tell them anything about what happened to me, although I can if I want. The counselor keeps quiet unless someone gets too upset or goes on too long.

CHAPTER 48

A class reunion is scheduled for a Saturday in September and for the first time ever I can get there without flying. After the first twenty-five years, the classmate who had been organizing the events cried uncle and said someone else had to take over. That seemed fair to everyone, but a few years passed before anyone got up the courage to take it on.

By that time, no one cared about dressing up and having dinner and dancing, or dragging reluctant spouses to picnics highlighted by rain, heat, mosquitos, or all of the above. We also stopped caring about whether it was an anniversary that ended in zero or five. After a few emails asking people to vote on dates and pass the message on to anyone she missed, Annamarie scheduled the reunion for a Saturday night at a pizza restaurant. No pantyhose, no angst, no drama. Well, no pantyhose for sure.

I guess there is always some angst associated with a high school reunion, especially if you've been far away and have missed most of them and were not all that popular to begin with. You get caught up in the idea of seeing old friends and you RSVP by checking the "Yes, I'll Attend" box. Then you regress into your insecure teenage self and panic just a little and think of one or two excuses to change your RSVP to "Sorry, Not this Time." Then you remember that everyone was insecure then and that everyone has grown up now and decide you will go after all. Or maybe you don't do any of that, but I do.

This year I am determined to go because (a) I need friends in Kansas City, even if they all are in the distant suburbs now, and (b) Angie is going and I can't expect her to not mention that I've returned to the area. We decide to go together and I leave my car at her house, which is closer to the restaurant, and she drives the rest of the way. Since our classmates have scattered to the far reaches in all directions, Annamarie has chosen a central place in the general vicinity of our high school, but far enough west of Troost that no one would worry about their cars or about walking to and from them.

I get a glass of wine and spend the first hour on my feet, moving around and being as superficial as possible in catching up with my classmates. I'm surprised to find that I'm relaxed and enjoying myself. Then the pizza arrives and everyone loads up their plates and finds places at the tables. I'm waved over to a table of mostly women who are sharing pictures of kids, a few even have grandkids. I'm off the hook for that and free to admire all of their photos. I actually enjoy looking at other people's family photos.

But these are kind and thoughtful people and they aren't going to force their kids on others forever. The question comes soon enough: "Hey, I just heard that you moved back to Kansas City." It's not technically a question, but we all know it is.

"Yes, I'm pretty excited to be back," I tell them, and they smile encouragingly. Then I try to steer away from the inevitable by saying, "I'm lucky to have a job where I can telecommute. I can really live anywhere with an internet connection." I know this won't work; no one really wants to hear about anyone else's job at this stage in our careers. But I've tried.

"You're so lucky. I wish I could do that," says one of the many

Marys in my graduating class. Then they home in on what is more interesting: What made you come back? Is your brother still in Kansas City? Where are you staying?

It's an interesting topic for them, a level or two up from small talk. These women were not my closest friends and probably won't analyze anything I tell them too closely. If I were to tell them I was looking in the Northland, the ones who live there would recommend neighborhoods or real estate agents. If I say "the Plaza area," they will say how cool it would be to live there, even if it's not really where they would live themselves. So I say "fairly close to Hogan, actually." Hogan is hard up against Troost, and from there, a few blocks west quickly gets into a very acceptable ZIP code.

That is enough for them, they really aren't trying to pin me down, and I'm able to reach back to the question about my brother, whom they were at least aware of, and we talk about the lake and who now has a place there.

Someone gives a little speech thanking Annamarie and recalling the loss of several classmates in the last year or two. We get more wine or pizza, shuffle to new tables. A few with very long drives home take their leave. I end up at a table with Angie and our closest grade-school friends. These are the kids in the social action club, the kids with whom we stood at the windows and watched the march on city hall when we were fourteen years old. We talk about that day in April 1968 and about the Sisters of Charity and their efforts to teach us social justice along with math and history and how to write cogent essays. "They made us who we are now, don't you think?" another of the Marys says.

So when someone in this group asks me where I live now, I know it's okay to tell them exactly where. They are surprised, and they don't pretend they are not. They read the papers, they know where the high-crime areas are, and they moved away long ago, to areas where they felt safe raising kids. They also know that houses are very small and inexpensive in my neighborhood, and they hadn't expected me to be in financial straits, given my class rank and college degree.

It would be rude for them to come right out and say, "Is that all you could afford?" or "Isn't it pretty dangerous there?" but it would be more rude to switch the topic to the weather, so they are kind of stuck.

Angie comes to the rescue with, "It was so cool being in that house again. I was there so much as a kid. I just couldn't get over it. I felt like I could just walk out the door and go to my old house again too."

No one has forgotten that Angie's house is gone forever.

"Yes, it's crazy," I say, using Angie's opening. "It's exactly the same but completely different."

Then I give them the short version: "We spent a lot of our savings on my husband's care before he died, and then there was a freak electrical system thing and the house burned down."

They nod and murmur their condolences in a way that means they care and will get back to that later but don't need to interrupt the current discussion.

"So at that point I had a little cash and no recent credit history. I was also an emotional wreck, as you can imagine." I make it okay to laugh at little about that.

"And somehow living in the old house just felt like something I could manage to do at that point. I really couldn't manage the decision-making it would have taken to choose a place and start cold."

That makes sense to them and they try to imagine what would have felt like safe choices if my story had been theirs.

"I might not stay there," I say, to make sure they don't have to feel sorry for me. "I wasn't thinking that far ahead when I did it." I sense their relief.

"But the longer I'm there, the better it feels." And I know that what I've said is true, mostly.

They ask a lot of questions after that, which is better than I hoped for. I expected silence, or half-hearted not-quite-encouragement, or at the worst, questions along the lines of, "Wasn't there a murder around there a few weeks ago?" and "Has your car been broken into?" and "Did you get an alarm?"

But they are truly interested and ask about getting to know the neighbors and is it hard to find contractors. I give them only slightly varnished answers, for example not mentioning that I have to shower in the basement. They didn't ask.

At this point I know I can redirect, so I tell them about going to St. Louis Church, how it has changed and how it hasn't, and then the conversation moves on. This group gets together on their own a few times a year, and they invite me to join them, which makes me happy. Someday, maybe, I'll invite them to meet at my house, but not just yet.

As the others start talking about going home, the Mary sitting next to me extends her sympathy. "I can't imagine what you went through last year, I can't even pretend to. I'm so sorry." And then she says what she really wanted to say, which is, "I thought you were crazy when you said you moved back to your old house, but now I think I get it. When I'm heartbroken about something, I picture myself in the kitchen of the house I grew up in."

Annamarie leans over the table. "Maybe you'll make a difference there, just being there, even if all you do if fill up one empty house and keep the roof on and the drug deals out. I think the people at that end of the whole East of Troost thing really try hard and deserve better than they are getting."

"Sometimes I think that, and then I think that's just do-gooder attitude. I don't have any idea if I'm good for the neighborhood."

"Those neighbors you talked about, the ones you've gotten

to know—they are good for the neighborhood, right?" another Mary says.

"Of course they are."

"And they like you, right?"

"They seem to."

"Then you are good for the neighborhood, so if you like living there, just stop worrying about it."

"You're right," I say. "I think Angie said something like that."

"Well, she has to because she's always been your best friend. But you know me—I'll just blurt it out."

"Yeah," another says. "We would be snarky and roll our eyes if we really thought you were off the deep end."

"And we could do an intervention, drag you out of there."

"But we're old now. Who needs the drama?"

By now we're all laughing, so I take a chance.

"Okay, you all can prove it by coming to visit me at my house."

They say that they will and we say end-of-the-party things and we all go home.

CHAPTER 49

I run into Henry and Matt at church one Sunday and meet Henry's wife and Matt's brother. Henry says that I'm not buying as much hardware and he might have to revoke my contractor's discount. I tell him I'll be in to talk about getting ready for winter, and he says that he's got a lot of excellent stuff in stock.

This is enough of a boost to get me to make a list, as in open a Word document and type "Winter Prep" on the first line. I add "snow shovel" even though I know that's not what this is about. "Shovel" makes me think of cold hands, so I add "gloves," and then make a separate "Winter Clothes" list and move "gloves" to that. My hands are busy, but I'm avoiding the real issue.

I type "Storm Windows." I know I can't buy storm windows, and that would be silly anyway. I actually need new windows. But that is even farther from possible. I use strikeout instead of delete because it uses up another second or two.

I type "Caulking?" I hate caulking, mostly because if you don't do a huge amount of preparing and cleaning before you start, it all falls out in two weeks. I go outside and look at a few windows and find that I could stand to do some caulking, but maybe not all the way around all twelve windows. I go back inside and remove the question mark.

Plastic film? I remember my dad taking down the screens

and covering each one with plastic, tacking it tightly with cardboard strips. I so don't want to do this. Maybe there is something better now? I Google "weather proofing windows for winter" and get a million results, all kinds of things I can buy. I don't click on anything because I don't want it to pop up relentlessly for the next six months. I close my laptop, get the leash, and Boris and I walk to Henry's.

"Henry, I'm at your mercy. What do I do about my windows for winter?" He absolves me of having to follow in my father's footsteps, and we discuss various problems and various solutions. I'm encouraged that I have no huge leaks. He tells me what to look for and sends me home to investigate and take pictures, then bring them back. He tells me to wait for the Columbus Day sale to buy the snow shovel.

"Snow on Halloween, maybe, but not enough to shovel," he says. "You don't need it before the sale. If you do, I'll give it to you for free."

In the end, I do have to do some caulking, but not all that much. I check Josie's windows on the weather side and do a little for her too. Hers are easier, being smaller and better cared for.

CHAPTER 50

Angie calls one day in early November, to invite me to Thanksgiving and at the same time let me off the hook for having Thanksgiving with her or anyone else. Thanksgiving with her clan means dozens of people, and she knows that's not the right place for me, but she wants me to know I'm welcome. I would love to get together with her siblings; I saw them all so much on Montgall that I remember many of their middle names and even some of their birthdays. But that can wait until a day less fraught than Thanksgiving.

She asks me how I'm doing, and I tell her that the griever group is helping and I'm not going to fret about how I'm feeling until after the new year. She's happy to hear that, and then surprises me with a suggestion.

"You know, it wouldn't hurt you to go to confession. I don't mean that any of this is sinful, but reconciliation is more about change than erasing some mark on your soul like they taught us in second grade. You know that."

I do know that. "You're right. I've never forgiven my husband for losing so much of our investment, even though I know it was the disease, not him. I haven't even forgiven him for dying and leaving me having to deal with everything by myself. Including clogged drains." She laughs at that. "And I'm greedy. I want what I used to have, even though I also don't want it and even though I'm surrounded by people who never had a 2,500-square-foot house, never got to go to Europe, never bought a new car with cash." I pause. "And I've been taking and taking and never giving back. I have never even asked you about your job."

I'm ready to cry, but she just says, "See? Do it."

This time I don't hedge and wait until she prods me again. Reconciliation is available before both weekend masses, so I finally go early instead of slipping in just as Mass is beginning.

The priest doesn't try to tell me that it's okay, it's understandable, that I shouldn't be so hard on myself. And thank goodness, or thank God, that he doesn't. He does ask if I'm getting grief counseling, and I tell him I have just started, and he tells me that my penance is to keep going. Damn, he's good.

After that, I think it's time I officially joined the parish. My fellow grievers have reminded me that volunteer work, no matter how trivial or infrequent, is a good antidote to feeling depressed. Exercise, social interaction, and helping others. I've got the first one down and need to work on the second and third. I fill out the form in the Sunday bulletin and leave it with the usher. He tells me there will be coffee and donuts today, and I think that will be an easy way to do a little trivial volunteer work.

"Do you think I could help with that?" I ask.

I can see him start to decline, to treat me like a guest, but he looks at the form I've given him and he says, "I'm sure help would be appreciated."

So I meet quite a few people whose names I forget as they say them. I give a few people the shortest version of my story: "Born and raised in this parish, just moved back." I get a lot of "Well, then, it's great to have you back" and some attempts to find common ground, but I've been gone a long time and we can't come up with names of any long-time parishioners whose names I remember. So I ask them about things going on in the parish now, and I leave after twenty minutes or so. Not a bad start.

CHAPTER 51

My mobile contract comes up for renewal and I decide to look into changing plans. I start with the closest provider for the simple reason that it's on Prospect and I can walk there. I get there just after they open on Saturday morning. Saturday morning must be a busy time because there are several employees, although so far I'm the only customer. One young staffer spins around in his chair, pushes off from the desk, and zooms over to greet me, all smiles and welcome. I explain that I want to compare their plan to mine.

We go back to his desk and are soon deep in plan features, when suddenly the chatter in the shop stills. We both look up. There is a police vehicle outside, lights flashing. No, two police vehicles. The big black imposing kind.

"What's going on?" I see that everyone has moved back a bit, away from the door. No one says anything.

The cops are out of the vehicles now, in helmets and vests, weapons visible.

The phone rings. No one moves. Customer service has dropped off the priority list.

The cop out in front holds up his cell phone, points to the storefront. Someone's brain is working well enough to read that as "Answer the phone," and he does.

"Phone store," he says into the phone, not in a customer-service voice. "Yes, sir. No. No. Everything is fine, sir."

He moves the phone slightly away from his ear, looks around. "Anyone press the silent alarm? He says that there was a silent alarm." Heads shake, just barely.

"No, sir. No one pressed the alarm."

I'm beyond puzzled, but caught up in the tension, so I'm as silent as the others.

"He says that the alarm was pushed and that the manager needs to step outside with his hands up."

My mind is racing. Is the manager a suspect in some crime? Did someone press the alarm to alert the police that a known criminal is in the store?

The manager has come out of the back room. He says, "I'm not going out there. They'll shoot me."

Okay, so they do want him for something. I wonder if he has a gun.

"No, man. You can't go out there. Is everyone sure they didn't hit the button?"

The clerk next to me startles. "It could have been me, when I shot my chair over here."

"Sir? We think we figured it out. One of us bumped into the button without realizing it." He listens for quite a while. "Yes, sir."

"They still want you to go out there." He's looking at the manager again.

The manager is adamant. "No way. I go out there, I'm dead."

I think I've figured it out now, and I've got a plan. "I'll go with you. They won't shoot you with a customer along."

They all look at me like I am a foreign object. I'm not a customer at the moment. I'm a liability. I just don't get it yet.

"Ma'am," he's respectful but also a little angry, as if I am a particularly stupid and annoying teenager. "If you go out with me they'll shoot me for sure. They'll think you're a hostage."

I stare at him. Then I realize that I am the only white person in the room, and the only female, and the only person over thirty-five. What's rational in my world is not rational in their world. All I can say is "Oh."

The manager takes the phone and repeats the story that this was a false alarm. He listens for a minute or so, and then says to the group, "He still says I have to go out there. I can't go out there."

"Tell him there is a customer, and ask him if I can leave. I'll explain what happened."

Again they look at me like I am a foreign object. They picture the police storming the building before they hear me out. "They'll shoot us all," he whispers. He looks so young, so vulnerable in his polo shirt and khakis, lips clenched.

But no one can come up with any other solution, so he relays the message.

After a lot more back and forth, the manager hands me the phone and the cop asks me if I'm okay, if there is a robbery in progress. I tell him that I was talking to one of the staff about a new plan and nothing else was going on and then they arrived. He tells me to give the phone back to the manager, who says "yes" and "no" a few more times and then tells me I can go out the front door. "She has to open the door herself," he adds. No one seems inclined to rush forward to open it for me anyway. There is no relief in their voices. I was a liability inside and I'll be a liability outside.

I walk to the door with my hands up, nudge it open, and walk out, still with my hands in the air. I feel like a criminal. A cop materializes, perp-walks me to a vehicle, and puts me inside. I don't know if it's for protection or if I'm being arrested. I think I might throw up.

They make me go over the entire incident, starting with why I am there. "To see about a new cell phone plan."

"Where is your car?"

"At home. I walked—it's only a couple of blocks," I say. *Why didn't I just answer the question? He probably doesn't believe I walked or that I live near here?*

He wants my driver's license, the license plate number of the car that isn't there, and my name, address, and phone number. They dial the phone and it rings in my pocket. I wonder if they are going to take me to the station.

They leave me locked in the back of the giant black SUV and confer in the parking lot. After a few minutes, I see the employees exit the store one by one. They are frisked and each one gets out his wallet.

Finally, they let me out with a curt "Thank you, ma'am. That's all." The cops leave and the rest of us are left standing in the parking lot, me out near the street and all of them in a bunch near the door.

The others recover before I do, and they go back inside. I am freaked out but I can't make myself just walk away. I walk over and open the door cautiously. They all look up. The looks are bland now, with a tinge of hostility. Why am I there?

I want to say, "That sucked," but that is too gross an understatement. I want to say, "I'm sorry," but I would be apologizing on behalf of whom? And for what? I would really like to say, "Whew, glad that's over. Shall we get back to it?" but this situation can't be lightened by anything I say or do.

Finally I croak, "Should I come back later?"

I brace for "Just get out," because that is what I would probably say in that situation.

But they look at each other. One clears his throat. Another plops down in his chair.

"Okay."

I sit down and the guy who was helping me an eternity ago says, "I think this is the one you wanted," pointing.

The manager goes back to the other room and we can hear him on the phone. A phone rings and someone answers it. I sign papers, ask a few questions. I can't make small talk. There is no space in the room for chatter.

I hand over a check and pick up my signed contract. He seems to rally. "Thanks for coming in."

"You're welcome," I say, and I stick out my hand. We shake and I say, "That sucked. I'm sorry."

I can't get to sleep that night, going over and over the whole incident, telling and retelling the story in my head. I try writing it down, thinking maybe that will get it out of my head. But I can't write down the feeling, and I give up. I finally make myself say the thing that bothers me most, or second most after the sheer terror of facing the police weapons. When the incident began to unfold, I was alone. Maybe no one meant me any harm and maybe no one saw me as a threat, and that separated me from the cops and the staff as much as did my skin color. But it's more than that. What is bugging me is this: When I moved here, I did it mostly for financial and emotional reasons, and I willingly admit that to one and all. But there was also the unspoken idea that I could "be the change" and have a positive impact here. Today's incident makes me face the naivety and presumptuousness of that whole idea.

CHAPTER 52

One afternoon, I see my concrete guy, Sean, working next door at the Saunders house and go out to say "hello." He comes over to the fence and sees my ersatz raised bed made of fireplace screens.

"Interesting look," he says, with raised eyebrows.

I shrug. "I was going for rustic but I think I hit squalid instead."

"That you did," he agrees. "Lose the galvanized pipe and set up some little brick posts. Might as well stick with the fireplace theme."

I think he's right and make a mental note to start scavenging bricks.

"What's up over there?" I raise my eyebrows toward the Saunders house. "That looks like quite the patio you've got staked out."

"Oh, that." He smiles proudly, chin raised. "I told them I would lay out the patio so that it can be used as the foundation for an addition later. I put it in the permit as an addition. They think maybe by next spring they can put up the walls. It's your fault—they saw all that stuff for cheap at ReStore. They don't care if the windows all match. I told them they can make it look okay just by where they put the windows. And there's insulation and all kinds of stuff they can use."

This is enough to lift my spirits for several days, not having to worry about them moving away. And it gives me an idea about my own house.

We've had some November frost and I'm back to thinking about winter projects. I realize that my California car has never needed antifreeze or even winter-grade windshield washer fluid. I start to read up and instead just drive to Jiffy Lube on 75th. I don't realize until I'm on my way that it's on west 75th, not east 75th, but it's raining and I go anyway, so I can check off oil change and antifreeze and windshield washer fluid. I go on to Cosentino's while I'm out so I can tell John that I'm eating my own arugula now, thank you very much. No peas yet, and I'm not sure they are going to win the race against the first hard freeze, but I'll be ready to replant in March.

Then I continue west to the ReStore on the Kansas side, just for a change and because Sean's comment about insulation has me thinking. I don't see why I can't cut lengths of rolled insulation batting, drag them up through the scuttle hole, and add four inches to the ceiling insulation. If they have some, I'm going to get a little and try it. And maybe pick up a few bricks.

This ReStore doesn't have a FReStore, so I don't have to agonize over whether the junk there is useful to me or not. I locate the insulation, which is mostly bags of loose fill. I shudder at the thought of doing anything with that and pick up a few ends of rolls of the batting style. I change my mind about bricks because I know I won't do anything with them for months.

When I get home I roll out the insulation on the basement floor. I measure the room and haul the first strip up into the closet. Right away I see why this is going to be harder than I thought. I'll have to crawl around on the ceiling joints without putting a foot through the ceiling itself. Someone has put plywood on top of the joints near the opening, but that's all. I think about buying more plywood, but realize that the pieces have to be small enough to fit through the opening, so there would have to be dozens of them. I get one piece of insulation in place and cut the second, which uses up most of what I brought home. By then I don't even care. I have pink fuzz in my mouth and my hair. I'm itchy. This is not a job I'm cut out for. If I get any more insulation, I'll have to first see if Matt wants the job of installing it.

The other winter project I can't figure out is the shower. To get one in the bathroom without a gut remodel will mean putting up a shower curtain that goes all the way around the shower, so that the window doesn't get wet every day and end up moldy and peeling. It will be crappy and it will leak and there will be mildew and paint will peel and I will be depressed. I decide that the shower in the chilly basement will have to do and I can stop thinking about it.

I've mentally prepared for thirty days of sunless gloom in November, so one Friday when the sun is out I put on my warmest clothes, put my rain jacket in a backpack just in case, and head out with Boris, a water bottle, and a sandwich. I want to see what's west of Troost and I want to see it on foot.

I live about fifteen blocks from Troost, and from there to State Line Road is about the same distance. After that you're in Kansas, which should be obvious. But it's not. People who have never been here are pretty solidly convinced that there is a river between Kansas and Missouri. That's true in the northland, because the Missouri River flows south between Kansas and Missouri until it gets to downtown Kansas City, at which point it changes its mind and makes a sharp turn east and heads across Missouri to St. Louis. Downtown Kansas City and most city landmarks are south of the river after the turn. No river to separate us from Kansas. At some point in every teenager's high school career, he or she has the brilliant idea of walking down the middle of State Line Road, one foot in Kansas and the other in Missouri. Or at least to walk straight across the street and make a wisecrack about being in two states of mind when crossing the center line. State Line is a pretty ordinary street, two lanes in each direction. Walking across it is no big deal. The big deal is, or was, that there were a lot of bars on each side of State Line because the two states have, or used to have, very different liquor laws. If you were age eighteen to twenty-one, you could buy 3.2 beer (meaning 3.2 percent alcohol instead of the standard 5 percent) on the Kansas side. If you were a Kansan age twenty-one or older and wanted to go to a bar that wasn't a "private club," you crossed to the Missouri side.

I don't care about beer or bars, though, or even about Kansas. I just want to see if the effects of the "Troost Wall" are obvious. My friends and I occasionally walked to Kansas just for someplace to go, so I know it's an easy walk. I probably did it barefoot then, and I have comfortable hiking shoes now.

I take Gregory the first part of the way, to get across the expressway and around Forest Hill Cemetery. It's not all easy going, since the sidewalks disappear shortly after crossing Prospect. When I cross Troost, it's immediately obvious that west of Troost is a different world. The sidewalks are back. The houses are bigger and mostly two-story, although they are too new to be in the classic shirtwaist style. Trucks are banned. There are street trees. People are out walking their dogs. People ride by on bicycles. It's a lovely neighborhood and much as I remember it. No wonder we used to come over here. No wonder our mothers didn't worry about us when we did.

I dogleg north a couple of blocks to skirt Holmes Park, an important high school hangout back in the day. The neighborhood gets even nicer as I go west, and everyone I happen to see is white. I stop at Ward Parkway, a block short of State Line, and turn north because I want to see the fountain at Ward Parkway and Meyer. Where the two boulevards come together, Kansas City has built one of its few rotaries, or traffic circles as we used to call this one. On our teenage jaunts, the fountain was as good a destination as any, and we usually spent some time wading in it before meandering home. It's a good destination for today, but too cold for wading, so I eat my sandwich and turn back east on Meyer Boulevard. One block east of Troost, the sidewalk ends at my old high school and I turn south and follow my old route home. Almost everyone I see is Black. The wall still holds.

Of course, both sides of the Troost Wall were white to the south of 63rd Street when I was born in the 1950s. I vaguely knew it existed north of 63rd Street in the 1960s, but it didn't have a name then, because it was still a sort of open secret among bankers, real estate brokers, and probably politicians. It became obvious to me as I grew old enough to notice. Laws changed, but you can't walk across Troost and not see that it's still a real thing. It's a bigger deal than State Line Road.

Kansas City is by no means the only city that has a color wall. When I moved to Saint Louis for college, I discovered the racial divide there almost immediately, and I lived even closer to it there. In San Francisco, the wall is the bay and their "east of Troost" is the city of Oakland. Even in Silicon Valley, there is a wall, although there are very few Black people to wall out.

I enjoy the walk in spite of the implications, because I discovered nothing I didn't already know, and it was a lovely day. I can't afford to live on the other side of Troost anyway. The only thing that suddenly spins my head around is the idea that I'm perfectly free to live wherever I can afford to buy a house, Troost be damned. I'm not sure that's true for everyone. It occurs to me that I'm lucky. My neighbors didn't panic when a white person moved in.

A few days later when I break for lunch, I go out to check for mail and see a For Sale sign in front of the two-story house on the other side of the street. I don't know the owners well, but I suddenly don't want them to move.

The next Tuesday, I make sure I'm taking my trash out when Josie and Dave are dragging their bags to the curb.

"See the sign?" Josie asks, knowing we have all seen it.

"I did. Do you know why they are moving?" The universal question when a sign goes up.

"He got a job at the airport. They're moving up around Platte City." Josie has the story.

We're happy for them, but worried that the buyer will be a property manager who will not take care of the house and yard.

"I guess we'll just have to wait and see."

I go inside and ponder. On this block, people used to worry that a new owner might be Black. In California, there was a period when we worried that a new owner would be a Chinese investor who would just hold on to the property, leaving it vacant; other times we worried that a new owner would tear the house down and we would endure two or three years of construction noise and dust. Now, here, we worry that it will be a faceless rental agency.

CHAPTER 53

In mid-November, Cathy again asks me if I would be willing to go back to forty hours. I agree because I'm not working frantically on the house now, and I'm hardly working in the yard at all. All of the administrative chores of death and insurance and taxes and moving are behind me. I'm still going to my griever group meetings. I know Cathy has picked up most of the slack of my absence, so I feel like I owe her. And I'm hoping that being more immersed in work will help get me through the dark months ahead. Besides, this means I'll get full pay for the five holidays coming up shortly. So I agree.

I call a distant cousin in the suburbs and break the news that I'm living in Kansas City. I tell him exactly where I live and ask if he and his wife would like to come for Thanksgiving. I love these cousins dearly, and they love me, I think, but there is no way they will come to my house. Instead, they kindly invite me to theirs. I expected this and I have to admit I was counting on it. My house is looking better and better inside, but it's not quite ready for people who aren't quite ready for it.

They have already invited relatives of my cousin's wife, so they aren't related to me, which is perfect. They are sort of family, and family means, according to my cousin Paul, that we have to love each other—it's required. But the once- or twice-removed status of the relationship means they don't have to know about all my recent tribulations and we can discuss ordinary things like the food and the weather and the Chiefs, and the day passes pleasantly enough. I can go home and be sad in the evening, with Boris for company, and then I still have a three-day weekend to do and be and feel any way I like. I let myself have a minor breakdown, a long crying jag that scares me a little. When that's over I feel a little better. One holiday down.

On the subject of the Chiefs, it's a tricky thing living in Kansas City if you are unable to make yourself care at least a little about football and/or baseball. For me, it's like drinking beer. It's an important social convention, but I just can't stand the taste no matter how hard I try. So, as with beer, if it's forced on me I take it, and then I leave it behind a potted plant. I probably should have developed this approach in high school. I might have been a little more popular, or at least a little more visible.

My knowledge of Chiefs football is limited but mighty. I did pay attention in 1967, when they played in the very first Super Bowl (losing to the Packers), and again in 1970, when they beat the Vikings in Super Bowl IV. I know that for both games Hank Stram was the coach, Len Dawson was the quarterback, and Jan Stenerud was the placekicker. I even know that the Vikings were expected to beat the Chiefs by quite a bit. In 1972, I went off to college and worried about the Vietnam War and apartheid and whether tie-dye was still the thing and I forgot all about the Chiefs. From 1970 until now, that knowledge was enough, and was occasionally impressive when someone needed one of those bits of data for a crossword puzzle. Now that I'm back in KC, though, my lack of more recent factoids may be a problem. My brother, however, has informed me that the Chiefs have not won or even played in a Super Bowl since I left town, and I'm hoping that I can use this as a distraction to get me through football-themed discussions for at least this first season.

During this year's baseball season, I didn't talk to enough people for it to be an issue. By the time spring training comes around again, I may have to read up or at least get a royal blue t-shirt. No yard signs, though. All I've got for baseball is that the last professional baseball game I went to was the Kansas City As, in Municipal Stadium, and that will just draw blank stares. The truth is that it's the only professional sports game of any type I've ever attended, and I was maybe eight years old. No one needs to know any of that.

CHAPTER 54

The first week of December brings an early cold snap that catches me off guard in spite of all my dithering about winterization. I take Boris for a walk—I'm wearing my fleece sweater and my rain jacket, and I am cold before I get the door locked behind me. I think I'll warm up once we get moving, but after one full block I turn around. I am cold from top to bottom. Boris is confused about going back. He's well dressed for winter.

I cruise the Eddie Bauer website for a coat, gloves, wool socks. My old friend Indecision is along for the ride and I almost break down in tears. Over outerwear. This won't do. A walk will clear my head. I can't go for a walk, it's too cold. I close my eyes and mentally walk to the coat closet and bury my face in the coats and smell my father's coat, my mother's coat. I cry after all. And then I go back to my laptop and choose a coat and gloves and socks, plus a robe and house slippers. At least I get free shipping. I don't get a stocking cap, though; Officer Carl's visual is still vivid.

Christmas is imminent and I put it out of my mind as much as possible, mostly by spending too much time at my desk working. I don't shop and I don't send Christmas cards. My cousins in Joplin text me asking when I'll arrive for Christmas and how long I can stay. They take it as fact that I'll be there, and it's easier to go along than to come up with an excuse and argue about it. My brother will be there for Christmas dinner, so no excuse will work anyway.

I go to ReStore for a bedroom light fixture so I can swap it for the old lantern fixture, which I'll give to my brother for Christmas. There is nothing interesting about any of the ones I see, but I don't care enough to keep looking and choose the least glittery one. I won't bother calling Jimmy to change the fixture. How hard can it be? When I get home, I take the ladder and my tool box into the bedroom and heave the heavy sigh of one facing a great injustice: the bed is in the way and the room is too small to move it aside. I roll my eyes, stand on the bed, and get to work. I find a paper grocery bag for the old one and wonder if I'll get around to wrapping it. I drop screws and don't bother putting up the new one. I tape the wires and tape the switch in the off position.

Christmas is low-key and relaxing. I've spent many Christmases with these cousins, so there is no need for pretending I'm better or worse than I am. We stopped giving each other gifts years ago, so that pressure is gone. We watch a few movies and look at old family photo albums. They have been going through some family things and have saved some for me in case I want them. I take a set of wine glasses and several quilts. We argue a little about the quilts because we all treasure them but none of us really wants them. We all want the others to keep them, though. So everyone is happy when I take a few and they assure me that I don't have to use them or even keep them.

When I get back home after Christmas in Joplin, the days are dark and damp and rainy. My first day back, I log into work but I'm feeling morose and have a hard time focusing. That night I tell myself I have a headache, which is almost true, and skip a griever group meeting for the first time. Instead, I log back into work and see an email from the president of the company. She is sending me to Australia as part of an acquisition team. She asks me to call her the next day. Moroseness morphs into something with an edge of anger. I thought that stepping out of my manager job eighteen months ago saved me from this sort of thing. I don't sleep well, lining up all the reasons I can't go.

The next day, I call her with the intention of getting out of this trip, which terrifies me for no good reason except that I hate long flights. I ponder my excuses while I wait for her to take the call. When she gets on, she starts talking about the acquisition, then notices that I'm quiet and says, "Are you not excited about this?" I prevaricate. She is kind but says that she knows I've been through a tough time but—and I wince, expecting "it's time for you to move on" and instead get "I really need you to do this. Would you be willing to go if it's only for two weeks instead of four?"

I realize that I don't have a choice. This is my job and I have to do it. So I tell her I'm just figuring out what I'll need to do to get ready and that I'll be happy to go. Then I staunch the flow of energy I've been spending on excuses and redirect it to figuring out what I'll wear. Two weeks of business clothes? Right now, I have two days of business-ish clothes, and that's if I wear the same pair of black pants every day, with different sweaters. It's summer in Sydney.

I've got only eleven days before I leave, so I shop online for classic mix-and-match sort of things. I find what I need in the tall sizes at J.Jill's website, but I'm not sure about sizes and fabrics and I don't have time to order a lot of things and worry about returning them. So the next day, I beg off my morning conference call and drive to the Kansas side.

As expected, they don't have tall sizes in the store, but I try on regular sizes and check color and fabric combinations. The clerk isn't busy and takes plenty of time with me, placing the order in tall sizes to be shipped to my house. She tells me that I can get 15 percent off the order if I open a charge account at the same time. I usually turn down these offers, but this one seems like a good idea. I don't have to use it ever again. So I agree to it and she enters my information and processes the order.

"Oh," she says about two seconds later. "Must be something wrong, it won't go through. Do you have a card we can put it on? I'll give you the discount anyway."

I am mortified because I know perfectly well that "won't go through" means I was rejected for the credit card. I give her my usual Mastercard and she calmly gives me the receipt, telling me I should have my clothes in about three days.

"Don't worry. It's probably just a glitch. It happens a lot—you can try again when you get home."

I do worry. I don't want the card. I want to know what's wrong that I can't get a J.Jill card. I own a house free and clear, after all, and I never miss paying a bill because they all are on autopay. Is it because of my address? Is there some deep secret box checked because my house burned down? Because I took personal leave last year? I want to yell at someone, but there's only Boris. He listens attentively but apparently hears a firetruck in the distance because he puts his nose in the air and lets out a long mournful howl, singing the song of his people. He then shakes himself, gets a drink, flops himself down, and falls asleep.

I tell him he's a poor listener and log in to check my credit, make sure I have not been a victim of identity theft. I find I've been denied because I have too few credit cards and no debt. I ponder this and remind myself that I am supremely lucky to have been able to buy a house for cash.

Clothes and credit settled, I make a new to-do list, most of which has to do with Boris. I think about having Matt house sit.

I trust him, but maybe I don't want to tempt a twenty-year-old who's been living at home. Besides, I really don't want anyone staying here when I'm away. I look into kennels, which are very expensive for a two-week stay, especially if it turns into four weeks. I can't put kennel fees on my expense report. Finally I ask Josie if she has any ideas, and she does. She wants to keep him at her house, for free. I say "no way" and that I'm paying her at least half the going rate, and she tells me that I will not, and we go back and forth until she diverts my attention.

"Why don't you hire Matt to check on the house and he can take Boris for runs?" This is a great idea, plus it ends the previous discussion. I tell her I'll give her a key and she and Matt can go in at least once a week to make sure the heat is on and the plumbing isn't leaking. And that no burglars have stopped by, but neither of us mentions that out loud.

CHAPTER 55

The Saturday before I leave for Australia, the forecast is for ice and snow overnight. I'm still a little nervous about driving on ice after so many years in California, even with my new snow tires, so I go to Mass on Saturday evening, feeling like a nervous old biddy. It's snowing by the time I get home, but I have no trouble on my hill or backing into the driveway. I've got my new snow shovel and broom ready, hanging in the basement stairwell, and I've got rock salt as backup.

By Sunday morning we have about five inches and it's still snowing lightly. It doesn't seem icy, so I leash up Boris and go out for a walk. We take our time, not because it's slippery, but because Boris is intrigued by the snow and I'm in no hurry. It's very very quiet out. I've forgotten how snow absorbs so much sound.

We meander around, avoiding the steepest hills just in case. In the 7000 block of Agnes, there are three churches. Two are on the corner at Gregory, one in a building that I remember being some sort of store and one across the street in what I think must be a new building. The third church is in what might once have been a house. Were these churches in the 1970s? I can't remember. I spin around, trying to get my bearings. I had schoolmates on this street, but can't locate their house. I haven't been down this street much since I moved back, and many houses are missing, and it's different in the snow. New Life Church, Temple of Faith Baptist, New Day Tabernacle Ministries. There are cars at two of them. One of the cars looks a lot like Josie's. I stand around while Boris sniffs, hoping to hear a little music and wishing I lived so close to my church. I try to imagine myself joining one of these, but I can't. I don't know why, or maybe I do know and I don't want to admit it.

The night before I leave, the Saunderses knock on the door.

"We just wanted to let you know that we've bought the house for sale across the street. We're so excited."

I'm excited for them, and I say so, and then I ask the obvious: "Have you sold this house?"

"No, but we think we can manage. We want to wait until spring to put it on the market, so we're looking for a renter until then."

"Oh, that makes sense," I say, but immediately I'm worried and then ashamed of myself.

"We thought we could just stay and add on next summer. But you know, we only have four rooms and you can't believe how much space the baby things take up. He's due in four weeks and we thought we should go ahead and do this."

They are nervous about the finances, so I make encouraging conversation and decide to worry about new neighbors later. Right now I have to lie awake all night worrying about lying awake all night the next night on the flight to Australia.

Because I'm allowed to fly business class, the trip to Australia is bearable. I fly to LAX, then walk to the International terminal and check in for the overseas leg. The flight is delayed thirty minutes and then another thirty minutes, and the TVs in the business lounge are full of a bombing in Europe. We assume we are delayed because our luggage is getting extra screening. I eat too much at the business-class lounge. Finally, we board, and the flight attendants tuck everyone into their pods and turn out the lights.

I don't sleep well on planes. Partly, it's that sensory sensitivity—the engine noise, people moving around and brushing against me, that loud Texan telling his life story three rows back. But mostly, it's because my lizard brain thinks the plane will crash if I'm not paying attention. I have to stay awake to keep the plane in the air. My human brain begs my lizard brain to take a break, but the lizard has had its way in a lot of things over the past year and won't yield any ground. So I manage to doze occasionally, but mostly I binge watch "The Middle," because it's almost amusing and it requires very little brainpower to follow the plot.

When we land, I stumble through baggage claim and customs and make my way to the cab stand, reminding myself to watch for traffic to the right. It's too early to check into my hotel, so I leave my luggage at the desk and go outside for a walk. It's a warm summer day in the southern hemisphere. I have a map from the hotel lobby and stroll down a street with coffee shops and Ugg stores. The cathedral is open and I sit for a few minutes, but I've been sitting for hours and hours so I stroll on, visit a museum. When the sun is low, I head back toward the hotel. I've lost my map but have a general idea where I'm going, so I don't panic. I make sure I have my wallet and passport, only to find that my passport is missing. Now I panic. The four-week stay may now be a foregone conclusion. I retrace my steps and find my lost map on the park bench where I had taken a break, but no passport. More panic. I get back to the hotel as fast as I can. The staff there is rather panicky themselves, wondering why I had left my passport at the desk. I decide I can't be trusted to go out to dinner alone, so I order room service and check in with Josie via

FaceTime. She's tickled about FaceTiming even though she has to go to my house and connect to Wi-Fi to make it work. All is well at home, and I'm asleep before it's even dark.

The first few days of meetings are grueling, with a lot of posturing and feinting and jostling for power between the acquired firm and the acquirer, which in this case is the firm I work for. We are the conquering heroes, but that's not what they said during the acquisition negotiations, so we have to pretend that it's "really more of a merger" and "we want to hear all your ideas." It's not and we don't, but we have to spend a day or so acting as if.

Worse, we all go out to dinner together those first few nights, and these Aussies are drinkers. We will eat and drink until ten or eleven at the restaurant and then go on to a bar. I've been through so many of these meetings that I know the drill and have developed my own survival strategy. First, I spend the hour or so between meeting and dinner in my hotel room with earplugs in and eyes closed, rather than going out for a pre-dinner drink with the team. I don't tell them I'm doing it. I just show up at the restaurant, in jeans and sans backpack. Next, at the end of dinner, when the rowdiest of the drinkers are choosing a bar for the next phase, I'm all in favor. In the confusion of cabs and sidewalk back-slapping, I disappear. No one ever notices that I have skipped the bar scene, probably because they were so drunk they don't remember whether I was there or not. By the next morning they are sober enough to know better than to mention it and have their memory lapse made public.

This trip, I decide to push my game a little. During dinner the second night, I implement my new move. When the waiter takes dessert orders, I demure. "I'll just finish my drink," I say. In the five minutes it takes to dish up desserts for everyone, there is a lot of movement around the table, calls for ouzo, the first suggestions for the post-dinner bar. I murmur "ladies room" and disappear, leaving my chair pushed back and turned a little. I carry one of those tiny purses to dinner, and of course it's summer in Australia, so I don't have a coat, and no one notices that I'm not there when the desserts arrive. I perfect this the next night, making sure that all my service items are removed with dinner plates and sitting at a corner where my empty chair is less obvious. I'm so pleased with myself that I almost want to stay and watch, make sure it's really working. But no, the whole point is to get out of there and get some sleep, so I leave. I go back to the hotel and text Josie to see if she can connect to my Wi-Fi from her kitchen so we don't have to set up FaceTime sessions in advance.

My strategy at the business dinners isn't entirely about avoiding people I've spent the day with and who are now drunk and loud and lewd. It's not just about getting some sleep, either. It's about steering the meetings so that when they are over, my part of the company integration can happen without months of arguing and recrimination. After three days and nights of making nice all day and drinking all night, everyone is pretty wasted and not functioning all that well during the meetings. Some call in sick or arrive hours late with a tale of a call they couldn't get out of. The integration of the newly acquired company begins to feel like a train wreck.

I've seen this train wreck before and I know we will sort it out. I'm not hung over, and I'm well rested, so I am cheerful and cogent and can pretty much control my part of the agenda and the outcome. What I want is reasonable after all, and it's what was always going to happen.

The downside is that by appearing to be effective when everyone else is feeling sick and cheated by the other side, I end up with way more than my share of the work to do. I need a strategy for this too, so I treat it like the train wreck my recent life has been. I focus on essentials, let the rest go, and rebuild.

I'm responsible for only a small-ish part of the integration. By this time, I know who I need to work with on my part, so I carve them out and find another place for us to meet. Everyone else can figure it out on their own, or stick with the posture-feint-drink routine. I don't care. I don't have a stake in integrating the financials or the HR policies or myriad other departments. I tell my group how it's going to be, which is a relief to them because now it's all out in the open. They whine about some details, and I let them, and I make some changes to suit whatever it is about their situation that is Special. After that, we're all fairly satisfied and can be friendly enough to go out for one drink after work instead of being so nervous that we have to go out for endless drinks.

By the end of the first week, we have an agenda for Week Two, and I've agreed to stay a third week to start implementing. I have FaceTimed with Josie to make sure it's okay with her to keep Boris one more week. She has connected to my Wi-Fi from her house and is tickled about FaceTiming from home. She's also tickled about keeping Boris for another week, which makes me think I'd better not stay a fourth week or I might not get him back.

I had chosen my hotel because it was one of the few that had rooms available when I booked and it has a washer and dryer in the room, something I had never seen before. This saves me from doing laundry in the bathroom sink with hotel shampoo. But the best thing about the room is that it is on the back of the hotel, away from the street, and quiet. The first night I am falling asleep in my room service dinner and I sleep the sleep of a person who had held an Airbus aloft the night before. The next few nights I sleep well from the pure exhaustion that comes from being bombarded by waves of tension in the meetings all day and straining to understand the Aussie accents and slang, never mind the acronyms of their soon-to-be-nonexistent company. But when I sleep well on the fifth night, I finally realize that I am sleeping well because my lizard brain is not staying awake to keep my house secure. It has left my security in the hands of the underpaid college student who is sitting at the front desk of my hotel, studying and trying to stay awake. My lizard brain apparently has more confidence in her than in my large and imposing German Shepherd at home. The lizard may be right. Nevertheless, I am sleeping well and waking up feeling almost good.

I have this realization on a Saturday morning, when for the first time since I arrived I have time to relax. Instead of rushing to the office for the seven thirty coffee-and-pastry networking time, I walk down the street around 9:00 a.m. and have breakfast at a sidewalk café. As I sip my latte, I realize that I've been so completely distracted all week that my grief and worries have been crowded out and the week-long break has been as restful as the extra sleep. I spend the weekend quietly and catch up by email with friends I've neglected for months.

The second week is easier than the first because I have my team and we are focused on planning. We sometimes have dinner together, sometimes not. The locals go home to their friends or families in the evenings and are not made to feel that they missed important bonding and decision making. We get finished with our plan by midday Thursday and rejoin the larger group to make sure our work fits with theirs. That was a good idea, but useless since they are far behind where we are. We surreptitiously take Friday off and climb the Sydney Harbour Bridge.

The third week is more fun because we are taking the first steps in implementing our integration plan and we are getting along well. I know this is temporary, that there will be issues, but I also am confident that we will solve our problems as they arrive. I'm also sad because I know that sooner or later, some of these people, some on each side of the merger, will lose their jobs because of the merger. I knock on wood; my turn could come. I congratulate myself on buying an inexpensive house.

By the middle of the third week, however, I am ready to go home. The break has been good for me, but I am a homebody and I need to go back to my own reality. I never mind a long flight home, and even the lizard is able to take short naps. I've made sure to book a flight that arrives in midday, partly so I don't go home to a dark house in midwinter and partly because I'm a little worried that a cab might not want to take me to my neighborhood after dark and I'll have to have a talk with the starter, which I am in no shape to do.

I underestimated the cabbies, at least my cab driver, who doesn't flinch when I tell him where I'm going. He is friendly but not overly chatty and we talk about the weather, which has been bad and good and bad again, since I've been away for so long. At the moment, the sun is out. South of the river, US 71 splits from the Interstate and we take the expressway all the way to my neighborhood. I tip the driver, tell him about the access point to the northbound expressway from 69th Street, and roll my luggage up my walkway. Josie's front door opens and Boris leaps out, barking and levitating. I am home.

CHAPTER 56

After three weeks in the southern hemisphere, being dropped back into winter is a shock. I know the days are longer than they were when I left in January, but they still seem short. One day it seems warm enough, or at least sunny enough, to wash my aunt's quilts and hang them in the sun to dry. That night, the weight of the cotton layers feels familiar and comforting and I sleep long and well.

On my first Tuesday morning back in KC, the Saunderses are putting their trash out in front of their new house and I realize that they have moved while I was away. By the time I get my trash together, they have disappeared, but I catch Josie as she is taking hers out.

I greet her with "I see that John and Liz have moved. Did they find a renter for next door? I haven't seen anyone."

"Yes, it's a woman who just got a job at Alphapointe."

"Up on 75th? Where Fairyland used to be?"

"Yes. I've talked to her once. She seemed nice. She's getting married in May."

It's cold, so we retreat to our houses and I'm grateful that I've got a neighbor who sounds great, based on Josie's six-word description.

I take a pan of manicotti over to John and Liz for a housewarming present, knowing they are too busy getting settled to cook. They are more grateful than pasta deserves, mostly because they are giddy about their new house, their new tenant, and their baby's imminent arrival.

"Thank you so much," Liz says. "You know, we were thinking about moving out of the neighborhood, but having a real neighbor next door made us decide to stay a while longer. I want to be able to stay home for at least a year, and we couldn't find a better neighborhood that we could afford on one salary."

I tell them I'm glad they are staying and that they are great neighbors. They show me the first floor of the house and I tell them about how their two-story house arrived in the one-story neighborhood, creeping down the street on a house-moving rig at daybreak.

In return, they tell me about when I moved in. They saw my car but never saw me and couldn't figure out who could be living there and why. They thought maybe the owners split up and one of them had to move in.

"I thought people might think I was here temporarily, to flip the house," I tell them, thinking this isn't the place for the witness protection joke.

"Flipping never occurred to us. That would be crazy in this neighborhood," Liz says. "Oh, no. That's what we are doing, isn't it?"

I assure them that if they were flipping the old house they would have built the addition first, and besides they have lived there too long to call it a flip. Not that I know how long they've lived there, but I want to defend them, even to themselves.

I wish them well and the next week the baby is born and John returns the manicotti pan, with thanks so sincere that I refill it with baked ziti and drop it off again along with a baby gift. I was going to make my husband's signature pesto-stuffed chicken breasts, but it's too intimidating. I prefer one-page recipes.

Angie and I go out to celebrate our shared birthday. We joke about getting a Coke at the corner diner, but that's a Church's Chicken now, so we meet at the Classic Cup on the Plaza and have a grown-up lunch.

Angie asks me about the drive from California. "I don't think I could drive across country by myself. Were you scared? I wish you had called me. I would have flown out and driven back with you."

There was never any question that I would drive to Kansas City. The logistics of flying were too much: selling the car, arranging for flying Boris, renting a car on the Kansas City end from a company that allows dogs in the car, and worst of all, buying a new car. Driving would leave me free to leave when I wanted and take what I wanted. And most of all, it would give me a time to detach from the past and mentally prepare for the first few days.

In the weeks before I left, I thought about the car trip when I wanted to avoid thinking about the present. Most often, this happened when I was trying to fall asleep at night. I kept a notebook by the bed to write things down: Get eyeglass prescription before leaving. Cooler? Sealed container for dogfood. Maps. In the mornings, these things usually seemed unimportant. I can always call the eye doctor if I need the prescription; dog food in a bag is fine. In the end, I just packed everything I had and headed south for the first night with my college friends. After that, I planned to avoid the interstates and stop driving by three o'clock to make sure I could find a dog-friendly motel. That was it.

I took Route 60, which went pretty much exactly where I wanted to go. It often looks like an interstate and sometimes it actually cohabits the roadway with an interstate. It was the best I could do without winding up and down mountains and risking flat tires out of the range of cell service. I usually woke up early, so I was ready to crash in mid-afternoon and really did start looking for a motel around 2:00 p.m. That paid off, since it sometimes took a while to find a likely spot to spend the night, someplace not too seedy but also where I wouldn't have to take Boris through a fancy lobby or up the dreaded stairs. And I wanted to be in a town with a park or some quiet streets where we could walk and recharge.

It was harder than I thought, not the driving, but checking into a motel room alone, figuring out dinner, walking the dog, planning the next day. I had made many business trips alone, of course, but that was entirely different from this and I missed my husband like crazy. Much of the trip was a fog of tears and worry. But I forced myself not to race across the country, to take breaks and stop at the scenic overlooks. It was for the dog, I told myself. He needed to stretch his legs, sniff at the fence line, post some pee-mail.

I made myself go into a café or restaurant at least once a day and sit down at a table and order, instead of doing what I wanted, which was to get take-out and eat in the car or a park or the motel room. This was easiest to do in the morning, when it was always cool enough to leave the dog in the car. On the first morning, I had to sit at the counter, and this turned out so well that I looked for counter service every day for the rest of the trip. The whole point was to talk to someone, and that was easier at the counter, where the waitresses (they were always women) casually pass by and pass the time while they are at it. At the counter, I don't feel like a pathetic, friendless solo diner or worse, someone hoping for a pickup. I feel like I'm having breakfast with my pal the waitress, even if I am paying her to be my friend.

A lot of the conversations started with "Where ya headed?" and I would say, "I'm moving from California to Kansas City." It has a ring to it, and sometimes they would say it back "California to Kan City" and follow that up with a story about a cousin or a friend from high school who went to Disneyland on vacation or moved to Wichita. I've never been to either one but that didn't hinder the conversation. The first time I heard that soft "Kan City," with the second syllable of "Kansas" so light that you had to know it was there to hear it, I knew I was almost home.

No one questioned my motives or my sanity or even my non-interstate route. No one gave me advice or sympathy. It was soothing and I stopped hiding in my room or car to eat. I sought out these people who cared about me just enough to say "hello" and refill my coffee cup, but no more. By the time I crossed into Missouri, I was calmer and sleeping a little better. I had stopped making lists in my head as I drove.

CHAPTER 57

March brings its usual warm days randomly mixed with sleet and tornado watches. I begin to think about spring and start some tomato plants. I know that buying seedlings will give me a head start in the race to have ripe tomatoes by the Fourth of July, but I like tending them and moving them from window to window as the sun moves from east to west every day. I watch for the tulips I planted last fall to show themselves. The yard feels bigger than it did last year.

By the end of March, most of the people who were in my griever group when I started have "graduated," and I decide it has done its work for me too. I keep in touch with a few of the people I met and we get together occasionally. I realize that it's hard to make friends in middle age, when most people have decades-long friendships and are busy with children and grandchildren. But the shared grief experience is also a bonding one, and we will give each other an outlet for grief in the months and years beyond what others consider the normal mourning period.

I stop at a Goodwill one day and realize that I can just browse now. I'm not here frantically trying to fill a gap in my little store of possessions. I find a lamp and take it home. I re-donate a lamp I don't like after all. The house seems larger now too. I think again about taking down the wall to expand the living room, and then I think about taking down the wall between the kitchen and the green bedroom to make a decent-sized eat-in kitchen. Both are good ideas, and I'm pretty sure I'll never follow through on either of them.

On the evening of Palm Sunday I feel like I might have a sore throat and hope it's just dust or pollen. I pick up Nyquil and cans of chicken soup and extra ice cream, just in case. On Monday I know it's a cold, which on Tuesday is worse. I miss Holy Week entirely. On Easter Wednesday I feel well enough to go to noon weekday Mass at St. Louis, where I hear the reading about the road to Emmaus, which reminds me that confusion and disbelief are pretty much the normal human condition.

CHAPTER 58

One morning Cathy texts me as soon as I appear online. She wants to call me. We usually chat online, so I am suspicious. I've been seconded to the integration team since Christmas, so I haven't actually talked to Cathy in months.

"Hey, I got a call from Deana a few minutes ago."

Deana is the company president who sent me to Australia and instigated my temporary assignment to the integration team. I hope I'm not losing my job now that the integration is almost complete.

"It was really just a courtesy call," Cathy says, "and I'm probably not supposed to talk to you about it. But she didn't tell me not to."

Okay, this is really worrying me.

"She's transferring you to a new corporate team."

Yikes, not what I was expecting.

"So I guess my little safe place on your team is over, huh? Is she asking or telling?"

"Asking, but you know she'll get her way. I just thought you should know, so you could get your game face on before she calls you."

"Which I see she is doing now. I'll get back to you. And thanks."

I end the call with Cathy and pick up the incoming call. It's Deana's admin, asking if I can talk to Deana.

"Of course," I say, wanting but not willing to ask for five minutes first.

I do get a couple of minutes on hold, most of which I spend wondering if I can ask for more money, and then she's on the line and talking before I can shift gears and listen.

". . . integration went so well, and now that we are a multinational we need to have Cathy's team focus on the US and you can pull the international plan together."

Maybe she's forgotten that I stepped down from my management job eighteen months ago, or maybe she's decided I'm ready to move on, or maybe she really needs to think about the whole business differently. I can see that I don't have much choice. So I act as excited as I can and tell her I'll be at her meeting in Santa Clara in two weeks. I don't ask about money or telecommuting or even who my new boss will be, but surely a move to corporate will mean a raise. Maybe enough to buy a less-needy house in a safer neighborhood. Would I do that?

Two weeks later I check into my Santa Clara hotel across the street from corporate headquarters and get a text from Susan Penta, a VP I've known for years but haven't talked to for months. She wants to buy me a drink.

"You're my new boss?" I type in a text. "Cool."

Twenty minutes later I'm sipping a margarita with Susan.

"I've been wondering," I say. "Are you moving here or staying in Baltimore?"

"Move? Here? Are you crazy? Do you know what I can afford here compared to Baltimore?"

"About one-fifth of what you've got. Which means one bedroom, one bathroom, one-fifth of an acre. What's not to love?"

"Shit. No way. Besides, you know I love Deana but I think she's just getting set up to sell the company. So why move?"

"Hmm. Interesting. But if you don't have to be here, I can still telecommute? You know I moved to Kansas City, right?" At least she's from Baltimore and doesn't have a whole lot of room to look down on Kansas City. She's not interested in that anyway, and we go on to plot strategy for the next two days of meetings. I do ask about salary, and she rolls her eyes.

"That asshole Delarosa says that since you live in a backwater—I think that was the word he used—it's cheap there and you don't need a raise."

Delarosa is the new CFO who wants to be CEO. He was CEO of a company we acquired two years ago and thinks highly of himself. I narrow my eyes and stare at Susan.

"No worries," she says. "We'll make it up at bonus time."

I have to be content with that. My two-week-old dream of a salary that would let me to consider a move to a better neighborhood evaporates like the mist it always was.

Two days later I go home exhausted but also energized. On the flight home I think about where I might have moved if the new job had meant more money. When I stand at my front door with my key in the lock and the sun warm on my back, I remember standing here a year ago. I remember the look and the smell and the feel of the neglected house. Today when I walk through my front door, I smile and wonder if I really would move.

CHAPTER 59

On a warm day in mid-April, I think about shade trees again and call the Heartland Tree Alliance to make an appointment. They are not dismayed when I give them my address. I call Josie and Dave and Carol and tell them about the appointment.

"Are you available on Saturday morning? If they plant a big tree, it will shade your houses eventually, and you'll have to look at it all the time. So I thought you might want to help me decide where to put it." I invite them over for coffee while we wait, and find they are amused, or at least bemused, that I included them.

"You can do what you want," Carol says. "No one ever asks first."

"Well," I say, "it's been a long winter—any excuse to get together, right?"

They admire the few improvements I've made over the winter and I tell them I'm thinking about doing something in the kitchen, not because I really am but because the linoleum floor and Formica counter tops are looking pretty shabby. The linoleum could date back to at least the 1930s and the Formica to the early 1960s.

"I like that painted floor you have in the bedroom. Maybe you could do that in here," Josie says.

"I hadn't thought of that," I say, but I will think about it now because it suddenly seems manageable, assuming I can get the lino up. My mother waxed it regularly and left it in good condition, but I doubt that it's been waxed since. By the time my parents moved, vinyl flooring was all the rage and people forgot about waxing the old-fashioned linoleum. I'm certainly not waxing it.

Boris goes to the door and barks, and the doorbell rings. We all troop outside with our coffee and stand around pretending that we know Latin and understand what the tree people are talking about. I want maximum shade in July and the others are agreeable to pretty much anything. We decide on a sugar maple and set a planting date. I sign a pledge to water it for three years and they give me advice on pruning back the overgrown shrub so that it continues to give me some shade while letting the maple grow freely.

As we are saying our goodbyes, a pickup truck pulls up and stops, and Boris goes over to investigate.

It's Charles, the neighbor who picked up my free door months ago. He seems pretty excited about something.

"Hi, Charles. How are you? We're just talking about planting a shade tree out here. I want to keep the house a little cooler in the summer."

"Oh?" he says. "Maybe I should do that." I realize I don't know where he lives.

"Well, these are the people to talk to. They'll give you a tree and even help you plant it."

He's clearly not interested in this distraction, so they give him a flyer and tell him to call any time, and they take their leave.

"I found something for you," he says, once the tree people are in their truck. "Come see."

We look in the back of his truck, and there is the double gate of last summer's dreams, the sort of gate I never got from Fern.

"That's perfect. Did you find it at ReStore?" I ask.

"No, I found it under a tarp in my backyard."

I raise my eyebrows. "Under a tarp?"

"Yes, my Aunt Fern had a stroke and had to go to a nursing home, so my wife and I moved into her house. We're doing a rent-to-own thing with her."

"Fern on Bellefontaine?" I ask.

"Do you know her?" Charles is surprised to hear this.

"Fern Grover?" Josie asks. "I know her from church."

"Sort of," I say, ignoring Josie for the moment. "She answered my Nextdoor post and I got some of my fencing from her. She said she had a gate too, but then she sort of went silent. I guess that's when she got sick."

"Oh, I wish I had known. We've been working inside all winter, and we had a baby in January. So I never even looked at the stuff piled up behind the garage."

We all stand around smiling idiotically, given that it's just a gate.

"Are you still interested?"

"Sure. Bring it on," I say, and I move toward the truck.

He and Dave lift it out before I get there, which of course I was counting on. There is no obvious place to put it, so we take it around back and lean it against the house. It's hung with cobwebs and bits of leaves and vines, and some of the wire needs straightening, but the frame itself is in good shape. No one has tried to drive a car through it, anyway.

"Thank you so much. I got the best of this deal," I say, and then think that I should pay him, and I try to think of how to offer that.

"Oh, no. Your door was nicer than this gate, and we really needed it to keep the cat out of the baby's room. She was born right after you gave me the door."

I'm willing to leave it at that. We both got a good deal.

He's on his way to the hardware store, so I thank him again and collect empty coffee mugs from my neighbors, and we go about our Saturday chores.

CHAPTER 60

May arrives, and with it planning for the block party, which is really a street party for the whole area. I offer to help, but it seems like the same people do the same thing every year and everyone else just shows up with food and drink. Then they decide I can get the permit. No one likes to do that. It's online now, and it's free, so I'm good with that. I read up and am a little concerned that the street has to be reopened by 10:00 p.m., and they tell me that they move onto the sidewalks by then.

I go to the party alone, taking my introverted self by the hand to walk around and talk to people. I'm better known now, although sometimes it's really Boris that people know.

"You're the one with the big German Shepherd, aren't you?" one woman asks when I am putting my plate of cherry tarts on a table. "He's a beautiful dog."

I thank her and we talk about the dog for a bit and I work in how much I like living here. "It's great for Boris too, since almost every street has sidewalks. We walk all over the place and he makes a lot of friends." Pretty banal, but I'm hoping for common ground to emerge. And it does, when some people I know by sight on Chestnut join us.

"It's funny, but when you took that house over so suddenly, we thought you might be a developer planning to buy up and tear down houses, like what happened on Bellefontaine," one of them tells me, and the rest of them nod. I'm amused that what we called Bell-Fountain is now Bell-Fon-Tane, but I don't say that because it sounds churlish, and I'm trying to restrict myself to talking about the old days to only maybe twice an hour.

A younger woman with a baby chimes in: "We were confused at first because of how you just showed up when the house wasn't for sale or rent or anything. Most people who move in here have some connection somewhere to someone who is already here, and you didn't. And yes, you were white—are white. Most of the whites here are the ones who have been here forever. They don't *move in* here."

I feel like I should take one of my twice-an-hour opportunities, so I say, "Remember, I did live here a long time ago, but I see what you mean."

"We did hear that, and we heard you went off to college and then went to California, which made it even more odd, your moving here." She considers. "Although there are more folks around here that have degrees than you might think." The others are nodding meaningfully when she says that, so I nod too. "Or their kids do." More nodding.

"So when Dave and Carol told us about how you joke around about witness protection, some of us thought—that must be it. She's hiding in plain sight and even telling us she's in witness protection to throw us off."

"Oh, I never believed that," the woman with the baby said. "You knew so much about everything, even things like that old zoo building story and what the kindergarten room looked like at Blenheim. So we kind of stopped thinking about what you were doing here. After a while we did notice that you stopped talking about California and your husband and what happened to you, so then some people went back to the witness protection idea. But we didn't really care by then. If you're in witness protection, we decided, we like it because it means someone is watching out for you and maybe some of that washes over on us."

I go back for more food and run into another group whose names I have heard but can't remember. They know me, though, or they know who I am.

"Glad you could come. We wondered if you would still be living here."

I'm briefly perplexed by this greeting, but apparently they've been discussing me.

"You had that break-in right after you got here, didn't you?"

"Yes, that did freak me out for a while," I say. I want a little sympathy but not too much. It's been a year now.

"They caught the guy in your house, didn't they? It was Bud Forsythe?"

"Yes, he parked in the driveway and I came home and saw the car and called 911," I tell them. "They got there pretty fast."

"He grew up on your block, I think. I don't know which house. My kid went to school with him, he seemed okay. Then he went in the Army."

"That didn't do him much good."

I haven't thought much about Bud lately, but I'm thinking about him now. So when I see the community relations police cruiser, I walk over to see if Officer Carl has come to the block party for a meet-and-greet. I find him getting iced tea and adding lemonade.

"I'm on duty, so this is the only mixed drink I'm having," he says when he sees me, adding, "I was hoping I would run into you here."

"You can always stop by the house," I say.

"You know how it is. People worry if they see a police vehicle parked on the street. This is better."

"That's true. I would worry. What did you want to talk about?"

"The next chapter of the Bud story."

I had hoped this story had reached its end and would have no more chapters, other than maybe a reassuring postscript saying something along the lines of Bud moving to Alaska, where he raises pumpkins in the summer and goes ice fishing in the winter.

"Does that chapter take place in Kansas City?"

"Ah, it does." I get the wry grin. "He has been at the VA being treated for PTSD. He has a service dog now, and he is seeing his girlfriend and daughter."

That all sounds good, and I say so, by way of delaying whatever bad news I see is coming next.

"He wants to apologize to you."

"Oh." That was not what I was expecting. "Um," I say, thinking, *No way.* "But . . . ."

"Yeah." He lets me sort out the noise in my head for another little bit. Then he puts on his cop face.

"The thing is, I've seen a lot of B&E cases. Solved some, investigated a lot. And this case is different. This is off the record, but I think Bud will probably straighten himself out. And if he can apologize to you, that will help him along."

I hear myself heave a big sigh. I came to this party for the food and drink, not to face a moral dilemma at the beverage table.

Officer Carl is talking again, still in kind-cop mode. "But no one wants to scare you into moving away, so think about it. It's up to you."

"Okay, I'll call you," I finally say. I'm thinking that I'll take it to the court of Josie, Dave, and Carol. And maybe Liz and John.

"I also need to know if you want to press charges."

"Okay, I'll figure that out too."

I go looking for Josie, but she's sitting at a table where she appears to be holding court, so I slip home and think it all over on my own. I know I'll let him apologize, and after that I'll decide about pressing charges. But I can't picture myself testifying in court, so I will probably let that go.

I decide to wait until Monday afternoon to call Carl back with my decision, in case I think of some compelling reason to change my mind. I stew about it, but it comes down to this: unless one of us moves to the burbs or west of Troost, I'll probably run into Bud sometime. I don't want to be afraid of him. So I can hear him out and then decide how afraid I am. I can always press charges and even get a restraining order.

Officer Carl says that he'll arrange the meeting in a community relations area at the local precinct. "It's not an interrogation room. It has windows and everything. We'll have coffee."

Nice touch, free police coffee. "Can we do it in daylight hours?" I don't want to go home in the dark if I get creeped out.

CHAPTER 61

Officer Carl schedules the meeting for 5:30 p.m. on Thursday and I show up at 5:29. I had planned to walk, but I'm feeling vulnerable so I surround myself with a metric ton of VW instead. Of course I have to leave that in the parking lot and walk in surrounded by a few ounces of denim and cotton jersey.

Carl meets me in the lobby and tells me that Bud is already there and that his girlfriend and daughter are with him. "Is that okay with you?"

I recognize the attempt to humanize the burglar and charm me with a toddler, but it would be rude to refuse and besides, meeting them all together might give me a better sense of how he is doing.

"No problem."

Carl takes me into the community relations section of the building, which is new and light and clean and not like any I've seen on television. I see that Bud has not only his family but also his service dog, who is lying under Bud's chair. The dog looks at me but doesn't move. Carl puts on his kind-but-business-like cop voice and makes introductions in a way that makes it clear to everyone that he is in charge. Even the toddler puts her thumb in her mouth and looks at him with wide eyes.

Bud wastes no time. He starts to stand up, looks at Carl, then sits upright on the edge of his seat. I had leaned back as he started forward, but now I relax and look at his face. What I see there is hope. He's blinking a little too often, but he's focused on me.

"Ma'am, I know you didn't have to do this and I really appreciate it." He sounds a little rehearsed, but that's to be expected. He takes a breath, lifts his chin just a notch, for courage, I think.

"I was wrong to break into your house." His eyes slide sideways, toward Carl, and his chin drops an inch. "Any house, actually, but yours is the only one I ever did break into." He's off script now.

I don't say anything, I don't even nod. I need to let him get back to the point. I'll let everyone be uncomfortable if necessary. Besides, I'm nervous and therefore likely to say something sarcastic if I'm not on guard. I glance at Carl; he's calm and relaxed and waiting for Bud to go on.

"So I want to apologize," Bud goes on. "That is, I'm sorry I did it. I know it was wrong, and I'm sorry. I just. . . ." He stops there, looks toward Carl again. It sounded like he was going to offer an excuse and thought better of it. Or remembered that he was advised not to?

It's my turn to say something now, but Bud's dangling sentence makes me miss my cue.

Bud's girlfriend sees that Bud has gone off script again. She hitches the little girl up closer to her chest and says softly, "He just wanted to get those presents. He hid them and I didn't know they were there when we moved out. He didn't know anyone even lived there. I mean, we moved out because the roof was leaking."

I probably should have let Officer Carl say something, since this was Bud's deal and not his wife's, but I jumped right in.

"So why was he upstairs?" I ask her, then pivot back to Bud—this is his problem, not hers. "Why were you upstairs eating peanut butter?" Somehow "peanut butter" makes it sound trivial and I feel petty. But I give him a look as serious as if I'd asked why he was stealing the silver. "And why was the back door standing open?"

"Upstairs? I didn't go upstairs. I didn't eat any peanut butter. Why would I open the back door if I was still inside?" He sounds believable, and I would believe him if it hadn't been my peanut butter and my back door. I scramble for some way to prove he was upstairs, something that he can't lie about.

"I didn't even open the basement door. I swear I was only in the basement."

I think about the basement door, but the police went down there so I wouldn't know if they opened it or he did.

"Once I saw the laundry I knew someone else was living there, maybe squatting, I didn't know. I just wanted to get my stuff and get out. I wouldn't have gone upstairs. It was too risky if someone was staying there, and besides I was a mess. I would have left dirt all over, and you would have known."

"So then," I started, and then I stopped.

Could I have left the peanut butter out when I made my sandwich, the milk out when I made my iced coffee? Could I have left the back door open when I took my backpack and Boris out the back door to go to the park? I don't want to think that I could have been so scatterbrained, but I know it is possible, especially that first week or so.

Everyone is waiting for me. There isn't much for anyone else to say.

"Daddy," the baby says firmly, a fact and not a question.

We all have to smile at that because there is nothing else to do.

I'm almost ready to concede, but I say to Carl, "Is it possible to verify with the other officers that he was in the basement when they went in? And that the basement door was closed?" At that, I grimace and say the obvious: "Although, if I really did leave the back door open, I probably left the basement door open too."

I'm thinking that Carl will say that he'll get back to me, but he just nods and says, "Let me check," and he leaves the room. Bud, his wife, the toddler, and the dog stare at me.

I'm unnerved by the four faces looking at me and by the idea that I could have walked out and left my door not only unlocked but standing open. I forget that I should sit quietly. Maybe the rules don't apply anymore.

"If the back door was open, why did you break in the basement window?" I ask, trying to feel like I'm on top of the situation. Surely any burglar would have tried the door first.

"I guess the storm door was closed and I didn't notice that the inside door was open. I just wanted to get in and get out. I had it all planned. It would only take a few minutes. But it was harder than I thought getting down in that window well and jimmying the window. It would have been easier to go in the window on the other side, where there isn't a window well, but I was afraid someone would see me. And I didn't know about the clothesline in the basement and I got caught on that, and when it broke then I fell and lost my sunglasses. I guess I shouldn't have worn sunglasses in a basement."

I'm picturing this movie in my head and I start laughing. We're all laughing when Officer Carl comes back in.

"Well, in case anyone still cares, I talked to the officer who went downstairs. Bud was on the stairs when the officers opened the basement door. He was sitting, not walking up. Or running away, for that matter."

Three sets of eyes turn to me, the baby having lost interest. The dog whimpers softly.

"Okay, I'm going to have to admit that it's pretty likely that I left the food out and the door open." I wonder if I should apologize for accusing him of eating my peanut butter and decide not to muddy the purpose of the meeting any further.

"I accept your apology," I say formally, and then I leave Bud a space to reply, even though it feels awkward.

"Thank you," he says, and his wife jumps up and might have hugged me if jumping up hadn't startled the baby, who squawked.

I want a little more reassurance out of this meeting, which has not turned out in any of the ways I had imagined. I'm not 100 percent sure I don't want a restraining order.

"What are you doing now?" I say. "If you don't mind my asking?" It's not exactly what I want to know, but it's the best I can come up with. I can't ask if he's stable, if he has a job, if he's moving to Alaska. I can't say, "So, how's the PTSD?"

He's happy with this question, though. "The VA helped me get an interview at Alphapointe, so I'm hoping to get on there. Right now I'm working nights at Church's Chicken. You know, on Prospect."

So he's very much in the neighborhood, at least during his working hours. I wonder if it's out of bounds to ask where he's living.

"We're getting married in June and we're looking for a place to live," the girlfriend says.

"We want to stay in the neighborhood, you know, because it's close to his work." She looks at Bud. "If he gets the job at Alphapointe, I'll only have to work part time while the baby is little, if we can find a place that's safe. And not too expensive."

I don't know what his income potential is at Alphapointe, but they seem to think that this neighborhood is safe enough and cheap enough. Isn't that why we all live here?

What can I say? I opt for "I hope you find the right place." And then add "Someplace that allows dogs. She seems sweet. What's her name?" I'm ready for a topic with no drama.

"She's a service dog, so we're hoping it will be okay. And we'd like to maybe buy a place."

If I can't get a J. Jill credit card when I own my house outright, it seems unlikely that they can get a mortgage. Well, maybe a VA loan. I resign myself to living near my burglar and then realize that it doesn't really seem like a problem anymore. Nevertheless, I've had enough together time.

"I hope you can," I say to Bud, then turn to Officer Carl. "Thank you for arranging this. I think it's all worked out well. I won't press charges." I say that last part to Carl but so that Bud can hear. He might as well know now.

Before I fall asleep that night I wonder if I've been stupid. Maybe I just proved to Bud that I'm gullible. But he also knows that I'm nice, or at least fairly nice, and maybe that will make him a good neighbor, since neighbor he will almost certainly be.

By morning I'm feeling okay about the whole thing. If he is a burglar, he's a pretty lousy one. I hope he gets the job.

On Saturday night, I sit down with a glass of wine to take stock.

I have made it through all the holidays and anniversaries, through the heat of summer and the ice and snow of winter. I am more financially secure than I was a year ago. My job is as safe as any job ever is. My house looks like a home now, at least to me. I still stop in at a thrift store now and then, but not so often, and sometimes as a donor, and never in desperation. I've got enough clothes to cover just about any situation. I've made friends. I have a garden and I am still hopeful that I'll have my first tomatoes by the Fourth of July. I no longer feel defensive when I say that I live east of Troost.

On the down side, I still have to shower in the basement. I'm occasionally lonely. I haven't met the neighbors behind me and I lie awake some nights, listening for trouble. I still live east of Troost.

My to-do list includes "go to a show at Starlight Theater in Swope Park" and "install gates." Maybe a rose trellis too.

CHAPTER 62

In July, I finally schedule the picture party. I send email to my closest neighbors, the ones whose houses can be seen in my childhood photos, although for the most part I'm the only one who can say which house is which. The invitation is to an afternoon Wine and Cheese and Pie Party. I've never offered or been offered alcohol when getting together with these neighbors, and I realize that I'm past the brand-new-immigrant period when I can be forgiven for being stupid about local customs. So I put the "wine" part right out there and give them the chance to decline or accept or whatever. All five accept and I agonize over what kind of pie to bake, what kind of cheese and wine to serve. But I don't agonize for long, and once I've been to the store I don't agonize any further.

I can now entertain six people comfortably in my living room, as long as they all don't try to get up and move around at the same time and as long as it's not too hot—in hot weather I'll have to entertain around the air conditioner in the back. I've got enough dishes and glasses and silverware for six too, and although they all have different patterns, they look nice together.

I've printed the pictures on photo paper, enlarged as much as possible without making them grainy. Everyone is interested in the pictures, but there aren't that many photos and there isn't much to say, so pretty quickly we move on to talking about the same things we always talk about: the weather, the Royals, the neighbors. The baby gives us more material. We talk about plans for our houses and our yards. An ordinary bunch of neighbors relaxing together, which was really the whole point.

We haven't seen a For Sale sign or a For Rent sign on John and Liz's old house next to mine, and Dave asks about it.

John and Liz look at each other. "Well," John says, "we have a renter for a few more weeks, and that's working out pretty well."

"But don't you want to get a new renter lined up? Or list it if you still want to sell?"

We all prefer homeowners to renters, but selling it doesn't guarantee a homeowner, so we are anxious either way.

"We might have a buyer. But it might have to be a rent-to-own arrangement. We're kind of nervous about it."

I wonder why they seem so hesitant to talk about it, but I have no room to question unusual arrangements, so I keep quiet. Josie has no compunction about wondering out loud.

"That sounds like good news. Who is it? What's the problem?" she asks.

"One problem is that we really need at least some cash out of it; our mortgage is just too much right now." This is Liz, who is possibly worrying about having to go back to work sooner than she planned.

"Who is it?" Josie asks again. "Maybe they can get something from family."

Liz looks at John again, looks at me. "And we're just not sure. . . ."

John sits up straight. "We might as well come clean. It's Bud Forsythe and his wife, Jennie. They came by and asked about it. They knew the current tenant would be moving out, and they know it's only four rooms, so they thought maybe they could afford it. Plus he's from this area and he feels safest here."

Silence. That got our attention and everyone is looking at me. I feel my face get red. I take a deep breath.

"Wow, I'm not sure," I say. "I get the safe thing, though." Crap. Why does his story have to be the same as my story?

"At least we could keep an eye on him." I tell them about the apology meeting, which I had kept quiet, although I was never sure why. I tell them about the therapy dog and even about the peanut butter that I'm now pretty sure I left out myself. I ask them if they would be willing to tell us how much Bud needs to come up with, and they say "five thousand dollars." I've spent that much on vacations, and although those days are behind me, it makes me cringe inside.

Dave says, "I assume he's working with the VA," and Josie says, "My church has a fund," and Carol says, "The city has a first-time home-buyer program," which reminds Liz that they used that when they bought their house.

We all think for a while, and I say, "Could this be a good thing? Better the devil you know, right? And he'll owe us."

"If it's okay with you, it's okay with us, but are you sure? Maybe he was just after that box of presents, but still—he broke into your house."

I tell them that I need to think about it, but I do want them to be able to sell the house to someone who will live in it. And his little girl is awfully cute.

"Do you think he can take care of a house, though? It's one thing to buy it, but if he can't keep it up. . . ." I think of the Barry family in the next block, which I am not going to bring up.

"I think he was in a construction unit in the Army," Dave says. "And we know he has a truck, so he can bring things home from ReStore." I think he is teasing me about my enthusiasm for

ReStore. "Plus, he came back and hauled off that mattress on the front porch after Josie called his mom about it."

"Oh. That explains something." I tell them about my puzzling phone call with the previous owners.

Things are quiet for a minute. I think they are giving me time to commit myself but they aren't going to force me.

"Okay," I say at last. "I won't object to Bud living next door." I take a deep breath, let it out. "If necessary maybe we can come up with some kind of co-investment plan to give him a lift." And I am pretty sure that I will be the one to come up with something, if it comes to that. I've saved him once before, after all.

John and Liz seem relieved that it's out in the open and that no one is upset. I look at Josie and suspect she knew some of this already. She catches my look and compliments me on the peach pie.

Carol is quick to pick up the new thread and says, "I won a bet. Dave was sure you would serve sweet potato pie."

I wait for the punchline, ready to laugh, hoping there is a punchline and I'm not the butt of a joke. I mean, I know they wouldn't, but what else could it be?

"Because your witness protection handlers would have told you to make sweet potato pie."

We all laugh because we've let the witness protection joke languish, and it's good to get it going again. We all make up more preposterous stories than ever about why I am in witness protection and when exactly they figured out that I am in witness protection. Finally, the laughter dies down and we have one of those silent moments that presage the end of a good party.

"Hey guys," I say when they are all safely down the front steps, "I just want to say 'thanks.' Some days I feel like I am in witness protection and you all are my handlers. That means we're in this for life. And you're the best."

I close the door, lean against it. The sun is going down and the door is warm and solid on my back. I smile at nothing in particular. I may not be in this for all of my life, but right now, my life is here, and right now is all I have to worry about. This is home.

ACKNOWLEDGMENTS

First, thanks to the denizens of East of Troost, past and present. In particular . . .

The Sisters of Charity, who really did teach us charity and were all-in proponents of social justice, no holds barred.

Louis Read, the English teacher at Hogan High who first made me think I really could write for an audience beyond the teacher who assigned the task in the first place.

Patricia Coupe, whom I have never, ever, called Patricia, for being my first best friend and sharing my birthday for all the years since first grade and for rehashing with me everything that went on east of Troost in the sixties. The site of her childhood home lies under the expressway now.

All the Marys and everyone else in my grade school and high school classes, who accepted me for the awkward nerdy kid I was.

Jackie Creel, who makes a cameo appearance in the story and gracefully allowed me to include her haunting song lyrics.

My parents, who bought the house east of Troost and raised me there, through thick and thin, and my brother Tim, who is sort of but not exactly the brother in the story and also sort of but not exactly the grocery store guy.

Also, thanks to the non-East of Troosters who were crucial to getting this book into your hands:

My husband Tom, who read and reread the manuscript and still claims to love this book, even though he says I killed him off before the story even starts.

Jamie Hansen, another early reader and inspiration for making this book more than just a memoir.

The anonymous scholarship donors to Washington University who unknowingly pried me out of East of Troost and flung me into a vast world of possibility.

The staff at She Writes Press, who believed in my story and who know all about the hard things that come after the manuscript is written, a process that makes writing the novel itself seem easy.

My cohort of She Writes authors, who have struggled along with me, learning that same difficult truth.

Josie Bongio, the consummate next-door neighbor who modeled the Josie in this story.

And finally, Boris the dog, who plays his best self in this novel. He still hates stairs.

ABOUT THE AUTHOR

Photo credit: Amy Sullivan

Ellen Barker grew up in Kansas City, where she had a front-row seat to the demographic shifts, the hope, and the turmoil of the civil rights era of the 1960s. She has a bachelor's degree in urban studies from Washington University in Saint Louis, where she developed a passion for how cities work, and don't. She began her career as an urban planner in Saint Louis and then spent many years working for large consulting firms specializing in urban infrastructure, first as a tech writer-editor and later managing large data systems. She now lives in Los Altos, California, with her husband and their dog, Boris, who is the inspiration for the German shepherd in East of Troost. This is Ellen's first novel.

Learn more about Ellen and *East of Troost* at
www.ellenbarkerauthor.com.

SELECTED TITLES FROM SHE WRITES PRESS

She Writes Press is an independent publishing company founded to serve women writers everywhere. Visit us at www.shewritespress.com.

South of Everything by Audrey Taylor Gonzalez. $16.95, 978-1-63152-949-8. A powerful parable about the changing South after World War II, told through the eyes of young white woman whose friendship with her parents' black servant, Old Thomas, initiates her into a world of magic and spiritual richness.

Beginning with Cannonballs by Jill McCroskey Coupe. $16.95, 978-1-63152-848-4. In segregated Knoxville, Tennessee, Hanna (black) and Gail (white) share a crib as infants and remain close friends into their teenage years—but as they grow older, careers, marriage, and a tragic death further strain their already complicated friendship.

The Cards Don't Lie by Sue Ingalls Finan. $16.95, 978-1-63152-451-6. Three desperate but spirited women of New Orleans—a voodoo priestess, a plantation mistress who has out-of-body experiences, and a prostitute—forge a unique partnership in order to save their city from the juggernaut that is Britain.

So Happy Together by Deborah K. Shepherd. $16.95, 978-1-64742-026-0. In Tucson in the 1960s, drama students Caro and Peter are inseparable, but Caro ends up marrying someone else. Twenty years and three children later, with her marriage failing, Caro drops the kids off at summer camp and sets out on a road trip to find Peter, her creative spirit, and her true self.

The Black Velvet Coat by Jill G. Hall. $16.95, 978-1-63152-009-9. When the current owner of a black velvet coat—a San Francisco artist in search of inspiration—and the original owner, a 1960s heiress who fled her affluent life fifty years earlier, cross paths, their lives are forever changed . . . for the better.

Shrug by Lisa Braver Moss. $16.95, 978-1-63152-638-1. In 1960s Berkeley, teenager Martha Goldenthal just wants to do well in school and have a normal life. But her home life is a cauldron of kooky ideas, impossible demands, and explosive physical violence—and there's chaos on the streets. When family circumstances change and Martha winds up in her father's care, she must stand up to him, or forgo college.